"*Play, With Knives* is a work of wondrous imagination—a dream from which I did not want to awaken."

—Elizabeth Gilbert, *New York Times* bestselling author of *Eat Pray Love*, *The Signature of All Things*, and *City of Girls*

"I love and admire the pulsing vitality of *Play, With Knives*. Horn's formal ingenuity and her exquisite prose—so precise, lyrical, rhythmically adept—make this book a delight to be inside of. It's a novel that seems to have been written with a genuine sense of pleasure, play, and possibility."

—Chris Bachelder, author of *The Throwback Special*, finalist for the 2016 National Book Award

"*Play, With Knives* is beautifully written, poetic—and surreal, in the inimitable way that life itself can be surreal. In a way that is difficult, if not impossible, to believe or even imagine until it unfolds. As Jeanette Horn puts it, 'But sometimes coincidences happened. Things happened and she wrote them, or she wrote them and they happened.'"

—Anja Snellman, author of *Skin* and *Continents: A Love Story*, the most widely read author of her generation in her native Finland

"What a wild ride! Jeanette Horn's new novel is part stage play, part novel, part freak out. Think of the comedic best best of Richard Brautigan and Tom Robbins and the unsettling, brilliant weirdness of Leonora Carrington, and you'll have a *little* idea of what you're in for. Have a seat in the bar car, and get ready for the show. Unforgettable!"

—Christian Kiefer, author of *The Heart of It All*

"Jeanette Horn's prose is as sharp and unexpected as a paper cut."

—Alia Volz, author of *Home Baked*, finalist for the 2020 National Book Critics Circle Award

"Working at the very limit of fiction, Jeanette Horn has conjured a wickedly alluring romance out of razor-sharp sentences and tricks of the light. Each page offers a magnificent illusion. Each page tempts to a shining edge. *Play, With Knives* is rare and dangerous, a novel so honed it slices as it sings."

—Joanna Ruocco, author of *Dan*

"Jeanette Horn's exquisite debut, *Play, With Knives*, is a meticulously crafted novel about art, love, trust, identity, the nature of reality, and 'the mission of living.' On this surreal train ride through a world outside of time, through an aspirational Midwest of European cities, we meet a cast of troubled actors and their obsessive playwright, who works on the knife's edge between artifice and reality. With lyrical sensibility, coy humor, and a Nabokovian sense of lexical gamesmanship, Horn gives us riveting plays within plays about the stakes of artmaking and the lives that we venture to live when we are prepared to risk it all—on the page as well as off it."

—Debora Kuan, author of *Women on the Moon*, *Lunch Portraits*, and *Xing*

"Jeanette Horn's *Play, With Knives* is a delightful and wry look at the many ways language conceals as much as it reveals. In Horn's nimble prose, we follow a troupe of actors (and a playwright) as they tour a Europe of the imagination (it's actually the Midwest) while their lives intertwine both onstage and off. At every moment, these characters' interactions blur the line between performance and the inner life, and the play of surface and depth reveals itself in jewel-like sentences I kept re-reading for their sheer beauty. It's a gift to find sentences of such fine detail in a book capacious enough to include recurrent passages from a physics textbook and an Abraham Lincoln lookalike who pours drinks behind the bar. *Play, With Knives* is a terrific debut by a seriously talented writer."

—Jared Stanley, author of *So Tough*

PLAY, WITH KNIVES

Jeanette Horn

Regal House Publishing

"Everything we call real is made of things
that cannot be regarded as real."

–Attributed to Niels Bohr

"Wherein I am false I am honest; not true, to be true."

–William Shakespeare

Sparta, Iowa

February 3

It was opening night. Edgar felt the night opening, saw its teeth. He was dressing himself as meat.

He slumped in the boat of his swan costume, its neck hanging to one side of his metal stool like an oar. One of the paint-spattered white tees he always wore stretched across his chest and shoulders above a diaper of swan body held by red suspenders. He swished whiskey around the bottom of a cut-glass glass swiped from the crowded prop table behind him. Before him rose the back wall of the black-walled dressing room, filled, floor to ceiling, with shelves holding rows of decapitated Styrofoam heads dressed in wigs of every era and description. Edgar read them, left to right, top to bottom, with an intensity that could only come from thinking about something else.

Will's disembodied voice from the next room brought Edgar back just in time. There were things he didn't think about.

"The prince ordered his head—ordered—ordered his head. The prince ordered his head chopped off."

Though the wall muffled the sound, Edgar could hear Will reading, enunciating every consonant, sounding each vowel. He knew the pre-show ritual so well he could paint the scene unseen. Will would have set the small slip of paper he'd read from on a stool and drawn another from a top hat turned on its head. His hands would be trembling, matching his voice.

"A joy—a joy to every child—child—is the swan boat," Will read. "Huh."

Footsteps approached the open dressing-room door, and Will's head appeared, the doorframe slicing it off like a guillotine. A red bow tie bled from its edge. His wavy brown hair was parted severely and slicked back with pomade, and he was still wearing the wire-framed glasses he took off whenever he went on.

"Did you hear that? It's a good sign for tonight, for your debut, don't you think?"

Edgar hoisted his lips into a smile. When Will's footsteps receded, he imagined more than heard the rustle of paper against silk.

"To have is better than to wait—better than to. To have is better than to wait and hope."

Edgar groaned. He'd been waiting and hoping since he joined the troupe as set designer three weeks ago, since the first time he'd seen Ava. Ava, he thought about.

There was a cough, retch, then honk as the stool leg skid on the concrete floor in the other room while—Edgar could picture it—Will lurched toward the trash can he'd have placed at his feet. A guttural sound was followed by a slop as Will vomited into it, spat, and rustled a new slip of paper from the hat.

"A siege will crack the—crack—will crack. A siege will crack the strong defense."

Edgar exhaled. Ava kept to herself whenever she had the chance, flitting in and out of focus at the troupe's margins. He'd hardly spoken with her beyond common courtesies. Whenever he approached, she bolted—left or locked up—or seemed to look through him. Her focus, when he managed to clip the edge of her attention, was always just behind him, as if someone else was there. Edgar wanted so much to be seen by Ava that when she'd knocked on the door of his sleeper compartment and drily asked him to take on a small, nonspeaking role in a play, just this once, he'd said yes.

The thought crossed his mind that Fallon might have asked her to ask. Fallon saw everything.

Edgar set down his now-empty glass, combed his black hair with a dollop of pomade, then fumbled a hand along the surface of the vanity until it stumbled into the fifth of whiskey. Lifting the bottle to his lips, he took another slug while swiveling feather-on-metal to face the mirror. He was blaming the drinking on nerves, but there were plenty of reasons, most he wasn't sure of. When the butt of the bottle lowered, his eyes in reflection were red-rimmed, haggard. They were sad, to be honest, as Edgar always was.

He rasped his eight o'clock shadow and rested his chin in his hands, elbows on vanity. When the loose skin of his cheeks pooled under his eyes, Edgar slid his hands back down slowly, stretching his lower eyelids, then kneaded his face into grotesque expressions in the mirror. It was nearly time for the play to begin. He knocked the top off a pot of white

face paint and used three fingers to scoop a cool glob, then poured
three more fingers of bourbon and downed them in one smooth swallow. Now he was ten fingers deep, two hands to the wind.

As Edgar smeared the first swipe of white across the crudely chiseled
planes of his brow and nose, he paled. Ava appeared in the mirror over
his reflection's left shoulder like a cartoon devil, her turn-of-the-twen-
tieth-century dress draping the doorframe in crimson. With her cloud
of dark hair, usually the largest thing about her, swept into an updo, she
was tiny. She hesitated on the threshold, then entered. An archipelago
of vertebrae erupted down her back as she turned her head, scanning
the room.

"My gloves seem to have wandered," Ava said, smoothing a dark
curl back under its hairpin and looking everywhere but at Edgar, who
wanted to be seen.

"Men think and plan and sometimes act," read Will on the other side
of the wall. "Act!"

Edgar jerked to a stand, clattering over the metal stool. Like a doe,
Ava started to a stop. Her gaze twitched on Edgar, then fled past him as
she continued toward the vanity.

"The kite flew wildly—wildly. The kite flew—flew wildly—in the
high wind."

Edgar met Ava in a two-step collision. She yielded, backing into the
prop table to let him pass, but he pressed her against it, pinning the
breast of his swan costume between his and her pelvises. He lifted his
large, calloused hand, and watched her eyes follow the motion, saw she
still wasn't seeing him. The skin at the hollow of her cheek was velvety,
less elastic than expected, the bone beneath like fine china. He ran his
rough thumb across her cheekbone toward her ear, then traced the line
of her jaw to the point of her chin, his hand at her throat.

Ava shifted her weight, refocused her eyes to meet his. The corner
of her mouth lifted da Vincian. Edgar felt the sear of her seeing. Pulling
her close by the nape of her neck, the small of her back, he dipped her,
kissed her.

ॐ

There is a moment after dueling rams rear, when they reach the peak of
their gathering: a split-second freeze-frame, an abeyance as the momentum collects. Then some unseen hand presses play, and they pour their
weight forward, brace for the blow.

There was some crash, some flag, some gunshot start. A cymbal—kiss—which held and held in one long note. Ava couldn't breathe, as if she was singing it.

Edgar's mouth was on hers, his broad cheekbone blocking her nostrils. She twisted, trying to break free, pushed against the brute of him while groping behind her on the table, grappling for anything, for air. Among teacups, silk flowers, and limp lengths of lace, her fingers grasped the handle of a knife. She pulled it to her chest, then pushed it into his.

The kiss broke. Air rushed to Ava's lungs. Edgar looked down at the hilt held against him. He covered her hand with his and slowly pushed away her white-knuckled fist. With a click, the blade sprang back out of the plastic handle.

"The boss ran the show with a watchful—show with a watchful eye," read Will in the other room.

There was a rustle from the rack of costumes closest to the door, and Ava looked up in time to see Fallon slip from the room. A dress trembled on its hanger.

From the dark of the wings, Fallon watched the love scene play out. Stage lighting limned the front edge of her haberdashered lank in silver, made a sliver moon of her. She ran a hand over her cropped blond hair to make sure it was still slicked back and, keeping her eyes onstage, shot the shirt cuffs farther from beneath the jacket of her three-piece suit, so that their margins just brushed her wrist's prominent knobs. Presently, the troupe had only one male actor, and as its owner-slash-manager-slash-playwright-slash-director-slash-actress, androgynous Fallon filled in wherever needed.

She waxed her face a touch further into the light, grew gibbous, to watch the audience watching Ava and Will onstage. The theater bled red, its shabby velvet seats mostly empty. Fallon ran a hand over her hair again. How could she determine if the play was a hit or not if no one came to see it?

"You're in a state, aren't you?" Chantal cooed, as though she'd caught the canary. Fallon turned to see her bounce a blond lock of hair over her shoulder, addressing Edgar. Although they were more than two feet apart, the fanfare of Chantal's bosom was nearly brushing the bow of Edgar's swan breast.

Behind them, a papier-mâché UFO hung from the ceiling above a rack of Beefeater costumes, and an upright piano stood back-to-back with its cardboard counterpart. Leaning against more dramatic detritus near the stage controls, Edgar could barely stand. His whitewashed face was framed by feathers at the base of the swan's neck, which rose above him like a periscope. Only his fingers emerged from the wrist-slits under his swan wings, all his muscle muffled. Chantal playfully punched his shoulder, and Edgar mumbled a grumble, whiffed a hand in her direction.

Fallon wondered whether it had been a good idea to write him in.

"I didn't think anyone could have worse stage fright than Will, especially now that he's playing lead," Chantal shout-whispered, loathe to lower her voice even while a performance was underway. "But here you are, all atremble." She toyed with a feather on his swan breast. "I don't understand what there is to be afraid of. It's just attention. What's not to love?"

Fallon waned back into the dark. "Not everyone likes being looked at," she muttered.

"Will told me once that when he steps out of the wings into the light and moves toward the beam of the spot, it's like dying," Chantal continued. "And I agree. But for me—"

"It's"—Fallon lifted the back of her hand to her forehead and raised her chin, dipping her hair into the light spilling from the edge of the stage—"heaven."

Chantal rolled her eyes. "Always putting words in my mouth."

"It's part of the job, my little puppet." Fallon shrugged. "But even when I haven't, I can usually guess what they're going to be."

"One of these days, I'm going to surprise you."

"I'd love that."

"Don't be so sure." Chantal turned back to Edgar, licked her lips. "Will the stage be death or heaven for you? I wonder."

In reply, Edgar let out a full-volume groan, and the women rushed to shush him. Writing him into the play may have been a bad idea, Fallon thought, but hiring him as set designer was another matter. His talent for trompe l'oeil lent veracity to the troupe's sets and productions.

Fallon turned back to the scene onstage, in which Will knelt before a seated Ava, pleading with her to be his. The sunlit tips of ripples in the painted swan pond center stage seemed almost to move, and the parkland on the backdrop was perfect: wild enough to appear romantically pastoral while groomed enough to demonstrate its high cost to maintain. Edgar had outdone himself. The light looked as though you could step into it. There was a boathouse stage right, constructed from repurposed timber. Stage left, a manor house's veranda swept nearly to the water, in which floated a wooden, swan-shaped boat. It was the start of the twentieth century, and everyone was dressed for dinner.

Ava stood and made her way to the veranda's white railing. This was the cue for sunset, but the light failed to shift.

Fallon turned back to Edgar, whisper-hissed, "Lights!"

His eyes were black and glassy, pupils dilated by dark and drink. After a beat of delay, he slapped a hand onto the control panel, bumping the brightness higher for a second before reddening it with a downslide. The red woke him. Fallon noticed Edgar notice Ava. He teetered a few steps, and his pale face rosied in the glow from the stage.

Overlooking the pond, Ava sipped ginger ale from her coupe glass. Will, not much taller and a bit soft in the middle, approached her.

HENRY

You can't get rid of me that easily.

ANNE

This is all so tiresome, Henry, really. I'm marrying Charles Darling in two weeks.

Will closed the gap between them.

HENRY

Until that happens, I'll wait. *Dum spiro, spero*: while I breathe, I hope.

Ava opened it again.

ANNE

Dumb is right. Honestly, Henry, you're as ridiculous as our swan. Just look at him—in love with a swan-shaped boat. He makes love to deafened ears, dedicated like a knight to a cause that can't love back.

This was Edgar's cue, but he didn't enter. He moaned, a sign of awareness, but with no time to await a second, Fallon and Chantal stuffed his hands deeper into his wings' wrist-slits, grabbed him by the plumage, and shoved him onstage. He entered the scene with a honk, having gripped too tightly the bicycle horn Chantal had sewn inside his right wing to produce swan sound. For a moment, he looked destined to trip; instead, he jogged a few steps, caught his legs up to his head, and regained balance. In the time he took to recover, blinking, several feathers wafted through the reddened light in a lazy pendulum swing to the stage. Then Edgar folded his wings at his sides, bent at the waist and knees to set the swan body parallel to the floor, and commenced a steady, skating glide across the pond, moving back and forth before the wooden swan boat with a grace and bravado that put Fallon in mind of a matador. She'd never seen this side of him.

Ava's mind seemed to go somewhere too, as she watched. Fallon tried to make eye contact, to reassure her that the scene was back under control, but Ava's attention was on Edgar. It took Will placing his hand on her shoulder, an impromptu addition, to return her to the scene.

HENRY
And I'll keep courting you, loving you, as long as that swan loves. We both mate for life, you see?

Ava sipped her ginger ale.

ANNE
They'll be putting the boat away for the night now. It will be good for you to see the pain that attends such a life.

At this, the doors to the boathouse were pushed open from within by an unseen stagehand, who slowly reeled the swan boat inside by its rope. Each theater on the tour had a small staff available for hire, but Fallon hated to use them. The troupe could hardly afford the help, and Edgar could usually handle the work. She knew she'd been indulgent, refusing a plywood or cardboard swan, but the play called for one with a heartbeat, one that could stand in stark contrast to the swan boat, which was now disappearing into the boathouse.

The doors closed behind it, leaving Edgar alone on the painted waves. His movements grew bolder, more flailing. He honked.

ANNE
See? When they take her from him—

Edgar honked once more, glided toward Ava, and spread his wings
wide before her. This hadn't been blocked.

ANNE
She doesn't struggle to stay.

Edgar flapped, beating his swan breast. Then he dropped his wings,
crouched to sag the swan lower on the water.

ANNE
She can't care, and neither can—

There was more to the line. There was more to the scene too, but Edgar
stole it. He lifted his swan head and breast and let out a series of honks,
distress crescendoing. Ava tried to continue with the scene, but even if
she could have been heard, its momentum was dead. Emotion, somehow, was killing the mood. The audience shifted uncomfortably, and
the creaking seats and shuffling feet brought them back to the theater.
Edgar flapped chaotically, then crashed the costume's breast into the
boathouse doors. He clattered against them, rattling the flimsy hinges,
went at them again, wingspan wide, then made one last crash and slid to
a kneel-slump, covering his swan head with a lifted wing before growing
still. There were several beats of silence, then a few unsure claps across
the audience, drizzle droplets scattered on the surface of a pond.

Upstage, Ava watched. Fallon saw her, saw something had happened.
She'd seen Ava look like this before. Since their former lead actor, Ben
Sterling, had left at the start of the season, Ava had somehow been bro-
ken, but now there was something else in her eyes, something asking.
Fallon hadn't seen this look in years.

Ava turned to the audience. Her voice wavered, tender but sure in
its scripting.

ANNE
Please—

For a second, Fallon thought she was addressing the house.

ANNE

Spend your love on someone worthy. Love—

She turned to Will, took his hands in hers.

ANNE

Should be a pleasure.

Cue Fallon. Relieved to be regaining control of the scene even in some small way, she strode from the wings through the visible portion of the manor house's interior and onto the bright veranda, somewhere both death and heaven, and opened her expression in boyish jest.

CHARLES

Give it up, Henry! Dinner's served. You can resume your wooing over trifle, where it's more suited.

Ava released Will's hands and followed Fallon's exeunt. The French doors closed, leaving Will to watch the swan alone. After a few beats of stillness, Edgar lowered his wing from his swan head and panto-mime-swam slowly away from the boathouse doors. Before exiting, he froze far stage right, glancing back at the boathouse, then at Will.

HENRY

We're true blue, aren't we, swan? But they're blueblood. How can we turn their wood to flesh?

Through the grid of the French doors' muntins, Fallon saw the theater's stagehand approach the edge of the wings nearest Edgar, as near the line of light as Edgar stood, teetering, from the dark. The man tugged on the curtain's rope several times to inch-worm it across the stage. When it closed, the audience smattered applause, tucked their programs beneath their seats, and stood, intermission drink orders already in mind.

Alone in the group dressing room, Ava removed the gold band from the fourth finger of her left hand—a place the Romans believed con-nected, via vein, directly to the heart. She dropped the band in a pouch

with her other costume jewelry, where it sank among tangled strands
of faux pearls, plastic cameos, knotted chains, and chandelier earrings
dripping with glass diamonds. She'd been wearing the ring in productions since high school whenever a marriage was called for. It was a real
wedding band (real gold and a real someone's, once) found cheap at a
pawnshop—a fake fake that made Ava's roles feel real.

She held out her left hand, bare fingers splayed. Where the ring had
worn, her finger was indented. The place looked weak as limb cut from
cast, with the close-pressed wrinkles of something newborn: a just-
hatched bird or just-dropped fawn, the feeling of air on it alien. Or
had its wrinkles been earned through experience? She'd certainly been
through enough.

Ava hauled her purse by its strap from where it hung on the back of
the metal folding chair at her vanity station. She unclasped it, unzipped
the discreet pocket in its lining, dipped in wrist-deep, and finger-sifted
past tampons, zit cream, a clamshell of birth control, a lucky charm—
things she carried but didn't want exposed. When her hand emerged, a
different ring dangled from her crooked finger. She swiped her thumb
across its face, clearing smears, and looked at it as though through a
loupe. Its sapphire, the size and color of an eye's iris, looked back.
Where stone met setting, the gem was crusted, set like a tooth in its
socket. Ava slipped the ring on her left ring finger and tried to push it
over the knuckle. It had always been tight, but now, once she wiggled it
over the bone with effort, it spun loosely where the costume band had
left its mark. Whichever way she turned her hand, the stone sank to the
bottom. Had she changed so much in four short weeks?

She'd been told the ring had been Ben's grandmother's; it had genuine history. However, whenever Ava put it on—including when Ben had
slipped it on her finger after proposing and again during their wedding
(playing the part of engagement ring and wedding band both)—she'd
feel herself slipping into character. Now was no different, except she
wasn't sure anymore what that role was. What could she say? Ben left.
Or he left her. Or he left her to decide, and she decided by not deciding,
left him by staying, by not leaving with him at the start of the season.
She hadn't spoken to him since, wasn't sure anymore if she was married
or not, except on paper.

Then there'd been Edgar's kiss. She hadn't taken much note of him
before, but the kiss and his lovelorn swan had sparked kind kindling,

tender tinder. His bruises had been flint. It had been so long since she'd felt. Was love beyond Ben possible?

Her heart fluttered. Fallon's voice strengthened in the hall, as though she'd turned up a dial, and Ava wouldn't be seen grieving. Fallon could read her so easily, and the breakup, if that's what it was, was still so new; she wasn't yet sure how to act.

Ava placed her left hand against her chest and fanned her fingers, stretched them straight. With her right, she tried to remove the ring. It wasn't so easy. She tugged, wiggling it side to side, but joint-stuck, it bit bone. Fallon's voice was nearly at the open door, and Ava had just enough time to plant her left hand in her lap and turn her back to the doorway before Fallon filled it, a black shadow in the tuxedo she always wore offstage.

"As you may have suspected, Edgar's out of commission, so the stagehand's helping us get him back to the train cars," Fallon said. "Would you like a ride?"

Leaning toward the mirror over a sapphire fulcrum, Ava peeled off her false lashes with her right hand and shook her head. "Thanks, but I'd rather walk."

Fallon leaned against the doorframe. "Are you okay? You seemed a bit distracted out there."

"I did?"

Fallon nodded, lifting an eyebrow. "While Edgar was onstage."

Ava continued to fuss surreptitiously with the ring in her lap. She could twist it from side to side, but it wouldn't move any farther toward the tip of her finger. "It was hard not to be distracted, really, what with him—the way he—his—all that melodrama."

"Right. It wasn't what we'd blocked, but it certainly stirred something up, didn't it?"

Ava couldn't meet Fallon's eye. She nodded lapward.

Fallon straightened, took her weight back onto her feet. "Enjoy your walk," she said, continuing down the hall.

Soon after, a wilted Edgar, face still pale and wearing only his paint-spattered tee and the black leggings that had served as swan legs, was half-dragged past the doorway between Will and the stagehand. The three barely fit the hall abreast. Chantal straggled past behind them.

When the door to the backstage exit slammed, Ava put her ring finger in her mouth. The metal clicked heavily against her teeth as she flooded the ring with saliva and worked it over the knuckle, then spit it into her palm. Her heart swelled at the bareness. Her future had been tied to Ben, but now Ava felt like Ava could be anything, become anyone. She couldn't imagine who.

She dropped the ring back into her purse lining's pocket and zzz'ed the zipper, snapped the clasp closed.

It was late. With her left hand, Fallon captured, pinning the wings of her black notebook open as if it was an insect on velvet. With her right, she created. The playwright wrote.

AT RISE

We are standing on the rail yard's gray gravel, three train cars camped before us. They're strung like pearls, ready to be lashed to the end of any passenger train headed the right direction. All it would take is a hook of the clasp.

We'll start far left, 'cause we're readers. The first is a windowless baggage car built in the fifties; this one brick red and built for theatrical baggage, of which we can all claim to carry. In it, characters and settings are created, costumes and props kept. Its fourth wall opens with the slide of a wide door for loading and unloading. The car is labelled Pennsylvania in gold, and it has a role, Romeo, billed beneath.

The second's the sleeper, and in it, anything can be dreamt. Above its stripe of windows, it reads Texas Zephyr. Dressed like a stainless-steel streamliner from the late thirties, it's in fact a Pullman heavyweight made in 1917, revamped to match the rest of the Zephyr, which crisscrossed the country from Dallas to Denver. With heavyweight steel painted silver and dark pinstripes to feign fluting, it's costumed in modern dress, guised in newfangledness.

The third one is our curtain call, the train's Fin or The End: an observation car from the tail of the century before last, as anonymous as audience, though a lot's been seen from its seats. It's wooden, painted a library green. Windows upon windows encourage observance, as does a platform at its end awned in green-and-white stripes. Its brim shades the view of two rails converging at horizon to an end point, period.

On the dot, the point of Fallon's pencil jolted a line. Out of the corner of her eye, she'd seen the other end of the observation car flicker with movement. She swiveled her armchair on its base at its place near the glass door to the observation platform. The car was a peninsula of window—everything not-glass, mahogany. A flotilla of wingbacks, club chairs, chesterfields, ottomans, and end tables of all styles and eras floated on its faded and threadbare Persian rug, and an antique sofa, wood-framed and upholstered in fox-hunting tapestry, lined one side of the car.

Fallon held still. There was a tinkle, and the crystal fringe on the farthest of three truncated chandeliers glissandoed ghostly. Keeping her eyes on the spot, she crept closer. When she was underneath, the fixture burst into music, and a sparrow slapped out from behind, landing on the center chandelier. It must have flown into the cars that afternoon, while Edgar was working with the baggage car's loading door open. The bird grappled for grip on the crystal, tilted its head to keep an eye on her. Fallon admired the precision of its little markings, the clockwork fold of its wings. Its breast bellowed with breath as it side-shuffled farther around the chandelier. Then Fallon noticed a ribbon of yellowed cloth tied around its pencil line of a leg.

A memory alighted. Standing in the center of the car, on the stage of its brightness, the playwright paged through her notebook.

The Russians tell of a queen who besieged a city. Eager to reach ceasefire, its residents offered honey and furs, but the queen assured them that all she desired was the trifling gift of a sparrow from each house. Once these terms were met, negotiations would begin the following morning.

On receiving the tribute, the queen gave a bird to each of her soldiers and ordered them to tie a strip of cloth dipped in sulfur to the birds' legs with a length of thread. As the sun set, they ignited the cloth and released the birds, which flew home to roost within the city walls, touching cote, coop, porch, roof, eave, and beam with flame. With every building burning at once, the fire was impossible to extinguish. The city burned to the ground.

Imagine, though, for a moment, the birds midair, pouring over the city walls, their wicks plumage-bright against the dusk. The scene set in motion, unstoppable. The city's gates still bolted fast. The place already vanquished.

Fallon lifted her eyes to the window but was confronted by her reflection. She'd written the passage at the makeshift desk in her sleeper compartment on the way to the troupe's first stop.

It was strange, the sparrow. The cloth especially. But sometimes coincidences happened. Things happened and she wrote them, or she wrote them and they happened. She chalked it to chance or hazard, pluck or luck, knew how easily the line of a story could be drawn between two points, how badly the mind desired a shape in the stars. Some people were readers. To them, life was imbued with meaning, begged interpretation. They looked overhead and saw Orion in the chaos, drew a bear or dipper. If Fallon had been a reader, she might have taken the sparrow as a sign, called herself a prophetess or witch, made meaning of it. But Fallon was a writer. When she saw a constellation, she saw the mind of the first person to point it out.

Fanning the ash of remembrance, she cleared the armchair from before the car's glass door, opened it, rolled her bicycle from where it leaned against the platform's railing, and propped the door open with its back wheel. The hum of the cars' generator seemed to warm the outside air, which was cool but not as cold as expected this far into winter. Fallon returned to the car's far end. Holding the wings of the book open to the bird, she flushed its pages in flight toward the open door. The sparrow thrash-flapped across the gap to the third chandelier and, pressured again by Fallon, flustered out into the night.

With the swan suit's head resting gently in her lap and lamplight haloing her long blond hair, Chantal almost looked innocent. Feather down floated in the air like dandelion fluff, or snow, depending on the season, like motes in sunslant.

It was night, though, and the baggage car was windowless. The space, packed with theatrical props, lent the feeling of being backstage. Painted scenery draped the wall holding the loading door. The rest were padded with racks of costumes, and a well-used, sturdy worktable filled most of the car's central space. It was strewn with flotsam: scraps of fabric, scissors, a measuring tape, spools of thread, wire hangers, and craquelured tubes of paint. Chantal sat on a stool behind it, and behind her, the wall was striped in shelves packed with all manner of items.

This costume meant more than most; Edgar had worn it. Chantal handled the body. Its head and neck had been dented by his performance that evening. She ripped the seams where the neck joined the breast and removed the batting. Where the fabric gaped like a wound, she dressed it. Running her hand inside the swan neck until she wore it like a sleeve, she puppeted its head toward her and reshaped the wire frame inside, then restuffed it with cotton batting.

Plumage flew free, and a draft churned up down, which drifted an updraft. Slow flakes swirled the inertia. As Chantal bobbed her heavy cleavage to the beat of the music piping through the earbuds connected to her phone, her robe parted, setting the stage for a specimen leg. From between terrycloth curtains emerged the hefty thigh's perfect surface, the calf's carved curve. Chantal uncrossed and crossed her legs. Stubble covered the revealed ankle's thick veins and bruises. The beat of the music picked up, and she leaned forward, drummed it onto her thighs—fleshy slap, hollow knock and back—then, wincing, ran her hands up under the robe, pulled her prosthetic leg free, and dropped it at her foot. The stiff neck of the swan costume hung from her lap, almost took its place.

Enter Ben. Ben stole every scene he entered, or so it seemed to Will, who, to better view his phone's screen, slid lower against the wall at the head of the unmade, narrow bed in his sleeper compartment. He'd washed the pomade from his hair but, with it still wet and its waves recombed into a side part above his round face, he looked virtually the same as onstage, except he'd added his glasses and wore only an under-shirt and striped boxers. Will's usual blue button-up and tan corduroy trousers hung from a hook on the opposite wall, and his dusty Chucks were strewn on the floor.

Ben's specialty was Shakespeare, and he'd committed fully to the Bard at the start of the season by joining The Rude Mechanicals, a Brooklyn-based Shakespearean troupe revered for its edgy adaptations. This had been surprising, but Will couldn't blame Ben for jumping at the chance to play somewhere so high profile and highbrow.

On the screen, Ben stalked the stage, halted, then hauled his body back. He wore an argyle sweater that reminded Will of a pair of socks—the ones he wore now. Will's left hallux thrust through the neckline of a hole in one. When Ben barked a line, something in furred and clawed Elizabethan English, Will repeated it, bowing the tip of his toe to each syllable. The performance was a toehold at homage, but he left off midline, regretted it as though Ben or God, or maybe even Fallon, was watching.

How would Will fill Ben's role—Ben's role in this week's play and every play, his place in the troupe? Will had only ever held supporting roles until his promotion at the start of the season, which he knew Fallon had offered him of necessity. She expected a lot, and the added pressure was making his stage fright worse than ever. He worried so much about flubbing a line, missing a mark, or forgetting a prop that he seemed to will disaster. This, in turn, made him worry more.

Onscreen, Ben started to swallow the next line, then spat it, snapping at the air as he let the words go, as though they'd been rent from him. A spray of spittle caught the stage lighting. Will sat a little straighter, backed up the video to watch the scene again. The struggle was exactly what he needed to add depth to his performance in the closing act of this week's play. He stood, swiping the script from his nightstand and rolling it open to the last act. As Will skimmed the lines and mentally blocked each scene, he felt a pulse of wildness ebb and flow within him. Then he let it loose, played the part of Ben.

Soft belly sucked in and head thrust low, Will paced the four-step length of his compartment. He prowled a spin-turn at the wall and re-traced his steps, ratcheting the pacing's pressure. At its apex, he halted, held himself still before the stage of the window framed in red velvet curtains, and tried to swallow the line which growled its way out.

"Rrrrrrrrrrrwhy," he shouted, then filled his lungs again with breath to bellow. "Not!" He held the last word back, lips closed, pushing the em but also restraining it. The hum tickled. It burned. He released the syllable. "Me!"

The still silence of the sleeper car was broken, and Will was shushed by the sound of Edgar rolling over in the adjacent compartment, dragging a limp arm across the wall above the head of his bed. Will looked up into the darkness of the window and, in its blankness, saw audience—all those black eyes, pupils wide in concentration, drinking in the light. His stomach lurched. When they'd leave the theater, they'd take some small part of him. Someone as vast as Ben could afford this, but Will worried there wasn't enough of him to give away.

❧

February 4
THE MIDWEST CHORUS | THEATER REVIEW
Cygnus Cygnus
The Troupe Adores
The Paramount Theater

Sparta, Iowa
Remaining performances: tonight at 8 p.m., tomorrow at 3 p.m.

In his *Gargantua and Pantagruel*, Francois Rabelais rated a litany of materials with which to wipe one's ass. The best he found was the pillowy down of a goose's neck, and on learning The Troupe Adores' forthcoming title would be *Cygnus Cygnus*, we daydreamed about the luxuriousness of using that swan as a torche-cul.

Long after our morning constitutionals, however, it's the swan we can't stop thinking about. Newcomer Edgar Cosentino, who heretofore remained backstage as the troupe's new set designer, stole the second act from swan dive to song.

As feathers float on the water but do not get wet, Mr. Cosentino's performance was both of the play and above it, his emotion unsullied by artifice, but like a fallen hero on some Viking battlefield, we too longed for some swan-suit-wearing Valkyrie to whisk us to a better world, or at least a better theater.

Morning sun glared through the small window in the sleeper car's bathroom, and Edgar glared back. Each press of brush on tooth made his head throb. He spat the paste into the sink with all the force of his regret.

The bathroom was hardly larger than a coffin. In its center, circumscribed by its door, a narrow shower stall, a pedestal sink, and a toilet topped by a plastic shelving unit, there was just enough room for one smallish person (which Edgar wasn't) to stand, crowded by the loofahs and makeup bags, blow dryers and robes hung and strung from every vertical surface. Edgar turned on the water, filled his cupped hands, and lifted them to his mouth to rinse out the toothpaste but, in doing so, knocked several heavy, wet towels from their hooks. When he turned to pick them up, his backside bumped the pedestal sink, causing aerosol cans to clatter from their spots beside the faucets. They rolled and clinked to a stop against the edge of the shower stall. Edgar's head pounded as he bent to retrieve them.

What he needed was coffee, fresh air, a paintbrush in hand. Only work would help him escape his poisoned body. He reached for the handle of the bathroom's plastic accordion door and pulled, but as usual, the door's bottom track stuck while the top glided fine, setting the door at a slant. Edgar struggled to correct it, then gave up. He stepped over the bottom half, wrestled the top as far back as it would go, and pushed his way through the diagonal.

The sleeper car was quiet. Edgar's head throbbed in time with his footsteps as he made his way down the corridor to his compartment, careful to close its door softly behind him. On the small table inside was a flaccid paper sack with just enough coffee beans for a cup and a half. Edgar didn't want to wake the others, but he had to run his small electric grinder; every atom of his body cried for caffeine. He gritted his teeth and pressed his thumb on the button. It roared three, four, five seconds. When he lifted his finger, he paused, heard no stirrings in the car save his head. Then his electric kettle binged. He poured coffee grounds and boiling water into the French press, sending up a whiff of wakefulness, and carried it and a faded mug down the sleeper car's corridor to the baggage car.

As soon as he crossed the vestibule between the cars, though, Edgar wanted to go back. It must have been later in the morning than he'd realized, for four heads turned from the battered worktable. Fallon was directing. She and Will, in slacks and white lab coats, stood before a tarnished, full-length mirror, which leaned against a tightly packed costume rack. Ava, in a spandex dress, stood on the pedestal of an overturned crate as Chantal stuck pins wherever the fabric sagged.

Chantal smirked out a singsong good morning.

Fallon made a low bow to Edgar. "Quite the debut. I had a feeling the role would resonate, but I never in my wildest dreams thought you'd dive so deeply."

"He dove clear to the bottom of that bottle," Chantal said.

Edgar freed a hand by hanging his mug from a finger beneath the French press. He rasped his stubble. "Sorry. I—"

"Don't be sorry," interrupted Fallon. "You were great. I should make all the roles silent. That way, no one could mangle my lines." She lifted an eyebrow at Chantal.

Edgar set the French press and mug on the worktable's scarred surface. "You told me the role would—" He cloaked his face in innocence, strained his voice falsetto, and tipped up his chin. "'Pretty much be scenery,' that 'no one will even notice you among the paint and feathers.'"

"He doesn't do a bad you," Chantal said to Fallon.

They laughed, even Ava. Edgar could see her teeth.

"Except her voice is a little lower," Will muttered, kneading a few fingertips into his doughy cheek.

"The swan shouldn't have been much more than a prop," Fallon said to Edgar. "But you made it something. I knew you could do this. Next time—"

"No, no. I'm done," Edgar said, backing away. "Don't count on me for any more roles."

"But you're a natural," said Will. "And with Ben—" He pulled himself up short, glanced at Ava.

"What he means is that it would be nice to have another man for small parts," Fallon said. "It would free us up, allow us to—"

"Look, I agreed to play this swan," Edgar said. "So I'll finish out the last two performances."

"Far more soberly, I hope?" Fallon asked.

Edgar gave a small nod, and Chantal shucks-snapped her fingers. "But don't count on me to play more parts," he said. "After this, I'm never acting again. Never again."

He'd said it again. He'd said it again, so she knew it wasn't true. Fallon watched Edgar slide open the baggage car's wide loading door, creating a proscenium unto the world at large. As he hopped off the edge of the car, she turned back to the full-length mirror. In the spotted reflection, a black cloud of damaged backing obscured the top half of Edgar's head. For a second, it hung over him like a wrong thought, then he turned and walked out of the frame.

Fallon set her notebook on the table to consult the table within it.

Grand Tour of the Continent

The Troupe Adores | Winter 2017

This will be an exploratory season. Each week, we'll perform one repertoire favorite, then give one new show the opportunity of weekend performances with matinees. In the way of Darwin, successful new plays will replace merely adequate standards in subsequent seasons. The tallest giraffe eats best. The brightest bird mates most. The fastest gazelle lives.

✓ *Tending Bedside, Besides*   Jan. 17, 18
The Notre Dame
Versailles, Michigan

✓ ~~(To be written)~~ *The Three-Piece*   Jan. 20, 21, 22
The Spyglass
Odense, Ohio

✓ *So Dreamt the Maharaja*   Jan. 24, 25
The Moonlight
Cologne, Ohio

✓ ~~(To be written)~~ *Le Deluge*   Jan. 27, 28, 29
The Paradise
Stockholm, Indiana

✓ *Sore Eros Rose*   Jan. 31, Feb. 1
The Premonition
Krakow, Illinois

~~(To be written)~~ *Cygnus Cygnus*   Feb. 3, 4, 5
The Paramount
Sparta, Iowa

St. St.   Feb. 7, 8
The Reminisce
Madrid, Kansas

(To be written)   Feb. 10, 11, 12
The Lyric
Lisbon, Kansas

The Aqueduct of Sylvius   Feb. 14, 15
The Gesture
Milan, Nebraska

(To be written)   Feb. 17, 18, 19
The Fox
Paris, South Dakota

Let Them Eat Cake The Midnight Rome, North Dakota	Feb. 21, 22
(To be written) The Mirage Lyon, Wisconsin	Feb. 24, 25, 26
The Singed Songbird The Conflagration Berlin, Indiana	Feb. 28, March 1
(To be written) The Looking Glass Warsaw, Michigan	March 3, 4, 5

Fallon placed a check mark beside *Cygnus Cygnus*. There were two more performances left, but it was time to start thinking about the next play.

She was supposed to be a bride, a wife. Ava sat onstage at the dining table in the slice of manor house that could be seen through the set's veranda. Behind her, center stage, Will rehearsed the third act. The scene felt different without her gown, lonelier. Ava felt like Ava. While her end of the table was set with cloth and china, silver and crystal, the half hidden from the audience was bare, chairless. A script with a curling cover lay on the naked plywood, lost or forgotten. The difference, Ava thought, was whether anyone would miss it.

From center stage, Will roared. "Rrrrrrrwhy! Not! Me?"

Why *not* me? thought Ava, then of Ben. She thought of him often in the theaters, the train cars, in bed, thought of him in every small-town diner, bar, and shop, places like those they'd visited together on tour, once and then never again. She thought of him most when she spoke her lines of the repertoire favorites to Will. The only place she could forget Ben was during the new plays. Ava didn't think of Ben where he'd never been. Eager to re-enter the scene, she looked back at it over her shoulder.

Fallon's clapping rang out in the empty theater. "That's right, my little coin toss!" she called to Will from a theater seat. "That's where you belong in this scene! There, between wanting and not wanting. Now once more, from the top."

That was Ava's cue. She rose from the table and moved into the wings, where she waited to go on, waited for the start of the scene that would let her forget. She could see Edgar on the other side of the stage, waiting in the wings opposite. The small lights illuminating the control board lit his face. He was handsome without his silly costume. His eyes met hers, and the French door's muntins felt like crosshairs.

On his motion, the lights came up, and Ava entered.

Fallon took a messy bite of gyro and wiped her chin with one of the two tissue-thin napkins she'd been given with it, turning the paper transparent with tzatziki sauce. There was one last sunny park bench in Sparta's busy town square, and she leaned her bike against its back and sat. An ocean of lawn stretched between her and the white-columned courthouse presiding over the square, and families marooned on pic-nic-blanket rafts were acting as though it were spring.

Fallon was part of the production. Her black tux jacket was folded loosely on the bench beside her, and although the air was cool on the skin exposed by the tank top she always wore beneath it, the sun was unseasonably warm.

The courthouse was filigreed with pediments, capitals, and cornices. Carefully setting the gyro in its wrapper on the bench, Fallon unfolded her jacket to extract a yellowed *Guidebook to Greece* from its inner pocket. Its pages frilled soft beneath her thumb and released a smoke-and-leather bookshop scent. When Fallon found what she was looking for, she held the book open on her lap, took a bite of gyro. She'd scheduled The Grand Tour for a reason: to see the world.

Start your day by stopping at Sparta's impressive neoclassical City Hall, a favorite of visitors and locals. Constructed in 1909 and designed by G. Katsaros, the building restores a glory the ancient town once held. The square is surrounded by cafés and restau-rants, perfect for enjoying a long lunch.

From City Hall, head north to the edge of town, where lie ruins of the Tomb of Leonidas, brave king who led Sparta in the Battle of Thermopylae. Beyond it, you'll find the ruins of the ancient theater, which dates from the second century BC. It was one of ancient Greece's largest, seating 16,000 spectators, and remains in use today.

A tzatziki-sodden piece of lamb dropped onto the page. Fallon negotiated the gyro back onto the bench and, holding the paperback open with her elbow, tore off a corner of the gyro's foil-like paper wrapper and used it to scoop up most of the sauce. Then she looked up from the book, letting her vision drift on a current of wind to the edge of town. She could see, ahead, a crumbling stone wall and, beyond, The Paramount's weathered sign.

There were a few last bits of lamb left in the bottom of the soggy wrapper. Fallon tongued them up and trashed the wet wad. Then she slipped her jacket back on, dropped the book in its pocket, swung a tuxedo-slippered foot over the bike, and coasted down the lawn toward the theater, serpentining to miss picnics.

In the dimly lit dressing room, Will drew a slip of paper from his top hat. His mouth filled with hot saliva. He swallowed it, took a deep breath.

"The walled town—walled town—" he read. "The walled town was seized—seized—without a fight."

All week every week, Will's stage fright crescendoed to a Saturday-night peak. More seats were sold for that performance, and more worrisome than the denser concentration of audience was that the audience, on those nights, concentrated more intensely. The air buzzed with a well-rested attention that never reared its head during weeknight or matinee performances. On Saturday nights, the audience was wholeheartedly there, the better to escape.

Will could already hear them gathering beyond the curtain, and he swallowed again, drew another slip of paper.

"The la-last sw-switch—sw-itch, switch—cannot be turned off."

Backstage, the playwright wrote.

WILL CONNAUGHT, a high-school senior, performs onstage in the echoing auditorium. His drama teacher, BUD MONCRIEFF, watches from a seat in the third row of an otherwise empty audience.

MONCRIEFF

No, no, no, no, no! (*Raising both hands as he rises from his seat and moves down the aisle toward the stage*) Will, my man, you are Danny Zuko! Danny doesn't hesitate! He doesn't wince!

WILL

I know. I— It's just—

MONCRIEFF

You've gotta be intimidating up there! You're the guy who calls the shots! Be a guy we wanna watch!

WILL

Right, but—but when I think about everyone watching, I—

MONCRIEFF

Perfectly natural. Perfectly. Everyone gets a little nervous about performing. But you need to channel that energy into the scene. Use it productively!

WILL

I worry I'll mess up. Forget the lines. Miss a mark.

MONCRIEFF

The line between fear and energy is thin. (*He shapes his hands into a pyramid, the tip of which touches his chin.*) What is fear?

WILL

Uh—

MONCRIEFF

(*He sits on the edge of the stage, and Will squats to meet him.*) Fear is a sign of life. It means you're alive and that you care. You have to embrace the fear, make it part of your truth. What are you afraid of? What's the worst that can happen up there?

WILL

I make a mistake: forget a line or start the wrong scene or forget to bring a prop out. Then my mistake snowballs, throws off the actor who has the next line, which throws off another. At that point, the whole scene's blown, which affects the rest of—

MONCRIEFF

You're not out there alone. If you make a mistake, you have the rest of the cast to rely on. They'll help you get back on script. You don't have to do it all yourself. (*He walks back to his seat, pulls a sun-bleached, cheaply bound manual from his messenger bag, and hands it to WILL.*) Here. I want you to have this. I think it'll help.

WILL

Telecom Wireless Signal Quality Testing Manual?

MONCRIEFF

I used to be on an on-the-ground testing team. My velvet voice got me the job. (*He cracks his knuckles.*) Even working actors sometimes need day jobs. We'd drive around, make calls from different areas, then (*opening the manual to a dog-eared page and pointing to the text*) we'd read these: Harvard sentences.

WILL

Harvard sentences?

MONCRIEFF

Phonetically balanced for testing certain sounds. We'd read them over cellular phones to ensure every sound was audible, able to be differentiated. Bees and vees, for example.

WILL

What am I supposed to do with this?

MONCRIEFF

Read from it! Read the sentences aloud! What you need is a vocal exercise. A sturdy warm-up ritual helps with nerves, settles the stomach. The sentences will also prepare the voice and tongue for the stage.

WILL flips through the book half-heartedly.

MONCRIEFF

Are you interested right now, or do you just *look* interested?

WILL

Uh—I—

MONCRIEFF

Trick question. (*He waves a hand dismissively, heading back up the aisle to his spot in the audience.*) It doesn't matter. If you look interested, you are, to the audience—maybe even interesting too, if you're lucky. Either way, they win; they get some truth. (*He props his feet on the back of the seat in front of his.*)

Truth is not necessarily reality, you know. Sometimes they're the same, but not always. When you add truth to reality, art happens; otherwise, you're just a guy speaking lines. Now try it again, from the top of the second act, please.

The dark teemed with eyes. A bead of sweat welled from a pore on Will's brow, rolled down the bridge of his nose and, from there, unchecked down his round cheek. In untucked shirtsleeves, hair mussed, he staggered along the edge of the pond at the front of the stage, holding a swan's long flight feather. Moonlight shone from a light overhead. Clenching his hand to his chest, Will boiled a wildness within and used the steam to dash on all fours up the steep embankment from pond to veranda. From there, he crept to the edge of its civilized tile and peeked through the railing.

The interior of the manor house blazed. Inside, Ava sat in white, a bride at a long table, with Fallon beside her in a three-piece suit suitable for a husband. With the audience, Will watched them dine as man and wife, then held the feather up for a second. He placed it at the edge of the veranda and, maintaining an air of defeat, rolled onto his back and slid down the embankment.

It was Will's moment. He held still so as to still the house, not rushing forward but propelling the thought of it, keeping himself back, letting his pot froth over. When he could hold the lid on no longer, he flung himself center stage and lifted his hands to the audience. There was a stirring, as though a breeze blew. They may have been moved.

"Wh—wh—why?"

The syllables stuck. He could loose them only as though removing a speck of tobacco from the tongue, bucking it forward with the lips to where a fingertip could lift it. Will tried to fill his lungs again, but his tight diaphragm allowed in only a little air.

"N—not-me?"

The third word fell out with the second, and the line was said. He could never have it back. The scene had ended, and with it, the play. The audience's applause beat too soon, as though they were brushing their hands of him.

&

February 5

Dawn yawned bluer. Edgar pushed down the narrow corridor of the sleeper car like the plunger in the French press he carried clinking against a dented aluminum travel mug. The car creaked about his body, and his body creaked about his heart, which hung as a clapper in the bell of him. It was time to work.

As he made toward the baggage car, Chantal's accordion door opened, and a man slipped out of her compartment in a rugby shirt. Its three buttons were undone, the cotton collar half standing and half tucked under. His feet were bare, and a pair of well-worn boat shoes dangled by the heels from the first two fingers of his left hand, the arm of which was draped in windbreaker. He lifted the shoes to Edgar by way of greeting.

It was no strange sight, even after such little time with the troupe, for a man to emerge from Chantal's compartment, but this morning it felt like intrusion. Although Edgar wasn't completely at ease in the private cars, they were becoming a respite, especially when he was alone. To have to don a public face before sunrise, and to do so to meet a man Chantal had only just met, tolled low notes within him.

Edgar passed the man in the narrow corridor. This forced them face to face, as though circling for a fistfight. The French press steamed between them. The man's eyes were bloodshot and crusted. He smiled a self-satisfied smile, and Edgar reciprocated with a tightening of his face that was closer to a sneer. After he'd passed, the man followed him down the corridor.

Every hair attuned behind him, Edgar crossed the vestibule's bright light and entered the dark of the baggage car, made darker, for a second, by the man's shadow. Then footsteps clanged down the vestibule's metal stairs, and the car grew lighter, stilling the clapper of Edgar's bell.

Having scored an equator on the skin of the orange, Fallon rotated the fruit and reset the knifepoint to cut a meridian. When the start of the line met its end, she tore a quarter of the peel from its pith in a single motion, releasing a citrus mist. The sound was matched across the observation car by Edgar's first long line of a sketch in pencil.

At his feet, Chantal painted the toenails of her prosthetic leg the red of the threadbare rug, knee tucked tightly at her throat. Will lay across the tapestried sofa behind the mask of his script, and Ava played solitaire in the armchair closest the end of the car. The troupe was killing the last hours until curtain, playing at leisure with work hanging over their heads.

Such rote work too. Fallon knew that by matinee each week, the troupe was ready to move on. They'd already performed the play twice before a full-price evening audience. The review had been written, its fate cast, and they itched to pack their sets and costumes and move on to the next town, next play, next day and chance to make a name for themselves.

Fallon placed half the naked fruit beside its piled peel on a paper towel set on the arm of the chesterfield. She lifted the other half to her mouth and pushed the tip of her tongue into the slit between two sections to peel one off. The air was misted again with citrus, and Fallon rubbed her wrists together as if she'd applied perfume, took a sniff. Will sneezed.

"You'd better stop memorizing," Chantal told him without looking up from her nail polish, her voice tight from the knee at her throat. "It sets better when you let your head rest."

"I know, I know," replied Will from behind the script. "I'm almost done."

"The *play's* almost done," she said, eyes fixed on the bristles of the little brush as she swept it from bottle to toe. "It's already matinee. It'd be more worth your time to start on the next one."

Will lowered his script. "You know it throws me when I—"

"I mean," she continued, "we'll probably never even perform it again. It didn't sell too well, did it? Not that I think that's any of *our* faults—at least, certainly not Edgar's." She turned her head toward him and rested her cheek on her knee. "They loved your performance. Besides," she said, turning back to her toes, "I'm hardly in the thing."

Fallon held up one long finger as she worked to rotate a too-large section of orange in her mouth. She chewed, swallowed, and started to speak, but a piece of the fruit lodged in her throat. She coughed, forcing it out, but before she could get a word in, Chantal had started up again.

"Shaken, not stirred," she said in a low brogue. "Shaken, not stirred."

Will's script lowered. "Shaken, not stirred—stirred."

"Not bad," Chantal acknowledged. "But it's more like, 'Shhhhaken. Shhhhaken.'"

Fallon swallowed. "The face comes first. Expression is key for turning impression to impersonation, or even possession."

Will pouted, cathedraled the back of his throat. "The name is—" He adjusted, tuning his features and testing the voice's pitch, stress, and rasp. "The name is Bond, James Bond."

Chantal lit up. "Oooh! That was a good one."

A pink blush rushed up his neck and spread across his cheek. "Right?"

"See?" said Fallon. She picked some pith from the fruit. "It's all in the face."

Chantal muttered something into her knee.

"What was that?" Fallon asked.

"Now a touch more gravel." Chantal lifted her face to Will. "The name is Bond."

"Shaken, not stirred. Shake—shaken not stirred. The name is Bond, James Bond."

"To become another, you have to hit it just so," Fallon said. "And when you do, suddenly the person's in the room, summoned—even the actor becomes spectator."

"If you know so much, let's hear yours," Chantal said.

"You know I don't do impressions," Fallon said, "only original material. Besides, I prefer to be stirred, not shaken."

Chantal shot a flat look. "Edgar?"

Edgar shook his head. "Not my thing."

"Come on, every man has a Sean Connery," Will said. "The name is Bond, James Bond."

Edgar kept sketching. "How about Ava? I'm sure she does a great Bond, or Connery, or whoever."

Ava's voice emerged from behind the dark fleece of hair that hung over her spread of cards. "If you'd been here longer, you'd know this is *their* thing."

A queen slapped a king, burying his heart with her spade.

Despite the matinee's score of crinkling candy wrappers and blown noses, despite the old ladies who, accompanied by more old ladies, spent the second act searching their purses, the warm spotlight was a greenhouse, and in it, Ava throve. In it, there was only thriving, for in a play, nothing is a setback—neither thwart nor war nor loss. Hindrance, too, is headway, advances the plot toward some predetermined end. In a play, everyone has a role, place, and purpose; everything's necessary.

From the veranda, Ava watched Edgar's swanning, became one more member of the audience. His later performances had been sober, but even so, she could still see the wounds. Onstage, he wore all his bruises, knocked a chink in her wall. It hurt but was worth it.

Edgar hadn't approached her since the other night. Ava ached, waited. She hoped for and dreaded such a moment. The closest he'd come was drawing her into the troupe's conversation earlier that day, but she'd snapped. Some instinct guarded against him. She'd watched herself react the way she'd watched, as a girl, her unbidden fist swing to strike a boy who'd startled her in a dark hallway. This afternoon, cringing and unable to stop them, she'd heard her words fire knee-jerk and strike. Maybe this cruelty was for his protection, maybe hers.

She wasn't sure he knew that she was married. (Then again, she wasn't sure she really was.) The close quarters of train and stage made the troupe value what little privacy they had, and Fallon frowned on gossip. Likely, no one had told Edgar about Ben. Ava certainly hadn't. How could she explain to another what she didn't understand herself?

Being married had meant the script of her life was written, but when Ben left or she left him, they'd torn the paper up. For the first time in a long time, Ava wondered what would happen next.

Night Travel

First, a spotlight. A spot to set the scene, lure the eye. Then, from the dark behind, a train enters with a wail. It floats the note—fermata-prolonged, lasting as an opera's last—through the air behind it like steam, its lungs afire with press of breath until none's left.

So often she was alone in someone's company. Ava looked up at Will from the open physics textbook in her lap. He was asleep on the observation car's tapestried sofa. Dreaming, he groaned and stirred, and she thought how odd it was that he could be anywhere right now, might be someone else entirely. Ava took a drag of her cigarette, then set it in a small brass ashtray and slid her spiral notebook closer on the end table beside her armchair. In the evenings, she liked to post up in the car's last seat, the one that looked out the back of the train, and solve problems.

For most of the day, she'd been spotlit, unable to escape herself. The stage lighting made it difficult to see past its edge, and now the reading lamp over her shoulder did the same to the dark landscape the train traversed. Night made a mirror of the black glass.

Ava returned her attention to the book.

> Newton's first law of motion states that, unless acted upon by an outside force, a body at rest will remain at rest and a body in motion will remain in motion.

She knew it to be true. Choice lent life inertia. A marriage is a body of two traveling together. When she and Ben wed, it gave them a push, made it harder to stop or change direction—like the train: once you boarded, you were bound to its destination. There was no stopping, no reversing (unless some stalled car or cow intervened). Once the journey was, it was.

> Newton's second law of motion states that an object's change of motion depends on the magnitude and direction of the force and the mass of the object, which can be described:

$$F = ma$$

Force is equal to mass times acceleration. Ava pressed the equation into the paper of her notebook, guided by its ruled lines. When Ben left her or she him at the start of the season, what force had knocked or drawn them apart? Something had changed. While Ben's trajectory took him to The Rude Mechanicals, she'd stayed on with The Troupe Adores' winter tour as planned. Was her inaction an action, a decision to live her life without him?

Unless—Ava lifted the cigarette to her lips, left it there, and leaned over the notebook. Unless there'd been another force acting on their marriage, one unknown to her. Had she grown too complacent, too happy to drift the same track indefinitely as he restlessly set his sights on another life, another—she dared think it—wife? A slip of smoke stung her eye, which welled—

> Newton's third law of motion states that for every action, there is an equal but opposite reaction.

—but she wouldn't cry. Ava forced the smoke out through her nostrils, closed the book.

When Ava's book shut, Will woke. He was laid amongst the hedges and logs woven on the observation car's tapestried sofa. Hunting parties on horseback leapt several, and he joined the hunt as the last grasp of sleep released him. As far as Will could tell, there was no fox. He slid the tented script off his soft chest, tented his knees. Before falling asleep, he'd been learning his lines for the troupe's next production. It was one from their repertoire, which he'd played before, but never lead.

To learn a role, Will would read a line, look up and recite it in his mind, read the next, recite, read, recite, recite, test himself against the text, read, correct himself, recite. He would recite again, committing it. Sometimes he would inject himself in the script, catch himself replacing a word with one he used more often or saying a phrase the way it felt more natural. Then he would stop, start over. When he thought he had it, he rested to let it set in. It only cemented when he rested.

Will turned to look toward the observation car's last armchair. Its back was to him, but he smelled smoke, could just make out Ava's bony elbow protruding over what he could see of the chair's arm. He slid the top of his phone from his pocket, saw it was nearly midnight, and took a deep breath. They were on.

❧

The relief he'd felt after the matinee was buoying, but it hadn't lasted. Edgar was on edge. He nested the last plastic boulder atop the stack of them in the corner of the baggage car and wiped his hands on his faded black jeans. Although the place looked a mess of costumes, backdrops, and props, there was a Tetris logic to its packed piles, ensuring every bit of space was used.

The long wall that held the loading door was thickly padded with painted backdrops hung from hooks on a ceiling track. They could be drawn like a curtain when the loading door was open. Edgar pried open a rusted stepladder. He climbed it with one end of a rolled canvas in hand and slipped the grommets on the ceiling hooks one by one, mounting and dismounting the ladder as he moved along the wall. When the last was in place, he dropped the roll, letting the veranda scene unfurl to the floor. Edgar was back in the swan pond, unloved. He spun around so he wouldn't have to face it, but as he did, a ghostly visage in the tarnished, full-length mirror startled him.

It was his own. He'd hastily wiped off most of his white makeup backstage before breaking down the sets, but smears still whitewashed his eyebrows and blanched his dark hairline. Edgar reached for a metal toolbox, dented and flaking army-green paint, which sat on one of the lower shelves on the wall behind the worktable. From it, he retrieved a paint-stained rag and a small bottle of rubbing alcohol. The makeup came off easily as he relayed the rag between the bottle's mouth and his face. When the work was finished, he looked about, empty-handed, for more.

Edgar dreaded the between-nights that took place after the last performance in one town and before the troupe's arrival in the next, travel nights they spent in the no-man's land between towns, between plays—between, even, days—when they met in the bar car at midnight. His one consolation was that meeting; it grounded him. For the others, it served as a wrap party, a time to relax and celebrate a closed show. For Edgar, it served as distraction. At the start of the tour, he'd tried to steer clear—he wasn't much of a joiner—but soon thought better. On between-nights, there was little work to take his mind off the things he didn't think about.

The rest of the troupe had already passed through the car on their way to the bar, and Edgar knew they were expecting him. After a glance at the baggage car's insular door, he made for the one at the other end that led to the public cars. Along the way, a vintage camera on one of the shelves caught his eye. He lifted it. Unsure if it held film, he tested a shot of a still life composed on the baggage car's worktable: Ava's crumpled red gloves on the battered, paint-spattered wood. It was loaded; he could tell from the click. Satisfied, Edgar left through the door that led to the train at large, stopping in the vestibule to snap a photo of the sign marked Private on the door he closed behind him.

The other end of the vestibule opened on a passenger car filled with a conversational hum that reminded Edgar of an audience's chatter before curtain. Rows of seats were filled with people sitting obediently in their assigned spots, looking forward to the spectacle of the train's destination. Edgar made his way up the aisle as if stepping onstage, rubbing a rough hand at the back of his neck where he felt the sightlines prickle. He expected relief in the next vestibule, but there, with the noise of the track and a cool wind whipping through the seam where the two cars met and separated with the train's movement, he only felt more exposed.

The next door opened on a dining car, bleached and starched and gleaming. As Edgar entered, the vestibule's clanking and clacking track was civilized to clinking where cutlery touched china, to tinkling where ice bumped glass.

Although the troupe ate for free on the train whenever the private cars were hitched, Edgar had only once made the mistake of dining here. During his first train trip with the troupe, he'd sat before the blank-canvas expanse of one of the car's smooth white tablecloths, painfully conscious of being alone. With no companion to gaze upon and the dark windows reflecting the car's interior, Edgar spent the meal dodging either the eye of the man facing him at the next table or that of his own reflection. The meal became a performance: too formal, too false, Edgar acting the part of someone who lifted from his plate the stiff peak of immaculate napkin, shook it from its shape, and spread it in his lap. Nothing on the fancy menu appealed, and when the food came, it wasn't even good. Ever since, he'd always grabbed a couple of sandwiches in the bar car when the train was in motion.

The bar car came next, hot with bodies. It was dim save the glow of wall sconces and tabletop votives as well as the faces they lit. The globes of light ricocheted in the dark windows, constellating the glass so that the outer space extended infinitely about the car's planet. The little air there was tightly woven with the warp of music and the woof of speech. Edgar floated into the crowd, scanning the room for a familiar face, and lit on Abraham Lincoln's.

The first time Edgar had entered the bar car three weeks ago, he'd done a double-take at the bartender behind the long mahogany boat of a bar. The man was the spitting image of an aged Honest Abe: tall and slim, with nearly the same haggard face, black hair, and chin-curtain beard. Even his bartender garb—a white button-up shirt, black slacks, and apron—while contemporary, on him looked especially of the mid-nineteenth century. There was something off about the likeness, something Edgar couldn't pin, but it was nonetheless impressive. Something else was off too.

On every train the troupe had hitched to, the passenger cars and dining cars and bar cars were uniform. The rail company was the same, so this made sense. What was strange was that in every bar car they'd been in on every train, whether crossing Ohio or Michigan, Indiana or Iowa, Lincoln had been manning the bar. This wasn't an impossibility; Edgar wasn't sure how the rail company scheduled its staff. Instead of assigning crews to daily round-trip routes, it may have been efficient to send a fixed crew on a longer regional round trip of a single train. The troupe, though, had been traveling on different trains, and although Edgar hadn't made it out of the private cars much beyond the bar, he also couldn't remember seeing any other railway employees more than once.

The crowd parted enough for Edgar to catch sight of Chantal flailing an arm at him from a booth against the windows farther down the car. As Edgar bumped through the crowd, chanting *excuse me* and placing his hand on a shoulder here and there to widen the narrow gaps between groups, Fallon cleared his seat of her notebook and tuxedo jacket. Edgar slid in, setting the camera on the table. He had to yell over the noise.

"Am I crazy, or is he always there?" Edgar flung a thumb barward.

Will stretched taller in his seat to see across the car. "Is he?"

"He does look familiar," Chantal said.

"Somehow that doesn't surprise me." Fallon shook her head.

Chantal flashed a bright smile to a group of men at the bar who had noticed her looking over.

Ava, temple to window, was out amidst the infinite. She hadn't acknowledged Edgar. All that could be seen of her was a nebula of hair that, against the black glass, erased her from her seat entirely. Edgar willed her to turn, then leaned further over his elbows and lowered his head to Fallon, Will, and Chantal conspiratorially. "Is it even possible?"

Fallon mirrored his hunch. "For people to find themselves on the same train over and over?" She grinned. "You're on every train I'm on, aren't you?"

"That's different," Edgar said. "You know that's different." He leaned back in his seat. "I'm just saying it's a huge coincidence, if that's all it is."

A match was struck, and Ava's lit face appeared in the window, hovering over the speeding fields and taking her place at the table like an apparition. "Coincidences happen all the time," she said.

"And so do happy accidents," Fallon said, throwing one lanky leg over the other. "Believe me, brighter minds than ours have failed at figuring the logic behind railway staffing, but if it means there's always someone on hand who knows how to make a proper martini, I'm all for it, whatever mysterious forces may be at work. Which reminds me—"

She downed the dregs of her drink and stopped a passing cocktail waitress, who carried a full tray on her shoulder like the weight of the world. A waitress was always on hand to help Honest Abe, Edgar had noticed, on Sunday evenings, busier nights that mixed business and leisure travelers.

Fallon set the empty glass on the waitress's tray. "One more for me, thank you."

The waitress locked eyes with Edgar, possibly to stop herself from rolling them. "Anything for you?" she asked.

Edgar glanced back at Ava's reflection, which gazed blankly in his general direction. He decided to feel lucky—"A Negroni?"—and immediately regretted asking. No one in any small town they'd stopped in so far had heard of the drink, let alone carried Campari. He'd tried liquor stores too, at least the ones that were open; most were closed whenever he went, no matter the time. The bar car was looking like his last chance before the end of the tour, but he hadn't so far dared to extinguish the option.

"A what?"

Edgar sighed. "I'll just have a whiskey, then," he said. "A double. Neat."

Ava turned around, lifted her empty wineglass.

"Another?" the waitress asked.

Ava nodded. She started to return her temple to the window, but paused, her attention drawn to the camera on the table before Edgar. "You're a photographer too?"

"I explore all mediums," he said. "But mostly I use the photos to paint from."

Before he could return a question, engage Ava, Chantal broke in. "For your tramp—tramp—"

"Trompe l'oeil," Fallon corrected, laughing. "It's painting something so it fools the eye, so it looks three dimensional—the way you felt you could sit down on that chaise in last week's backdrop."

Chantal lifted an eyebrow. "So you trick people?"

"Well," fumbled Edgar. "It's art, so—"

"We should be careful," Ava said, then turned her face back to the window and, putting out her cigarette, went dark.

Chantal leaned closer to Edgar. "What's a Negroni? What's in it?"

"It's a classic," Fallon answered. "Equal parts gin, vermouth, and Campari, with an orange-peel garnish. Very good. A bit bitter, but good."

Chantal glared at Fallon and addressed herself again, with emphasis, to Edgar. "And where did *you* hear about it?"

Fallon ignored her. "I assume it was a fairly standard drink in Rome?"

"Yes, but that's not where I first learned of it. My Sicilian grandfather drank them." Edgar fiddled with a cardboard coaster. "I grew up wanting to be the kind of man who drank Negronis."

"So *that* was the draw to Rome, to Italy," Fallon said, leaning in. "Your heritage."

"It's different out here, on the road," said Will. He peeled the wet label from his bottle of beer in one pull. "You've got to be happy with whatever you can get. The bar car only stocks trendy craft beers now, so here I am, drinking whatever *this* is."

The waitress returned with the troupe's drinks and passed them out, setting down a second cosmo beside Chantal's still nearly full one. "From the men at the end of the bar," she said.

"How sweet!" squealed Chantal in a rocketing pitch. She raised the glass to the men, who jostled and sloshed their scotches in return.

Fallon took a sip of her martini. "The game is afoot."

Standing, Chantal scooped a pink drink into each hand. "Don't wait up."

As she moved away, Fallon slid Will's sopping beer label toward her, painting a wet streak across the table. It bore a Viking ship. A bowsprit dragon's mouth gaped with teeth, and the sea leapt up in points to meet them. Fallon straightened in her seat, as though an idea had bitten.

She turned to Edgar. "Think you could paint the arctic?"

"I can paint anything, but surely you don't mean for the next show?" He could feel his blood pressure rising.

She shook her head. "The one after. Gives you almost a week. If God created the universe in six days, I'm sure you can create a sliver of it in five."

At the threshold of her sleeper compartment, the reel of Ava's daydream cut. She had arrived from the bar car to find something out of the ordinary: a long white flight feather lay on her bed.

As she lifted it by the quill and soothed its barbs, a new movie queued. Ava imagined the feather drifting in on a draft through the crack her broken accordion door left between catch and latch. She pictured a rabid fan slinking in from the public cars, then dismissed it as something that could only happen in one of Fallon's plays. She saw Edgar placing it here, then Fallon, then Chantal, then Will. His character, after all, left a swan feather for hers in the play, but it wasn't like him to do something like this unscripted. Fallon, however, had written it.

Feeling exposed, Ava turned and pulled the door closed, tried to make catch meet latch, but it wouldn't. The door sprang back, leaving an open slit. It had been broken for weeks, and whenever she raised this with Fallon, she was told it was difficult to find someone to repair vintage items, especially in the small-town Midwest, and that it would be expensive to boot. *Besides*, Fallon would add. She would smile. *We all know each other so well, and we keep to ourselves. We have no need for locks.* Ava wanted to say then that yes, she knew Edgar; she knew Fallon; she knew Chantal and Will; she knew them all far less well than she'd known Ben, and he'd blindsided her. But she didn't admit it.

She set the feather on the Carrera marble of her nightstand. Ben had a hard time carrying the rococo-style piece back to the private cars after they'd found it at a flea market several seasons ago. It was the only thing of worth in the room, which also held, besides the built-in sink, counter, and cabinets that all the car's compartments had on the wall holding their accordion doors, a full-size bed bare of head- or footboard. All the other compartments had twin beds, but the double was a luxury that had been afforded the couple. Ava wondered now if Fallon would reclaim the room, the car's largest, for herself. Maybe she too couldn't quite believe Ben was gone.

Ava unbuttoned her jeans and went to pull them down, but could feel the slit between catch and latch watching. She tried one more time to close it, but the accordion door sprang back. She switched off the light, undressed in the dark.

Edgar squinted. With the lights on, he had to lean close to his compartment's small window to see out. The train flew through fields, and he watched the crops change as it passed each square of land. Each plot had its expected farmhouse, its rotting barn, its rusting tractor. Speed blurred the furrows, but if he focused on looking far along their lines, a gap would open, letting him, for a second, see down an aisle of corn or soy, clear across the acreage.

The tiny bathroom down the corridor shushed with the flushing of water. Edgar leaned back on his bed against the wall where a headboard should have been. Between the window's red velvet curtains was an identical spartan compartment. It held his built-ins and sink, navy-blanketed bed, and small table stacked with sketchbooks. There was just enough floorspace to take four steps. He watched himself there on its set and placed his hands behind his head, displaying the muscles of his arms to their full advantage, as though he knew what he was doing.

So this was what it was to be an actor. To see yourself as another. To live at once in your body and outside it. Edgar wondered if he'd ever find his place in the troupe. He wondered mostly about Ava, made her his own creation.

Racing after the train's headlight, in the heart of its howl, Fallon wrote at a makeshift desk she'd built from a thrift-shop plant stand capped with a gilt-framed mirror. There was only room between its legs for one of hers, each of them straddling the other's. Her director's chair hunched her into a hunter's crouch, head low over the glass, and when she paused in her writing, she'd look herself in the eye, becoming aware, then, of the car's vibrations, the track's rattles, bumps, and squeals.

Fallon's clavicle cut the paper white of her neck. Her elbow bent. Her slant handwriting had edges. Between her and her reflection, the pencil lead moved across the page. To create, all she had to do was listen. Words had a touch of the farouche; to rush them would spook. The hunt was a wait, and she held out the bait in her hand. Patient, alert, she took down anything that came her way, dressed up the same stories again and again. There were so few, with infinite trimmings.

Every play could have been written any way. Any play could have been any other. It depended on what landed in the traps. A watchmaker was as likely as a pearl diver, bull rider, coal miner's canary. It could be quince, quartz, hat stand or cricket cage, a set of spurs, an orchard or orchestra. Tomorrow it would be different. Fallon was an angler, a tinker, a thief, a shuffler of cards. She was a writer. She cast line, plucked, and pocketed, and what she caught she transported in the boxes of words.

Fallon scried, conj(ect)ured.

EDGAR always wanted to be the kind of man who drank Negronis.

    Rome was a quest to discover some root of himself, a part unintelligible, in a language he can't speak. He didn't find it, but whatever happened battered the core of him, made a fist of his heart.

    EDGAR's history is one of heartbreak, of a thirst for something— something he can't have.

In the dark stillness of the bar car, the bottles on the backbar shifted, sloshed, made room for one more.

Madrid, Kansas

February 6

In the scene unfurled along the inside of the baggage car's fourth wall, a forest encroached on a rocky beach. The train shuddered as it decelerated into the station, but after several weeks of travel, Edgar had sea legs. He bent his knees, planted his feet on the floorboards and, because he'd learned the hard way, lifted stipple brush from canvas.

The train, though slowed, was still traveling too fast to stop, and for an instant, time stood still, as if there was still time. Edgar risked it—he tapped green along a span of branch, the sound of brush on canvas like dry pine needles underfoot, like boughs on trousers. Then he went deeper into the woods, where it was darker, daubed into the umber.

It was the stopping that brought him back. The train's brakes came on with a screech, and Edgar hissed, "Shit!" as he lifted the brush too late, dragged a shadow into the light. There was the sense of something slipping then, a shift or slink back to shade. He turned his head just in time to see, vanishing into the vestibule, a red tail tipped in white.

The words blurred, looked on coolly from their black and white at Will's alarm, as though they, in some forties film noir, had slipped him a mickey. He hadn't enough time for this. This, even. There wasn't enough time. He straightened his spine from its slump on posh ottoman, opened his legs, and dropped his script between them to the stage's parquet, where it half slipped beneath the bang of gold fringe that rose to his seat's green brocade. At the sound, the others looked up from their pages. Everyone was waiting on Ava so they could start the morning's read-through.

This week's theater was a historic gem, gilt and filigreed, every edge carved or painted with pattern. Unlike others they'd played, the glitz didn't stop at the stage—even the dressing rooms were done up, and as male lead, Will had his own. The vanity was marble, the light fixtures crystal antiques. He wanted to lounge on its cushy club sofa forever; however, he memorized better onstage.

Will ground his elbows into his thighs and lamented his forehead to his hands, sighing onto the script below. The troupe's pace had always been breakneck—to be expected, if each season was to be profitable—but it was especially so during an exploratory tour. Two plays a week—one old and one new—would have been doable, if Fallon delivered new scripts even a week in advance. Instead, she'd wait nail-bitingly long for inspiration, sometimes nursing the script until nearly their arrival in the town where it was to be performed. Will had complained on numerous occasions, but Fallon didn't listen. It was how she was.

Even compared to previous exploratory seasons, though, this winter's was setting Will a-sea. Fallon didn't usually hire new actors during them, and Will saw why. The tour was grueling, almost cruel. Now that he was lead, every role was new, even in plays he'd been putting on with the troupe for years. He was familiar with the leads' lines from playing supporting roles, but on top of exact memorization, there was blocking and staging and, hardest, getting a feeling for character. Instead of making the roles his, Will had been playing sorry impressions of Ben's. He hadn't time to consider how they could be improved, if it was even possible. Worst of all, Fallon said the troupe's funds were low. The pressure was on.

The straight-backed dining chair Edgar was sitting on creaked. "I think—" he said in a rare moment of unprompted conversation.

But Fallon interjected. "Therefore, you are."

Edgar smiled weakly. "I think I saw a fox in the baggage car."

Fallon and Chantal burst out laughing, and Will threw up his hands, groaned. "Now he's in on it too? Edgar, please admit they put you up to this. We men need to stick together."

"Put me up to what?" asked Edgar. The laughter redoubled.

"See?" Fallon said to Will. "There *is* a fox on the train. Now everyone's seen it but you." She turned to Edgar. "Will's convinced we're making it up."

"He calls the fox Ben's ghost," Chantal said.

Edgar crossed an ankle on his knee. "Ben from last season? The lead actor?"

"Their *story*, which I'm sure you're already very familiar with, is that the fox was found near the tracks," Will said.

"Was it a puppy—or—" Edgar stuttered. "Or whatever you call a baby fox?"

"Kit or cub," Fallon answered.

"Oodle," added Chantal, rising from her seat and curtsying to Fallon.

"Gesundheit." Fallon bowed soberly in return.

"Anyway—" Will's wire-framed glasses were slipping low on his nose, and he boosted them with his middle finger. He worried for a second whether anyone thought he was passive-aggressively flipping them off. "Legend—and I cannot emphasize that enough," he continued. "*Legend* has it that Ben was trying to tame it. This was before my and Chantal's time."

"Except it never took," said Fallon. "The taming, I mean. Even as a youngster, the nasty little thing was terrible—all needle-teeth and claw. It would scrabble and gnaw and scratch and snap at anything within reach. Ben kept it tethered, and it chewed through its tie several times before he made one of chain, at which point it nearly gnawed through the leg of the bed it was lashed to."

"That's what happened to my leg," said Chantal to Edgar, massaging her left thigh. "I chewed it off to break ties with the terrible town I grew up in."

Fallon grabbed back the attention. "*Eventually*, the fox somehow took its teeth to the leather collar buckled around its neck. It's been loose in the cars ever since."

Chantal riffled the top corner of her script. "It doesn't have as much fight in it, now that it's free."

Edgar uncrossed his legs and thumped his foot back to the floor. "It's not free, though, is it, as long as it's trapped in the cars? A wild thing should be wild."

"For one thing, my little rock star, it has every opportunity to leave," Fallon said. "The baggage car's loading door is often open, as you well know." Her attention was drawn to the lights and catwalks above the stage. "Besides, every time we've tried to set the fox loose, we've found it back inside. I'm not sure it could survive outside the cars. It's not truly wild, but not tame either." She shook her head. "It's best to let it be."

Edgar ratcheted his script into a tight pipe. "Why do you call the fox Ben's ghost?" he asked Will.

"Because the fox was Ben's," Will answered, returning his elbows to his knees. "Or the myth of it, at least, was his."

Chantal smirked. "Ben left part of his spirit behind to keep an eye on you, Will, now that you've taken his roles. Two beady black eyes, in fact. You'd better do a good job." She tightened her voice. "Or he'll seek his revenge."

A wheeze shuddered through the theater, ending in the proscenium arching over them. Footsteps followed, growing louder, then a clatter of chains. This echoed about the building, so it was impossible to tell whether the noise came from backstage or the empty house before them. Will turned up his face to look uneasily across the darkened mezzanine, both hands now over his mouth.

"Ooh!" said Fallon. The crest of her blond pompadour seemed to rise. "I love a venue with history!"

Will heard her inhale deeply and knew she was preparing to project. "Don't!" he fretted. "Please?"

She smiled wide and, as he gnawed a thumbnail, spoke out across the empty theater in a loud, clear voice. "If there's a spirit present, make yourself known!"

There were more footsteps, then a heavy bump of some sort, and a figure (Will gasped)—Ava—(he relaxed) entered from the wings. She had a takeout coffee and a cardboard tray with four more. As she crossed the stage toward the chair left empty for her, she offered a drink to each of the others.

"Why didn't you say it was you?" Will asked as he wrenched a cup free of the tray.

Ava shrugged. "I wasn't sure there was a spirit present."

There was something to what she was saying, no matter how dryly. Ava had somehow dulled, since Ben left. She was thinner, frayed about the edges. Will assumed she'd just been missing Ben, but now, for the first time, considered something Chantal had asked him soon after the start of the season: whether something had come between the couple.

This question could never be posed to Ava, however; it wasn't done. The one time Chantal wondered aloud to him about Ava and Ben—a rare late night early in the tour, when Chantal hadn't met any men and the rest of the troupe had long gone to bed—Will had grown so worried that Ava or Fallon would overhear, he'd changed the subject.

"Was there a ghost?" asked Ava. "I thought I heard you say—"

"We were just talking about the fox," Fallon said. "But now, we're all here. Let's begin."

The afternoon warmth made it still feel like fall. Edgar loosened the noose of his scarf and dropped it on the rail yard's gray gravel. Clad in his usual tee and black jeans, he stepped back to survey the arctic scene draped across the outside of the baggage car. It had to be finished for the next play, and used to working under pleasure, not pressure, Edgar felt the tight deadline looming.

From the corner of his eye, he saw Fallon's bicycle drop from the observation platform at the end of the parked private cars. Then a long, tuxedoed leg came over the metal railing, and she dropped down after it. With her left arm winged over a stack of flyers, she stiffly righted the bike and mounted it. A roll of tape braceleted her wrist.

Edgar called out. "Hey, Fallon?"

She twisted to look at him, one foot poised to pedal. Though his room and board and some meals were provided, Edgar was worried about money. Fallon hadn't doled any out since the third tour stop. His funds were dwindling.

"About getting paid? I was—"

Gravel crashed behind him, and he turned to see a small flock of doves scatter before Ava, as though she were a predator. A bird flapped up between Fallon and Edgar and, taking the canvas for woods and beach and open air, collided with it. The baggage car rang with the impact, and the dove dove into the rocks, raising a puff of dust.

Fallon tipped back her blond shock and laughed. "You couldn't ask for a better review," she said.

As Edgar scratched the back of his head sheepishly, the bird righted to a squat, wings held loosely at its sides.

Fallon called back across the rail yard, her voice coming and going with the wind. "We get paid when we get paid. As I keep telling Chantal: if you want to earn more, help me promote the next play." She waved the stack of flyers in the air. "Post some of these around town, spread the word."

"Will I get paid to do that?" Edgar asked.

"It certainly doesn't pay not to." The flyers again under her arm, Fallon untwisted her torso and pushed off on the bike, adding, "Don't spend too much paint on that backdrop!"

As she picked up speed across the rail yard's gravel, the dove burst up, the slap of its wings ricocheting off the car's metal. Its line of flight, the same as Ava's in the distance, drew Edgar's eyes after her. Fallon was after her too. He watched the bike catch up with, then overtake Ava on the dirt road into town, the dust from it marking her position overhead like a map pin.

જી

As Fallon coasted on her bike, the wind flapped her open tuxedo jacket like a flag and rippled her tux trousers' cool silk lining against her shins. There had been more to the town than she'd expected; more than three blocks of storefronts had gone by before dwindling to fields. Still, every Midwestern town she visited was a repeat performance of train station, post office, gas station, young mothers with babies, old ladies, and blue-collar men. The people were the same. The streets, the same. The lawns, the same before the same houses.

In the distance, above the amber waves of grain, rose a white church spire. Fallon started to yawn, but a second spire cut it short. Then two more appeared. She stood on the pedals, stretched her chest tall. What couldn't be was: amid the alien corn, a temple, intricately carved of what looked like ivory. Two full-sized gold elephants curled their trunks—one on each side of the building's entrance.

Fallon braked, set one foot on the ground, and pulled a guidebook from her jacket's inner pocket. She flipped through its heavily highlighted pages and, finding what she sought, folded back its cover and held the book out in one hand to survey passage and temple simultaneously.

Within Madrid proper, the unsuspecting tourist will be surprised to find themselves swept away to another place and time—

Fallon nodded, reassured.

—when they happen on an ancient Egyptian temple. Originally constructed in Devod in the second century BC as a small, one-room structure, the temple was later expanded by the Egyptians and then again by the Romans.

When construction began on the Aswan Dam in the sixties, the temple stood squarely in the forthcoming flood plain. World-wide efforts were made to save the structure. The city of Madrid agreed to take it, and in 1969, the temple was disassembled and shipped there, where it was reconstructed in 1972 in the Parque del Oeste. It has since been determined that the arches leading to the temple entrance were erected in the wrong order, making it Madrid's temple—something new.

Fallon shifted her focus beyond the horizon created by the top of her guidebook and looked at the temple without seeing it. In its place stood hewn stone and clean Egyptian lines stripped of spire and fauna. For all her careful planning, the tour retained the power to surprise.

When Ava tired of the train's closeness, its closed-in-ness, she would climb the narrow ladder on the side of the observation car and spend an hour or two on its roof.

The hood of her oversized sweatshirt hung down her back. In it stole a rolled-up script and pack of cigarettes. Ava reached up, wriggling her hands free of the too-long sleeves, and grasped the ladder's cool metal. She ascended it the way a train trucked along its track, the only decision propulsion. At the peak of her ascent, her hands stopped at the top of the car, and her feet stepped up the rungs to meet them, making her take a bow. When she looked up into the long, late-afternoon light, she saw, sitting at the car's edge, Edgar.

Ava's heart sank to her stomach, which was expected, but from there (for some reason), it fluttered into her throat. He was at the end closest the sleeper car, with a sketchbook in his lap. For a second, Ava considered descending, like her heart but, like her heart, reconsidered. This was *her* spot. She deepened her squint, halfheartedly hoped he'd read it as a glare. These days there was only half a heart to muster.

"Now you're *here*?" She threw up her hands. "Well, why not? I've run into you everywhere else, sometimes literally."

Edgar continued to sketch. Part of the page was visible over his shoulder, a view of the cornfield beyond. The lines were rushed and crude, but it somehow lent a sense of life. Framed by his rough hands, bruised or bruised with charcoal, and with either dirt or paint beneath his torn-short nails, the sketch's skill took the wind out of Ava's sails. She was pitching into doldrums.

The pencil halted. Edgar swiveled, looked through her every stone. More nights than not, a crowd of eyes clutched Ava, but she hadn't been seen in ages.

"I can leave if you'd like," he said calmly, in one motion turning back to the sketch and replacing her mortar.

Ava shrugged. "It's not like I own the place. It's not my place to say."

Edgar misheard. He repeated the end of what he thought she said. "So stay?"

She took it for a question. Then somehow, she decided. Or her half-heart decided. She nodded, stepped from the rung onto the green of the car's roof, and sauntered to its opposite end, nearest the platform. As Edgar continued to draw, Ava drew the scrolled script from the hood behind her head like an arrow from a quiver. The pack of cigarettes, however, had sunk to the hood's peak. She twisted and strained to reach them over her shoulder, then took another bow to flip the hood over her head and knock the pack loose. At its clap on the roof, Edgar didn't stir.

Ava lay back on the sun-warmed wood, hood playing pillow, and held up the script, adding one more cloud to the sky. Others scrolled behind it, lazily changing shape as they clipped along on the wind. A wineglass slipped into a beehive, a barbell to a fox. Another was bed then ship then fist. Ava turned from a third taking the form of a riven heart. She should have been rehearsing what the troupe had read, blocked, and played through several times that morning, but she couldn't concentrate with Edgar nearby. She forsook her lines for the scratch of his pencil on paper.

Although Ava's faded skinny jeans were looser than usual, her hand could still only be worked into the front pocket flatly. Inside it, she retrieved her lighter by sandwiching it between her index and middle fingers. When she reached across her body for the pack of cigarettes, her sleeve swallowed her hand. She shoved the fabric up to her elbow as she put a cigarette between her lips and bruxed the lighter's rusty wheel once, twice, three times into flame. Cigarette lit, she looked up at the sky again and sighed smoke, which momentarily made whole the split-heart cloud.

When Ava's lungs were empty, Edgar spoke. "Can I bum one?"

"You smoke?"

"I do. Well, I have."

Edgar scooted closer along the car's length, and she slid him the pack, lighter stowed inside. A cigarette between his lips, he came close enough to hand the pack back. There was heat coming off him, the smell of turpentine. The lighter's rusty wheel bruxed once, twice, then he shook it, tried again, produced a spark. Ava gave in to impulse. She leaned in and touched the tip of her cigarette to his. At his small gasp, it lit.

Ava's pulse raced. This sort of play was dangerous. It was playing at being single, and she was married, wasn't she? Ava wasn't so sure. Besides, she liked being looked at, and seen. She needed that now. She and Edgar gazed over the cornfield, breathing fire. He was quiet, but she was more so, had nothing to lose but him.

"All these weeks, only a few thin walls between us, and I know nothing about you," he said at last.

Ava's eyes squinted to slits. The sun was setting behind Edgar, and to look at him, she had to hold a hand up to the glare.

"You're just as much of a mystery to me," she replied. "Why would anyone leave Rome for these godforsaken towns? Was it love? The end of love, I mean."

"Something like that." Edgar rasped his dark stubble, then stopped, deliberative. "You can make a good living in Rome as a painter, if you don't mind churning out shit: paintings of ruins and lovers, wine bottles and cobblestone streets. Some artists don't mind. They can compartmentalize. I had a hard time doing that. Rome wasn't the place for my style, the realism," he continued. He moved closer to her along the roof. "Tourists don't want the real Rome. They want the dream. And what they buy is almost never art: something with guts and thought and polish, something asking to be met halfway."

Ava tapped ash from the tip of her cigarette. "You like what you're painting now?"

"This troupe is a haven. I can create whatever I like, so long as I stick to the script."

"Quite the caveat, you must admit."

"It could be worse. It has been."

Edgar lifted one knee and rested his elbow on its summit. Trying to make it look casual, he swiveled his body toward her until the shade of his hand fell across her face, relieving the glare of the sun. Ava relaxed her squint. They were silent for several beats, inhaling and exhaling. The gates of her city were giving, but Ava barred them. She pitched her cigarette off the side of the car into the rail yard's gravel and shifted from Edgar under the pretense of reaching for her script.

"So, tell me," she said. "What's the point of painting realistically now that the camera exists? It's unnecessary. Nowadays, painting should be about something else: feelings or fantasies, visualizing the unseen."

As she gestured, Edgar adjusted his knee to keep the shade across her eyes. "There's still subject, composition, craft," he said. "A photorealistic or trompe l'oeil painting can be more life-like than a photograph—the texture richer, the highlights brighter, revealing more."

"But real is real, right? Nothing can be more real."

"But it can be truer, you know? Something can appear one way, but be quite different, and the artist will reveal that in the work. Then, the painting shows a truth about its subject in addition to its resemblance."

"Like how?"

"Well—" He looked into the distance. "Let's say I painted a portrait of you backstage, when you were preparing for this last play. A photograph would show you wearing a wedding band, but if I painted you, I'd show you without one, because it's truer. It better represents the truth of the subject, if that makes sense."

Above Ava, the heart-cloud unraveled in the wind, went up in smoke. She gathered her cigarettes, lighter, and script and scrabbled her feet beneath her to stand. "Not really. No. It doesn't."

At that, Edgar dropped his hand, blinding her with the light.

Bralessness was bliss. As soon as Fallon had closed her compartment door, she'd reached under the back of her tank top, unhooked the clasp of her bra, pulled its black straps down her arms, and drawn the thing out through one of the shirt's dingy armholes. Now it dangled from the back of the chair at her makeshift desk, where she took a breath unfettered. A mug reading *ad vitam æternam* was abob on the lap of her silky midnight-blue pajama pants. She lifted it, sip-kissed its lip, and bent over her notebook.

A life had only so much time and energy, and Fallon's was invested in art. She had never wanted children, yet she still had the urge to create something that would survive her. To put it simply, her biological clock was ticking. The troupe was her only hope of procreation. She didn't deign to think herself a Homer or Shakespeare; all she needed was a spot on the record, a shot at resurrection—something more than a gravestone's eroding name and date. That way, even if she went forgotten for centuries, there would be the chance that someone someday would read an act of a play and breathe life into her, raise her voice from the grave. The more of a mark she made while she was here, the better the chance of that. She was writing for her life everlasting.

Each day, though, was one day closer to death and the end of the tour. This was Fallon's last shot to come up with a hit. If she didn't before the end of the season, she'd have to shutter the troupe, accept being forgotten.

Her pencil was poised above the page, but nothing came. Fallon swirled loose loops in the top margin for momentum, but it wouldn't kick over into script. The mug traveled to and from her lips. The seconds ticked. So much of writing was waiting, but even so, tonight something was off. She was seated at her makeshift desk as usual, everything aright, but somehow the scene couldn't come to life without the motion of the train.

This put her in mind of a recent dream. Fallon was canoeing across an ice floe when, a little way away, the smooth white back of a whale parted the arctic waters. Trainlike, it fogged a blast of breath, rolled forward the arch of its back as it dove, and lifted its flukes above water to make the shape of an open book on a lectern. Despite the blankness of those pages, Fallon could read them. She felt the ache of the story, each word right and in its right place. It was her dream play. She paddled frantically toward the whale, but it resubmerged with a lobtailed slap on the surface of the water. Fallon woke scrambling for pencil and paper only to realize she could remember nothing of the play, only the feeling of it. Ever since, she'd been haunted. Although each word she wrote was a stroke toward it, the dream play was always just out of reach.

Tonight, she hadn't come one word closer. Fallon harpooned her pencil into her notebook's white flesh, breaking its lead, and kept pressing until the pencil cracked in half.

As if one act precipitated the other, there was a knock. The accordion doors to the car's compartments absorbed most of a fist's force by merely wobbling in their tracks, and their plastic didn't resound, but it was a knock all the same. Fallon shielded a hand over the split pencil, called for whoever it was to come in.

It was Edgar, his stubble scruffier than usual and dark circles under his eyes. He pointed toward the observation car. "Will made spaghetti, if you want some."

"Maybe in a bit. Don't wait for me."

Edgar pulled the door closed, rattling it along its track, and when the latch clicked, Fallon lifted her hand from the pencil, a bit surprised by her impulse to hide it. She picked up the sharpened half and positioned it once more over the page.

People were rife with drama; they would knit it from nothing and hoard the stuff. She had a habit of using them for fodder, spying a river of injury and tracking it back to its source. Now Fallon wondered again about Edgar, about why he left Rome. Therein lay the danger. She scried, conjectured.

> *EDGAR is hungry. It's that simple. He enters his Roman studio apartment, checking the hall behind him before closing the door, and flips the light switch. Nothing happens. Flips it again. Nothing. His hands are clammy and trembling, and he grabs his hair, roots and uproots through cupboards and drawers, upturns coffee tins, tosses boxes, guts pants pockets—all the usual caches for cash. The drawers hang out like tongues. He delves between couch cushions up to his elbows, drops to his knees, reaches deep underneath, and scrapes up one euro. Not enough for a bite of anything, let alone light.*
>
> *There's a knock at the door. EDGAR freezes, then stands, the knees of his pants patched with dust. There's banging: the landlord, cussing in Italian. EDGAR understands just enough to know that. He pockets his precious coin, lifts the window, and climbs out onto the ledge. Then he leaps across the narrow gap to the next building.*

In the baggage car, Chantal picked a stitch. Once she got it started, the rest would unravel.

Every hem had to be taken in, now that Will was filling Ben's role, and how barely. In Ben's shoes, padded with thick socks, Will's footprints would be the same, his steps different. His lines would be the same, delivered differently. Will's only hope of playing a part as well as Ben was in playing Ben playing the role. The thing was, only Ben was that good.

From the sleeper car came a single, somber chord that struck, resonated and, from its haunches, launched into symphony.

"Uh!" Chantal threw the white lab coat she was sewing on the baggage car's scarred table. "I'm so sick of this shit Fallon listens to—music from the days of kings and queens."

Edgar, standing on a small stepladder, was working along the tree line of his arctic backdrop. "I like her music," he said without turning his head.

"Really? I guess it's nice, sometimes, when I'm *in the mood*." Chantal shifted her eyes to Edgar to ensure he wouldn't miss the innuendo, but he wasn't watching; he was working.

"I wonder who it is," he muttered into the backdrop as he dappled an area at the edge of the woods. The shadows had more depth there, and the painted light made the canvas, from the corner of Chantal's eye, glow as though it were a window.

"It's always some Russian whose name sounds like a bunch of scuffling," she said, twirling a lock of her long blond hair.

"Rachmaninoff?"

"No, but I'd know the name if I heard it."

Edgar turned to Chantal. "Dvořák? Tchaikovsky? Shostakovich?"

"I think you had it with tchotchke."

"Speaking of Fallon, I know she's a *she*, but is she—? Does she—? I mean, the short hair, the tux—"

Chantal hadn't expected this of Edgar. She glanced toward the sleeper-car door, leaned closer, and lowered her voice. "Right?"

"Of course, I support whatever, but—"

"She'd kill us if she overheard this." Chantal giggled. "But I'm not sure any of us really knows. Will swears he saw her kissing a man."

"Okay, so maybe—"

"But it's Will, so who knows what he really saw. I once saw a woman leaving Fallon's room, and things looked intimate, but sometimes I wonder if she's asexual. She's never been in a relationship, as far as I know. All she does is write and ride that bike. It's not healthy."

As Chantal spoke, she massaged her thigh in a practiced way. It ached where the prosthetic met it, and the pain snaked down her phantom limb to her nonexistent foot.

"How did you lose your leg?" Edgar asked.

"I'm very absent-minded." Chantal smirked. "I must have left it somewhere when I was a girl." She looked at the painting, at its shadow and light, its dense woods and stone. The pain in her phantom foot fisted, and she winced.

"You okay?" Edgar asked.

"My foot's cramping."

"But there's no—"

"Tell that to my brain. That's where pain exists, and mine believes the leg's still there. The foot aches and cramps, and there's nothing I can do to relieve or release it."

"Have you seen someone about it?"

"I've tried, but these small-town doctors just prescribe pain meds."

"But the pain's not real."

"I beg to differ." Chantal smile-grimaced, bit off a length of thread, and motioned to the painted backdrop. "You know, you don't need to spend so much time and effort on these sets. This isn't Broadway. The people who come to our shows are happy just to see a few new faces, put on a jacket or lipstick, and skip haying for a night. All this caring is shattering my first impression of you."

Edgar wiped a hand on the thigh of his jeans. "Which was?"

"You looked like you'd be at least a little trouble."

Chantal dropped the lab coat and came at Edgar with a purse to her lips, but he was already looking past her to a crystal decanter on the shelf beneath the worktable. He sidestepped her, took the decanter from its silver tray, and poured a bit of its whiskey into one of the matching glasses beside it. Then he gestured a question.

"None for me, thanks, but be my guest."

Edgar tossed back the drink, and all the features of his face pulled downward. As he doubled over coughing, Chantal doubled with laughter.

"What *is* this stuff?"

"Iced tea," she said. "Made last year. It's a prop."

Edgar sputtered a few more coughs. As he replaced the glass on the silver tray, it clinked, doubled in reflection. The complex minors of the music swelled.

Chantal's face mirrored Edgar's as, spurned, she returned to her stool, draped the lab coat back across her lap, and pressed earbuds into her ears like a child shutting out a reprimand. Taking up the needle again, she glared in the direction of the sleeper car, of sleeping Ava. When she resumed her sewing, her thread was so thin it went unseen. It was as though she was conducting.

❧

February 7

Backstage the next morning, Edgar pressed his tee-shirted torso against the cold edge of a stainless-steel table. Opening his arms wide to grasp the table's ends, he lifted it. The table and another, identical, were on loan from a second-hand store. Borrowing props helped the troupe save on costs and storage space, and most people they asked the favor of were eager to be helpful, to play some small part in the production.

Edgar carried the table onstage, and as soon as he entered the light,

Fallon leapt on him from where the rest of the troupe was huddled for rehearsal.

"Ah, Edgar! I was looking for you. Since Will's taking Ben's usual part and I'm taking Will's, I need you to cover my usual role today."

Edgar's jaw tightened as he set the table on the boards of the stage.

"Which is—" She paused, and the anticipation made Edgar squirm. "Out there, in the audience. I need someone to tell me how the blocking looks."

They were laughing at him now. Without so much as glancing at Fallon, Edgar scrape-scooted the tables together end to end, then dropped off the edge of the stage.

Fallon winked at the others. "He must have been gunning for a bigger part."

The theater's carpet and velvet upholstery were soothing shades of deep blue, and even the aisle's rising slope was gentle. Edgar already regretted the damage he may have inflicted on the stage in anger. He selected a seat mid-house, kicking his boots up on the back of the seat before him, but doing so carefully, so as not to harm the fabric.

Fallon addressed the troupe from center stage. "Okay, this scene takes place after the doctors switch their wives' minds. So remember, Ava, you're playing Chantal's character, and she's playing yours."

Stage right, Fallon pulled a pipe from her pocket, removed her tux jacket, and tossed it into the wings. She placed the pipe's stem between her teeth and approached Ava—beautiful Ava, Edgar couldn't look away—gripping her upper arm and walking her toward the table. Will lifted a finger.

DR. HAMLET
Sexton, I don't appreciate you grabbing my wife like that. She can walk well enough on her own.

Fallon stopped the scene, broke character. "More impassioned there, Will, more force. Remember how Ben played it? 'I *don't* appreciate you touching *my wife* like that.' This woman is *yours*. Mark your turf more firmly. Remember the way Ben would snatch Ava's arm, as if meat was being taken from his plate?"

Will nodded, started the line over.

DR. HAMLET

Sexton, I *don't* appreciate you touching *my wife* like that. She can walk quite well on her own.

DR. SEXTON

This isn't *your* wife, man. It's mine.

DR. HAMLET

What do you mean? That's *my* wife's body, isn't it?

Edgar had a thought. Unsure if the theater's acoustics worked audience-to-stage, he yelled, "Fallon, why don't you just learn Ben's part? Then Will wouldn't have to learn all these new roles."

"Will needs to learn them eventually, now that he's lead," Fallon said. "He may as well do it this season, while we're experimenting." She nodded to Will, who began again.

DR. HAMLET

What do you mean? That's *my* wife's body, isn't it?

Will grabbed Ava's arm slightly less gently, and Fallon rubbed her forehead, which may or may not have been part of the play.

Though Ava hadn't spoken a line, she held the audience rapt. Edgar couldn't stop watching her. He shifted in his seat, unleashing a squeak that reverberated around the theater and proved its audience-to-stage acoustics were just as good as the other way round. The sound caused a beat of reality in the rehearsal, a reminder that they were playing parts.

Fallon gave the next line.

DR. SEXTON

But the woman within—the brain, I should say—is mine. Everything that's ever happened to her has happened inside that brain.

DR. HAMLET

Her brain today is different than yesterday. She can hardly be called the same woman. Besides, that *body* is *mine*.

Fallon and Will began tugging Ava back and forth between them, until Fallon took up another of her roles.

"And scene," she called, sweeping her eyes across the bare-bones stage setting and the other three actors, who looked to her for approval. "It'll have to do," she muttered, running a hand through her hair. "It will simply have to do."

❧

In the dressing room, Will read his part and said it back to himself. He read it and said it, learning by heart the part of Hamlet. As he turned the pages, he pictured the flip book of Hamlets, all the actors who'd filled the role, taken a breath in that beat between "to be" and "or not to be." That was the question: to be or not to be Ben. Even if he wanted to, could he?

The upturned top hat sat before Will on the wooden desk that served as his vanity. Its lining's stitches were loose. He lifted the hat by its brim and jerked his wrist a few times to toss its contents, then drew a slip of paper.

"The show was a flop—" he read, but before he could get out the rest, his stomach flipped. Will spun toward the trash can near the door, but it was too far. Vomit hit the tile and splattered across the tip of his shoe.

Outside the dressing room, the hum of the house was picking up. Will scanned the room for paper towels but settled for a week-old newspaper, wiping his chin and shoe before covering the mess. Leaning over the vanity, he painted the backing of a false mustache with beard glue. His hands were trembling; the best he could do was stick it on askew.

It was time. Will swapped his glasses for safety goggles, left the dressing room, and took his place onstage behind one of the stainless-steel tables on the otherwise stark white set. Fallon was wearing the same goggles, mustache, and lab coat, standing behind the other table that, like his, was covered in beakers and vials. His blurry vision made him feel he was looking in a mirror.

Edgar nodded to Will from the wings, then the curtain rose, revealing the meager audience. The house churned with a strange, disgruntled energy, as though demanding the truth. Will felt faint for a second, took a deep breath. When the stars subsided, he shifted the goggles to his brow, held up a test tube with a gloved hand, and let fly the first line.

DR. HAMLET

Abracadabra!

❧

A young woman appeared, contrapposto against the dressing room doorframe. Fallon froze, one Oxford shoe halfway off. The woman's look was lit.

"Excuse me, sir? Sorry to bother you?" she said, everything a question. "I just wanted to say—your performance? I felt—I've never felt?"

She took one awkwardly certain step into the room, as though someone had pushed her, and ran a finger down the bust of her dress in a motion stolen from a movie.

"Maybe we could go somewhere?" she suggested. "For a nightcap?"

Fallon stood. Maintaining eye contact, she moved closer until she could feel the woman's nearness on the skin of her face. Then she reached up to her pencil mustache, grasped its curling end between thumb and forefinger, and slowly peeled it off. At exactly the same rate, the woman's eyes widened.

❧

February 8
THE MIDWEST CHORUS | THEATER REVIEW
St. St.
The Troupe Adores
The Reminisce Theater
Madrid, Kansas
Remaining performance: tonight at 8 p.m.

Before st-st-stuttering to a st-st-st-stop, *St. St.* (*Saint Street*) really took off. Sometimes one word makes the rest of the play possible, and in this one, it's *abracadabra*.

Uttered, the term summons. From the Aramaic *avra kadavrai*, it means "I will create as my words," making it every playwright's favorite.

This isn't Adam's naming of beasts, mind—a sound bestowed on something existing. We're talking let-there-be-light-style manifestation from word, a spell from spelling, something leaping from page to stage.

Considered magical since at least Roman times, *abracadabra* was written on protective amulets in the triangular form shown below, the word diminishing along with the evil it protected against, the arrow it shot.

$$A - B - R - A - C - A - D - A - B - R - A$$
$$A - B - R - A - C - A - D - A - B - R$$
$$A - B - R - A - C - A - D - A - B$$
$$A - B - R - A - C - A - D - A$$
$$A - B - R - A - C - A - D$$
$$A - B - R - A - C - A$$
$$A - B - R - A - C$$
$$A - B - R - A$$
$$A - B - R$$
$$A - B$$
$$A$$

In this, we can't help but see an ancient amphitheater's seating chart, a genome of audience as creature. See the DNAish bases, sequenced? How they couple to create? Seeded—excuse us—*seated* are five distinct types, an odd number, yet fret not; none are alone long.

A: Amour
B: Beloved
R: Rake
C: Companion
D: Darling

Abracadabra: a bra and a bra brawling, twirling about a cad. There's a lie in the core of it from which everything else unreels.

We'd be remiss if we didn't cite a second theory, that the word may instead derive from the Aramaic phrase *avada kedavra*, meaning "let the thing be destroyed." It's a fine line, but we can't advise how to walk it. Must there always be destruction where there's creation?

Outside, the afternoon light was likely lengthening, but Edgar was working under yellow lamplight in the windowless baggage car. As he pulled a sheepskin taut across the skeleton of a canoe, the door to the sleeper car creaked open, then softly clicked closed.

"I really can't convince you to catch the acting bug, can I?" Fallon asked, stepping from the shadows. She sauntered toward him down the length of the arctic-beach backdrop that hung ready for the next play.

Edgar continued his work. "I'm not an actor."

"And no one expects you to be, my little dissident—not *just* one, at any rate. We need you free to build the sets and change the scenes, to light and stage-manage our productions, but it would be nice to count on you for small roles here and there." Fallon paused. "Like the swan."

The force of Edgar's answer pelted the canoe. "I can't." Edgar pulled the skin tighter over the canoe's body. It didn't quite fit. He shot his staple gun three times, breaking the skin to secure it.

"But you can," said Fallon. "You can, and you have. Most of us take on several roles; otherwise, the troupe wouldn't be feasible. I write and direct and act and manage. Chantal does costumes and makeup in addition to acting, and Will and Ava— Well, let's just say they're special, or maybe *specialized* is better. I need them focused."

"I can't. I can't lie."

Fallon made a sweeping gesture at the beach behind her. "My cozy little kip, isn't your trompe l'oeil a lie?" She laughed. "Now there's a sentence." Her eyes followed the line of her arm to the top corner of the scene. She peered closer, then closer still. "I think there's a fly"—as Edgar stood, trying to see what she was seeing, Fallon shooed her hand at the backdrop—"stuck in the—" She prodded a spot of black on the canvas with her finger.

"I always paint in a fly. It's a signature of sorts," Edgar said.

Fallon raised an eyebrow. "And that's not a lie?"

"It gives away the lie of the illusion, reminds the viewer that what they're looking at is two dimensional."

"Fantastic," Fallon muttered as she peered closer, then spoke for Edgar. "And like a signature, it points back to the artist, reminds the viewer that this is *your* work, not God's." The corner of her mouth lifted. "I knew you'd fit in with our little group."

That night they played the play again, but it was seen with different eyes, different minds. If the troupe succeeded, they would say the same lines. Fallon watched from the wings, white-knuckling the edge of the velvet curtain. The theater was one-third full, a graveyard of curved seat backs. She held her breath as Will stepped forward from the lab table center stage to deliver his soliloquy.

"To breathe"—he proclaimed, the pitch of his voice rising into silence. He inhaled.

The house hung for a second, suspended between birth and death, each person like another, one filling one hundred seats. Fallon couldn't tell them apart. This person they all were talked alike, looked alike, made their way to work each morning along the same roads. All day they mostly did what was expected, then clocked out at five and drove home to fix dinner, watch the show, put the kids to bed. The next day they did it again. They were aimless save the mission of living. And in living this way, they were dead.

The audience knew how the line of the play would end, how their lives would end. It was inevitable, and yet they pushed the thought to the backs of their minds, held some meek hope it would go another way. They pretended to forget.

Fallon was different. It was because she kept death over her shoulder that she lived. She was someone created, a work of art. How strange it was to have been someone other when she was younger, she thought, almost like them. How strange to live this way or that, to love, to be anyone at all, really, a being in a body.

"Or not to breathe." Will inhaled. "*That* is the question."

Night Travel

The train cut across the country, severe in its sever, a machinated vector splitting (exacting task) nature's imprecision: the woods and the fields fallen fallow, a raindrop's crooked path, streams following the current of the landscape. All decimated by a line manmade: so sure, so true, like a zipper down the curve of a woman's back.

Edgar left his compartment for the bar car, smoothed his tussled hair. It was early—half-past eleven—but he couldn't help but hope he'd meet Ava there before the others arrived.

When he passed her compartment, he saw the accordion door was open enough for an eye, and there was one: one dark iris to match his. As soon as he saw it, Ava's accordion door slammed with a rattle, bounced open a blank slit.

The question was what to show and what not to. Chantal wanted to garner attention, which wouldn't necessarily have to be from Edgar, but she wouldn't mind either. Because she wasn't sure what kind of women he liked, only that he hadn't so far fallen for her, she figured she'd try being a different kind, maybe more like Ava. Chantal had a hunch.

She turned to the mirror in her compartment, smoothing her hands over her hips and distractedly rubbing her thigh to assuage her aching foot. Her black wrap dress had sleeves. It covered her knees. Ladylike, it left much to the imagination, but it was a turncoat, working for any man she met by revealing a thigh via slit, a bra strap when its shoulder slipped. The fabric hugged her curves, shifted and slid over them, requiring her to keep touching her body to adjust it. It was a dress that could be opened completely with one tug on its fabric-belt bow.

Chantal's stomach growled. She fluffed her blond bangs higher, checked her lipstick, stretched her neckline lower, and leaned forward a little to test it. It gaped. She slumped, leaned back in laughter, lifted her elbow to the angle it would rest on a bar, tippled a pretend drink.

The dress was perfect, revealing a hint of her black-lace bra any time she moved.

Sitting on the edge of the bed, she nudged a pair of stilettos closer with her foot, then slipped one on and used the tip of her finger as a shoehorn to wriggle her prosthetic foot into the other. With one last look at her backside, she left her compartment.

Edgar ran a hand along the carved curve of the bar car's mahogany bar, which was deserted of both flies and tender. It had a warmth, like a body, and his elbows fit nicely in slight hollows at its edge where others had worn down the wood.

With a tinkling, the storeroom door at the other end of the bar swung open, and the bartender backed out, holding it open with his shoulders as he maneuvered a plastic rack of glassware through the narrow doorframe. He had on the same white button-up, black pants, and apron he always wore, and when he turned, Edgar was slapped by the past. Here again was the famous face of pennies and fives—now of bar cars.

"Sorry about the wait, boss," said Honest Abe. "Thought I'd restock while I had the chance. You're lucky, though—just missed the rush." The glasses clinked as he set the tray on the bar. "What'll it be?"

Edgar had to try. Although he'd asked the bar-car cocktail waitress, he'd never asked the bartender himself. He winced the question. "A Negroni?"

"A classic!"

Edgar's face slackened. "You know it?"

"Of course! Just let me make sure I have Campari. I haven't seen it here before, but that's not to say—" The bartender turned to scan the backbar's liquor display. "Aha!"

He reached a long arm to the dusty bottles on the back row and carefully tipped one forward, retracting it from its spot. He wiped the bottle with the dishcloth slung over his shoulder, then twisted the metal cap to crack the seal.

Hearing this made it real. Edgar's mouth watered.

"Not a common cocktail, though it's a standard Savoy," the bartender said as he dropped a large ice cube in a crystal stirring glass, poured in the aperitif, and reached for gin. "A lot of folks don't like it. They say it's too bitter."

"I'm surprised anyone out here has an opinion on it at all. I haven't seen Campari in weeks."

"We tend to be a bit uncivilized," the bartender said, stirring with a long metal spoon. "But we're good folks."

He switched the spoon to his left hand and extended his right to Edgar. "Arthur Conan-Doyle."

"Excuse me?" Edgar asked as he shook the man's hand.

"Don't worry—everyone calls me Art."

Edgar gave his own name. "Any relation?"

Art shook his head as, in one motion, he lifted the stirring glass and poured its contents through a Hawthorne strainer into a lowball glass. "My mother was a huge fan. She was also a Conan. When she met my father—a Doyle—she couldn't resist, though there weren't many other reasons to be with him, that's for sure. Even his name was only interesting when joined to hers." Art picked an orange from the bowl of citrus on the bar top and, with a knife, peeled off a strip of rind. "When he took off shortly before I was born, she figured she could name me whatever she wanted. That's how this piece of art"—he swept a gesture top to tail—"came to be."

He spritzed the orange peel over the glass, wiped the rim with it, and pushed it in beside the ice. "That'll be ten," he said as he slid the drink toward Edgar.

Edgar listed to retrieve his thinning wallet from his back pocket and set down three fives, glancing between Art's face and Lincoln's as the bartender collected the cash. Albeit not exact, the resemblance was incredible.

"Keep the change," Edgar said, and Art nodded. Edgar lifted the drink to his lips. Behind the bright scent of orange oil, the Negroni was aromatic, perfectly balanced. He took three long swallows. For a split second his mind drifted to Rome, to the wobble of cobblestone under his boots, but he tore himself back to the bar.

Projecting the trajectory of the drink's decline, Art started making a second. As he poured, he motioned his chin toward the paint splattered across Edgar's worn-thin tee. "You a painter?"

Edgar nodded.

"Tough trade. My dad was a bricklayer. Worked his body until it fell apart and then some." Art stirred, whirling the spoon around the ice.

"No, I'm a *painter*—an artist."

"Ah," Art said. "Invaluable work, creating worlds, but not so different from bricklaying, is it?"

"Especially what I'm doing now, building theater sets. The sheer scale is backbreaking, not to mention the pace."

"You The Troupe Adores' new guy?"

Edgar nodded. "You know them?" The warmth from the wood of the bar was bleeding up his arms.

"We run into each other now and then." Art smiled. "And I like chatting with artsy folks. I'm a bit of a performer myself, actually, though nothing so grand as the troupe. I'm strictly an impersonator, played Lincoln for fifty years at historical sites and public events but never once considered myself an actor. You probably didn't recognize me, though, without my stovepipe hat." He winked. "As I always say, 'Don't worry when you are not recognized, but strive to be worthy of recognition.'"

After sliding the second drink toward Edgar and collecting a ten, Art removed a handful of glassware from the plastic rack he'd entered with and began shelving it under the backbar. "Looks like you're worthy of recognition right now," he said. "And by no one less than Miss Ava Vale."

Before Edgar could swivel his head toward the private cars, Ava slid onto the barstool to his left in a kelly-green, sleeveless jumpsuit and white sneakers, her dark curls tangling over her shoulders. They were almost always between him and her, enclosing her, wrapping about her self-satisfactorily, like a cat's tail. When they weren't, she crossed her arms, palmed her cheek, kept him at bay with a bent knee.

Edgar took another swallow of Negroni.

"Isn't anyone else here yet?" Ava asked. Art set a glass of red wine before her, which she lifted to sip. From the purse slung across her chest, she retrieved a pack of cigarettes and a crumpled ten. This she smoothed on the bar top for Art. "Even your camera's late tonight, huh?" she said to Edgar. "I thought you explored all mediums."

This rankled him, as he guessed was intended, which rankled him more. He kept his eyes on his dwindling drink. "Right now, I'm working in gin," he said.

"Well, that's easy, isn't it? But I thought whiskey was more your thing." Ava took a look at his glass. "Wait—did you finally get that fancy drink you've been asking for everywhere?"

Edgar gave an almost imperceptible nod.

"Does it transport you back to Rome?" Ava continued. "Remind you of strolling ancient streets on cool summer nights? Of candlelit tables?" She smiled as Edgar rasped his stubble. "Of gelato stands, crumbling ruins, tiny espresso cups clattering in their saucers?"

He ran his hands along his thighs, wiping the sweat from his palms. To spite her, he finished his drink through his teeth, though he could barely stand it now for what it evoked.

Ava must have sensed the rift, for she let up the roller shade of her front. With her window glass exposed, her voice softened. "Do you miss it? I've never been."

"I don't talk about Rome."

"You did before."

"That was a mistake."

Ava raised both hands. "Just trying to make conversation. It's the only thing I know about you."

Neither of them noticed Art slide a third Negroni before Edgar.

"You've seen my art, so you know me," Edgar said, his irritation extinguished. "There's nothing more to know. My question is: who are you?" At last, he looked at her. She was so beautiful, it hurt.

Ava sipped her wine. "I could say the same thing. You know me from my art."

"It's not the same. Your art is being another."

"Everything you see onstage is me." There was a beat of silence, which Ava broke. "Can I try it?"

"Try what?"

She motioned toward Edgar's drink. "I want to see what all the fuss is about."

Edgar handed her his glass. It was ice cold, but the warmth from the wood of the bar now radiated from his arms to his chest and legs. His teeth were somehow numb. He tapped them together.

Ava tipped the drink to her lips and swallowed, wrinkled her nose. Her little nose wrinkled.

"It's an acquired taste."

"I'm not sure I could learn to love something so bitter." Ava smirked. "But you never know." She slid the drink back, overturned her pack of cigarettes, and slapped it twice against her palm.

There was a crystal ashtray farther down the bar, and Edgar stretched to reach it, grabbed a matchbook from a nearby tray of them. He tore, struck, held the flame between himself and Ava. They watched it quiver, moved by draft or train or charging heart. Edgar could feel the warmth of the flame, of their bodies, the warmth of the wood and the drinks within him. Then Ava, lifting a cigarette, puckered her lips, leaned toward him.

Edgar saw only rosebud, kiss come nigh and nigher. It was time. He leaned to meet her, but before he could land or plant, she touched the cigarette to her lips, dipped it in flame, and breathed in. Its lit tip brushed Edgar's cheek, and an arc of sparks showered down. Then so did he, unable to check his momentum. He tipped forward on his barstool until his brow bone hit the knob of Ava's shoulder. She smelled of juniper and sage, a landscape. Edgar moaned with the burn of the missed kiss. He traced her clavicle with the tip of his tongue.

She sighed smoke. Then, looking toward the door, pushed him away. The rest of the troupe had come in. Fallon, seeing Ava and Edgar, led Will and Chantal to the other end of the car.

In her compartment, Fallon dressed the back of her director's chair with her black jacket. Without a body, the chair wore it blankly, unable to give it shape.

In the flowery china teapot she'd filled with steaming water from the kettle on the observation car's hot plate, Fallon added two spoonfuls of Earl Grey tea. She set the pot on her makeshift desk with a matching cup and saucer and sat. Then Fallon scried, conjectured.

Enter AVA, who interrupts BEN in his study. Enthroned on a saddle-brown, cracked-leather armchair, and with his mop of light-colored curls haloed by the reading lamp over his shoulder, he is surrounded by his attributes: a thick, hardback volume of the collected Shakespeare and red wine of an excellent vintage.

AVA

I'm not going.

BEN sets the wineglass on the end table beside his chair, methodically marks his place in the tome with its bound-in red ribbon, and closes the book in his lap.

BEN

Why not?

AVA

It's not what I want. I want to stay.

BEN

With me?

AVA

With the troupe. I want you to go. And I want to go—on tour with the troupe this season, as usual. This will be good for us. I need some time. Some time alone, I mean.

BEN

(*Looking down, pressing the pad of his thumb against the book's sharp corner, and speaking almost to himself*) Mean indeed. (*With renewed vigor*) Are you worried about working? The Rude Mechs said they'd take you on as well, but if you don't want to do Shakespeare—

AVA

It's not that.

BEN

(*He stands, nesting the book in the dent of the cushion, where the leather still holds his shape, as though some version of him still sits there. Then he approaches Ava, hugs her.*) Come with me. I need you. Some new scenery will do us good. (*He slides his hand down her arm, then takes her hands in his.*)

AVA

All we've had is new scenery, countless towns panning across the windows of the cars.

BEN

But there's so much more to be seen.

AVA

Give me till the end of the season. In the meantime, you know where to find me. (*She squeezes his hands, lets them go, and crosses the stage, turning back once before exiting stage left.*)

ॐ

All things bend toward disorder. That's the bent of it, of us, thought Ava.

She was sitting among the moguls of her mussed comforter. The best part about not having a husband, or not having a husband with her, should have been having the bed to herself. But Ava didn't even have that.

Nightly since this season's start, since Ben left or she left Ben, the fox, cautious even in the dark, slinked into her compartment. When it was certain Ava was asleep, it jumped onto the foot of the bed, scratched at the coverlet, circled a few times, and lay, its tail curled about itself.

Sometimes the slight weight of it settling on Ava's ankles startled her awake, but by the time she looked down the length of the bed, the fox would be gone, a few red hairs proof she hadn't dreamt it.

Ava rooted one hand in the drawer of her nightstand among coins and keys, checkbooks and chargers, feeling for her phone. When her fingers gained purchase on the pocket-sized *Romeo & Juliet* Ben used to read to her from, she found the phone lying quietly beneath it, like a corpse beneath its gravestone. She cradled the phone in her lap and bowed her head over it as though she was at a seance, willing.

Ben hadn't called. He didn't. It wasn't that Ava missed him. It wasn't so much. It was that she wanted to be wanted, wanted the choice of not being with him, anything but this coolness. What was she, after all, if she wasn't loved? She wasn't sure who she was without an other.

On the bed, her physics textbook spelled it out.

The measure of molecular disorder, or randomness, within a macroscopic system is called entropy. As a rule, all ordered systems gradually decline: ice melts, wood burns, sugar dissolves, and a pendulum slows.

The Second Law of Thermodynamics states that in an isolated system (one that is not taking in energy), entropy never decreases.

$$dS = \frac{\delta Q}{T}$$

Originally, the Second Law referred to the process in which usable energy in the form of a difference in temperature between two bodies is dissipated as heat flows from the warmer to the cooler body.

Every Sunday, to start the week, Ava would fight entropy, mostly because no one else in the troupe would. She'd dust and mop her compartment, bleach and scrub the sleeper car's small bathroom, straighten and vacuum the observation car. When all was in order, she'd shower and shave her legs, file and paint her nails, pluck her brows.

From that point, the week dismantled. Each day, her nightstand grew dustier, the tapestried sofa's throw pillows more disordered, the bathroom mirror spattered with soap. Her nails became ragged, and hair sprouted where it was unwanted.

Her workweek pattern was similar. It started orderly, with the troupe's two repertoire shows. Because Ava knew these standards by heart, they required only a walkthrough of the blocking and a refresher on the script to make the lines fall back in line. But on Thursdays, the troupe would move on to new plays. Everything was unfamiliar, then, as they scrambled to finish the script, memorize lines, block scenes, build sets, and set characters in time. Ava would finish the last matinee in shambles only to restart the cycle.

She was already tired, and it was only Wednesday. There was always something to do, something that could be done to beat back the hard lean toward chaos. And she'd do it, make the effort. Why, then, hadn't she done so for her marriage? She and Ben had acted passion five times a week, not including rehearsals. Onstage, they worked to keep each night fresh, to see each other as if for the first time. Why hadn't they cleared the cobwebs offstage?

There was a long zipper down the side of her kelly-green jumpsuit, which Ava undid. Her compartment's narrow closet was usually packed tight, but with Ben's things gone, her dresses and coats swung sparsely on the bar. She hung the jumpsuit beside them and slipped a baggy, faded tee over her head. It had once been Ben's, but she'd considered it hers for so long she'd nearly forgotten.

Ava picked up the textbook. As she set it on her nightstand's cold marble, a sentence leapt out.

Without new energy—a whack from the outside, a shake, a kiss of flame—isolated systems become less and less structured as they inevitably slide into an eternity of tepid monotony.

She yawned. As soon as you stopped sweeping, trimming, dusting, she thought, the porch filled with leaves, the grass overgrew, the motes set-tled. Marriage, like life, was one long fight against falling apart. Could Edgar be a build toward order? Could he deisolate her system, add heat?

Ava retrieved her phone from the bedding and looked at its blank black glass. Ben hadn't called, and she wouldn't. Let the coward work up the balls to tell her it was over, she thought. Why should she have to do it all?

The change in the drawer chattered when she dropped the phone into it and slammed it shut. There was a flash of red, then, from be-neath her bed as the fox burned across the compartment and slipped out through the gap where the accordion door didn't close. Ava's fingers tingled from the startle.

LISBON, KANSAS

February 9

Rolling thunder half-woke Ava from her dream of fisticuffs, of either throwing or taking a punch. The sound brought her comfort. She rolled over in bed, pulling the sheet taut across her shoulder, and balled her fists beneath her chin in fetal position, in basic boxing stance.

But behind her window's red velvet curtain, the morning was cloudless. The sun was lighting the sky. In the rail yard's gray gravel, Edgar and Will walked by, a sheet of tin between them. Each step rumbled a wave that pushed the same shape through the air to Ava's ear.

Hours later, Chantal woke lazily, stretched and sighed, slowly opened her—*shit*. The light was too bright. She'd overslept. She grabbed her phone. Rehearsal was ten minutes ago. Until she made enough of a name to try her luck in Hollywood, she needed the troupe; her role in it was crucial for moving beyond it.

Chantal scooted toward the foot of the bed, the only way out with the man beside her pinning her in. He was a family man, probably retired, who'd been taken with her conservative dress. All evening, he'd talked about what a lady she was, repeating, "They don't make 'em like you anymore." He'd been all right, fun enough to pass an evening with, but she remembered now with a sinking feeling that Edgar hadn't so much as noticed her, what with Ava beside him.

When Chantal walked into the bar car, the two had looked cozy, but for some reason, Fallon had steered her and Will away, then Edgar left soon after. Ava had never known how to close. She'd been married, sure, which was more than Chantal could claim, but Chantal credited that to Ben. Ben was a closer.

At the foot of the bed, Chantal woke the man by placing her hands on his thighs and pumping her weight on his legs, bouncing him violently on the mattress. He snorted, startled, and took a kick at her, but the blanket didn't allow his leg enough reach.

"Sorry, sorry. I thought you were an intruder," he said, rubbing his eyes.

Chantal flung his Chicago Bears jersey at his chest. "Get dressed, and get out. I've got to go." The man blinked. "Now."

Hopping on the compartment's small square of flooring, she popped on her prosthetic leg and stepped into the nearest pair of crumpled jeans. Then she raked her hair into a ponytail. As she twisted the elastic around it, she looked in the mirror and was glad she did. Her eyes were raccooned with last night's mascara. She was late, but wasn't one of those women who didn't care how they look.

Chantal rummaged in her makeup kit for a wet wipe and erased the smears under her eyes, coming too close to the lashes. Her right eye stung with soapy sop, and she held it closed as she swigged mouthwash from its bottle. Swishing the wash in her mouth, she wriggled her feet into a pair of white tennis shoes and walked briskly from the room, down the hall, and into the rail yard, where she twisted and spat an arc of green liquid on the way toward town.

⇛

February 10

From inside the observation car, the cars creeping past on the yard's parallel tracks made it look like the troupe's were moving. Ava wished it were true. The tour had been dragging, no part more than the long afternoons between dress rehearsal and first performance. The middle was always the hardest to get through.

They were filling time. Ava hadn't so much as glanced at the textbook wilting in her lap. On the tapestried sofa, Will flipped to and fro through his script. Chantal and Edgar occupied the wingbacks that grazed on the red Persian rug—her picking a zit in a small round mirror, him scratching halfhearted crosshatch on a sketch. The only one toiling was Rachmaninoff, whose furious chords sparred on the CD player in the corner.

Fallon sat sideways in the chesterfield, knees flung over one of its tufted arms, her back braced against the other. She was practicing her sleight of hand. She held up an ace of spades, made a chopping motion, and the card disappeared. Another chop brought it back. All this while staring blankly out the window.

"What's the difference between a magician and a god?" Fallon asked.

Will set his hands on his script, blinked himself back from the scene he'd mentally been in. "What do you mean?"

"I mean, what's the difference?"

"Exactly," said Chantal. Ava saw her catch Edgar's eye before rolling hers.

The card came and went, came and went. The generator hummed heat into the room. The course of Ava's thoughts had been changed. This furrowed her brow. "Where is this coming from, Fallon?" she asked.

"We're in the observation car, my little diamond," Fallon said. The card disappeared. "I'm just making an observation."

"We don't like to admit—like to admit"—Will spat—"our small faults." He set the slip of paper aside and drew another from his upturned top hat.

Distracted in the wings, Fallon refocused all her attention onstage. There, it was arctic spring. A thaw had stripped the snow to pelts, striped them with slate. Where she stood holding a sheet of tin in one hand and a light in the other, Fallon could see Ava as the Inuit princess Tuuluuwaq, supine beside a beached sheepskin canoe. There was an arrow in her chest, pointing to her heart.

Fallon heard Edgar pulling the ropes in the trap room beneath the stage, and Ava's heart-wound bled a length of red silk. It was the only color against the snow, the slate, the woods, the gray-beige of the furs.

The scant audience mumbled approval, and Will as the Viking Hrodgeir, Tuuluuwaq's forbidden love, entered stage right, where boulders blocked his view of the princess. He let out a gull call, listened. He called again, coming farther downstage.

Will cried out. He knelt beside Ava's body, then jumped to his feet and looked about for the archer. Assured no one else was there, he knelt again, lifting Ava's head and resting it in his lap. A key light lit her fur-framed face, its blue-black tattoos striking above the blood.

Will snatched a fistful of slate pebbles from beside his knee and threw them to the stage full force. He let out a sob, stopped himself, then launched into a speech. Spittle caught the lights, each syllable ballistic.

HRODGEIR

Coming to leave with you, I find you already gone! My love for you filled my heart, and I poured it out to you, so it could fill your heart too. I had enough for us both. With your blood, your life, and your love spent, mine too seeps into this land. I am nothing now but melting snow, erased by wind and wave.

Fallon held her breath as the audience vanished in rapture. They were perfectly silent, absolutely still. Will looked up.

HRODGEIR

I swear—

Will looked at Ava, whose head was still in his lap. "I swear—"
He looked into the wings at Fallon, who could feel her jaw clenching. She whispered the next few words of the line, but he couldn't hear.
"I swear—" Will repeated, unable to go on.
Ava's eye slit open. She muttered through a corner of her closed lips, "You swear a hronis eel-ard—"
At that, the words rushed back.

HRODGEIR

I swear a promise steel-hard as this black slate, as this fine sword, that before the next full moon, this land will run red with the blood of your murderer. For you and I were one, and your death is the death of the man I once was. I once was Hrodgeir of the Vikings. Now I am yours.

A single sniffle broke the audience's silence. Then another, from the mezzanine. A third made a constellation, then one by one, the stars switched on—a tissue rustle here; there, the clearing of a throat—connecting the dark swaths between them.
Fallon wielded a flash of lightning, shook her sheet of tin. The curtain lowered for intermission, and as soon as it touched the boards, she rushed to peer out one end.
When the house lights came up, eyes in the audience were reddened, avoiding others'. Hands not clutching clutches clutched tissues, and some, rosy-nosed, swallowed the lumps in their throats. Fallon hoped they had to remind themselves it was just a play.

Ava lifted her heel to the edge of her bed and leaned forward against her tightly closed knee, hooking her toe in the toe of a rolled-up black stocking. Then she leaned back, pointing her foot and straightening her leg in the slowest cancan kick. The stocking stretched taut, and she let the length pull through her fingers like kite string.

At the bottom of her tiny closet, tucked between boxes and dropped clothing, the fox slept in a curl. As Ava's bare leg lifted for the next kick, it yawned, its bared teeth a line cut with pinking shears. It arched its back, ellipsing its curl, and stretch-straightened a black-stockinged leg so hard its small paw shook.

When Ava stood, the fox flip-twisted to a crouch. It froze, ears swiveling. A nostril twitched. Then it scrabbled among boxes—gnawed, dug, scratched, clawed, chewed farther back into the under-umber.

With a click, the scene was captured. It was unusual to find a place in town still open after one of the troupe's performances, and from the way the bar's patrons seemed to be there simply because they could, Edgar would bet it was the only one for miles.

The room was hazy with smoke, the product of a thousand sighs over love or money or simply the end of a long workweek, exhalations that intensified the multicolored lights of a jukebox and cigarette machine in the corner. If Edgar didn't know better, he would have thought he'd time traveled. The evening had begun in seventeenth-century Greenland, was now in 1970s middle America, and would conclude in the train: a world outside the world, spanning decades. He was never sure where he was within it, where he was with Ava.

Edgar lowered the camera, swiveled his stool back toward the bar, and took a maiden bite of burger. The well whiskey he'd ordered had been too sweet at first but now satisfyingly cut the salt and grease.

The couple seated at the bar beside him were gathering their things. As they stood, the man dropped a few crumpled bills beside his plate. Then Ava, in heels and earrings, dropped onto the stool next to Edgar. The silk robe she wore open over a black turtleneck ended far beyond the shredded cutoffs she had on over stockings.

"You shouldn't drink alone," she said. "You'll set a precedent."

She motioned to the bartender for a drink, crossed one leg over the other and, leaning back, clasped her hands just below her kneecap, underlining the spot where the stocking stretched sheer.

But she couldn't sit still. Ava leaned forward and placed her elbows on the bar, fanned her fingers across her mouth, dug in her purse. For once, Edgar felt like he had the upper hand.

"I can't believe they allow smoking," she said to him, or maybe to no one, setting a cigarette between her lips. Her lips. Her skin. The line of her cheekbone gilded by the cigarette machine's amber light. She was a strike-anywhere match. She held up a matchbook. Edgar lifted the camera from his lap.

From her fingers came a rasp, whip crack, flash, radio static, then flame (that silent, wavering eye of the storm), heat, and a reflexive scolding out as Ava gave the match a shake, unspooling smoke, which unraveled to linger. The camera clicked.

Ava took a deep drag and exhaled, the last of it clouding what she said next. "Can't we just have a drink without making something of it?" She stood pointedly, and her lips twitched a smirk. "Besides," she added, gesturing to Edgar with the lit cigarette's tip. "Your lens cap's on."

Edgar turned the camera around to check but, no sooner than he had, glass crashed. He swiveled his stool.

Ava, trying to make a quick exit, must have tripped. Her weight hung limply from her taut arms, which were planted elbow-deep on a tabletop crowded with left-behind pint, wine, and lowball glasses. Where her palms rested on the wood, the glassware had been knocked over. Red wine, Edgar hoped, bled from the edge of the table. Her dark hair smudged out her face. As he watched, she turned her head slowly to look back at him, opening the curtain of hair with her cheek, and released more smoke. He tore the lens cap from the camera and—click—captured it.

Ava stepped her legs back beneath her, using the table to regain her balance, then returned to the bar. She took it from the top.

"You shouldn't drink alone. You'll set a precedent," she said, sliding back onto the barstool. Then she touched her hand to his chest, kissed him.

❧

Ava and Edgar lay in bed—separate beds in separate compartments, restless. All night the night psst. The moon circled like a shark.

❧

At her mirrored desk, Fallon scried, conjectured.

Swaddled in the lamplight of her sleeper-car compartment, AVA rifles through BEN's drawer, paws like a cat in a litter box. She slides the weighty cologne bottle toward her, sprays it in the air to parachute a mist of scent over his things. He's left odds and ends: a screwdriver, tape, a clothespin, paperclip, and pin—things to fasten. Things to sever too: scissors, a pocketknife, a corkscrew, and pliers.

She lifts a wrinkled receipt—for condoms, which they never use. To fasten or sever? It is dated during the troupe's last hiatus, just a week before he told her about leaving, about his new position.

For a second, AVA sees herself driving, shotgun riding shotgun. Then the feeling drops. She feels punched in the gut, numb, but she wants to know. She picks up her phone, listens to it ringing his and, as she listens, wonders who he is. Her husband, but who else? How much of what she knows is true?

❧

February 11
THE MIDWEST CHORUS | THEATER REVIEW
Vikings, Like Lightning, Pillage Villages
The Troupe Adores
The Lyric Theater
Lisbon, Kansas
Remaining performances: tonight at 8 p.m., tomorrow at 3 p.m.

Latin for "I shall please," placebos have—in study after study—proven an effective treatment for a slew of disorders, physical and psychological. Sugar pills work nearly as well as antidepressants and morphine drips, perceived allergens can cause reactions, and perceived ergogenic aids can improve athletic performance. People under the impression they are consuming alcohol show sensorimotor impairment, and those coming off supposed addictive substances suffer severe withdrawal symptoms. After one man took twenty-six harmless placebo pills in an attempt to commit suicide, his blood pressure dropped dangerously low.

Strangely, a placebo's effectiveness cannot be confidently pinned on belief or trust in medical professionals. In fact, even when people are told their medicine is a placebo, they show marked improvement, reporting twice as much symptom relief as patients receiving no treatment.

This could explain the audience's reaction to the opening performance of *Vikings, Like Lightning, Pillage Villages*. We weren't surprised that, yet again, Will Connaught was no Ben Sterling, forgetting his lines mid act on the very night Sterling debuted in *King Lear* to rave reviews halfway across the country. But Connaught's got beginner's luck; like the faithful citing God's mysterious ways, the audience's willingness to believe transcended his failures. They saw through the artifice to a deeper truth, and when the lights came up at intermission, there wasn't a dry eye in the house, including ours (albeit for an altogether different reason).

Will's stomach churned. He pushed past Chantal to one of the green plastic trash bins lined along the alley.

"Watch it! My leg's not on," she said.

As Chantal leaned against the brick wall and hopped herself into balance, Will ripped off the trash bin's lid and vomited inside. A cloying whiff of rotting flesh met the acidic scent of sick stinging his nostrils and burning the back of his throat, and he heaved again, a passenger to his body's animal reaction. He replaced the lid and drew another slip of paper from his pocket.

"A chicken leg—chick—" He coughed, spat on the asphalt. "Chicken leg, chicken leg—is a rare dish."

"That's a good sign. Both of us are in that one."

Will looked at Chantal without lifting his head, could feel how bloodshot the whites of his eyes must be. "How so?"

"You're the chicken, and I'm the dish, see?"

"Are you sure this is a good idea? I'm not sure Fallon would approve."

Chantal massaged her thigh. "She's always asking us to help spread the word, so she'd better approve. I'm tired of not getting paid, aren't you? You've got the flyers?"

Will nodded, patting the stack clamped under his arm. While he lifted the trash bin's lid again, riding another heave, Chantal cut the empty sleeve of her pant leg off just above the end of her residual limb. Her prosthesis was leaning against the wall behind her, and she slipped the pant leg over it. A train horn held, its sound growing louder.

"Here it comes!" she said.

Will left the alley and rounded the corner of the building just before the train drew its curtain between them and the busy shopping center on the other side of the tracks. The horn's note lowered as it passed, and they hurried out, Chantal hopping on one leg. She bounced to regain balance between each jump forward, the prosthetic leg flailing in her hand.

When she was as close to the tracks as the passing train allowed, Chantal squatted on her leg, then fell onto her backside. She tossed the prosthesis a short way away and lay on the weedy margin. Will opened a bottle of stage blood. He poured it over the ends of both prosthetic and residual limb, splashing the ground between the two, and they waited for the train to pass. Its momentum created a wind and caused the ground to tremble, making their proximity to it uncomfortable. Then the caboose slipped by, and the curtain of the train opened, revealing them to the townspeople across the way. For a moment, the stillness was relieving. Then Chantal started screaming.

An ancient snow machine hung dusty in the theater's rafters, among the lights and fly system. Edgar leaned out over the railing of the catwalk, flipped the machine's red switch. Nothing happened, at first, but a buzz. Then a few motes of snow floated down to the stage, disappearing as soon as they touched it.

Walking as quickly as he could without breaking into a jog, Edgar left the theater through its stage door. He crossed the small town, the road that stretched into the fields on its outskirts, the railroad tracks, and then the rail yard's gray gravel. When he blustered into the observation car, each member of the troupe had half a sandwich on a napkin in their lap, the other in their hand. One, as yet untouched, sat on the end table nearest Ava, presumably for him. Edgar's thigh muscles twitched from quitting their exertion, like the ticking of a cut engine.

"You did what?" Fallon was asking.

Chantal's laughter filled the car, making it feel smaller. On the last peal, she slapped her magazine on her prosthetic knee in delight.

Fallon turned to Will, who lifted his script across the lower part of his face like an outlaw's bandana. She eyed them both. "Run it past me first, next time."

Will submerged himself underpaper.

"Your flyers aren't exactly selling out shows," Chantal said. "We took matters into our own hands. You should be proud of our initiative. After all, we're here to make a living, right?"

Edgar tried to break in, but Fallon held up one long finger without so much as looking over. "We're here to make art, first and foremost," she said. "I don't want my troupe associated with cheap stunts, no matter how many tickets they sell—or don't, in this case."

"You're telling me we didn't see a sales bump from Will's and my performance?"

"I know this will come as a shock to you," Fallon said. "But people tend to hold a grudge when they find out they've been lied to."

Edgar couldn't stand it anymore. "Why didn't you tell me the theater had a snow machine?" He tossed up his hands.

Fallon had been targeted, such an easy place to aim in her black, with that white bullseye on her chest. "I didn't know they had one," she said.

"I could have been using it this whole time. I could have—"

Chantal puffed her cheeks and lips and squinted. Barely moving her mouth, she squeezed a deep, hoarse voice from the back of her throat out over the faded, white-bread-blotted lipstick on her lower lip. "You don't understand," she croaked, eyes nearly closed and chin raised. Her hand turned micro-circles under her chin. The effect was that of a ventriloquist without a dummy. "I coulda had class."

Were they making fun of him? Edgar looked from one face to the other, uncertain.

Will crafted a similar expression. "I coulda been a contender. I coulda been somebody."

Chantal set her sandwich-laden napkin on the nearest ottoman, then stood. "I coulda been somebody, instead of a bum, which is what I am. Let's face it."

They were. They were making fun of him. Chantal motioned in Edgar's direction. Then Ava laughed.

Spurned, Edgar spun on his heel, put on a performance. He left the car by way of the vestibule, but halfway down the sleeper car's narrow corridor, he remembered the sandwich, which he'd never even touched.

When Edgar stopped and looked back—considering whether or not to return for it—he saw Chantal mutter something to Ava, saw Ava shrug.

༺

It had happened. Will had forgotten.

He coughed with the will to empty, only he already was. Will wiped his brow with the back of his hand, then leaned back against the wall behind his bed and swaddled the paisley robe tighter across his soft middle, knotting its cloth belt. So many times others had assured him his fears were unfounded, that he'd get used to performing, that the nerves would fade onstage. *What's the worst that could happen?* they'd say, or *Don't worry, you'll do great.* But trying to believe them was where he'd gone wrong.

Will had been lucky this time. He'd recalled his lines at Ava's prompt. But what if he hadn't? What if he'd been out there alone? What if she hadn't remembered?

The corners of his script were curled with use. "For you and I were one," he recited once more. It was something he'd never forget again.

He rested his script in the sheets, then dressed and walked to the theater, where he swapped his clothes for costume. As his stomach churned, Will pulled a slip of paper from the upturned top hat.

"At night, the alarm—alarm—alarm—roused him from a deep sleep." He pulled another. "It is hard—it is hard."

That one, he couldn't finish. Another cough punched him in the gut. His faux-fur coat was clammy with sweat. He pulled it away from his chest, tried vainly to fan a breeze beneath it, then drew one more slip of paper, for luck.

"The birch canoe slid on the smooth planks—the smooth planks."

Fallon—also in faux fur, her face ticked with blue tattoos—swung into the dressing room with one thickly mittened hand around the doorjamb, as though it were a lamppost in the rain.

"That's apt," she said. "You ready? We're on."

Will dashed a hand into the hat, gripped one last slip of paper, and rushed through the sentence as he headed for the stage. "The crunch of feet in the snow was the only sound—snow was the only sound."

The lights dimmed. The intermission din died down. Above the crowd, Edgar flipped a switch, and the snow machine whir-purred to life. He could see Will in the wings, whispering his lines over and over, waiting for the first flakes, his cue to enter. But no snow fell.

Edgar rasped his stubble. The snow machine was loaded with fluid; it should have been blowing soap. Leaning over the catwalk's railing, he tinkered with its dials, gave its side a tap. When nothing happened, a thump. Another. Still nothing, save some knocked-loose fuzz that dusted the stage.

Will wrung his gloves. He raised his eyebrows to Edgar in question as the audience shifted, coughed, and scratched. This shifted to whispers. There was actually a decent turnout.

Edgar stood, lifted a leg over the catwalk's railing, and gave the machine a good kick. It purred dryly on. He kicked the machine even harder, but this time, the purring stopped. Edgar shook his head, waved Will on.

February 12

Clip-clops tattooed the asphalt. Fallon let go of her bicycle's left handlebar mid-pedal and, wind ruffling her hair, looked back over her shoulder. A black horse and buggy turned onto the road from a dirt driveway she'd passed. If it weren't for the noise, she'd have sworn she'd seen a phantom. Then something struck familiar.

Fallon squeezed the bike's brakes and set a foot on the asphalt. From the inner pocket of her tux jacket, she pulled out a water-stained guidebook, opened it to a page blemished with marginalia.

> The National Coach Museum, Lisbon's most visited, is housed in the former riding arena of the Belem Palace, which now serves as the residence of the president of Portugal. Within lies one of the finest collections of historical coaches and carriages in the world, the jewel of the collection being a pompous and ornate baroque carriage gifted to King John V by Pope Clement XI.

The silhouette approached, all shadow. The horse's dark knees lifted like pistons. Blinders sidled its eyes. The driver, as he passed, tipped his hat, and Fallon watched the back of the buggy, packed with black trunks, drive on. She wondered what was in them.

A gift, Fallon thought. Clip, clop, clip, clop. Then a gust of wind blew her hair the wrong direction, against the part. It lifted electric.

The final performance was underway. The cast couldn't act the plot. They could only act a moment, relying on the audience to string the moments together, put them on.

At any given time, the house was attentive; some of them to the painted lichen on the backdrop, some to the wisp of faux fur sweat-stuck to Fallon's cheek, some to the spittle frothing from Will's lips. Others focused on the seduction of their date or on an argument at dinner—what they should have said, would say later—running their lines.

Likewise, the players paid attention—to a pebble in their boot or a childhood dog's death, the better to summon emotion. But mostly they attended the audience—every cough, throat clearing, phone notification, blank face, and sniffle in the right and wrong places. The house was a creature, a beast the savage music soothed. Like any animal, its danger was its I. An I that couldn't speak but in laugh and scratch, growl and howl and flee.

Worse, this beast was made of many, each with will and wandering minds, wanting what they wanted. Its rest was beast rest: no rest at all. Its tenterhooks kept the cast tiptoeing some verge between conquer and loss.

Sometimes, Fallon would near the edge of the stage and feel the front row withdraw when her world touched theirs. Each line was feed in the palm. She held it out, gingerly.

Astride Fallon's bike, Edgar coasted down the empty, rain-slick, small-town street. He'd already unloaded the last of the set in the baggage car and returned the theater's pickup truck. Even Fallon, citing fatigue, had been returned to the cars like one more stage dressing.

Balancing on the inch of width the bike's tires afforded was as natural as he remembered from childhood. It was something to be done, unlike train travel, where the landscape seemed to pass passive him. This was a relief, as was his solitude. He still felt out of place in the troupe, an interloper.

Traffic picked up at this end of town, where the highway ran through, and the wet road shushed each rushing car. As Edgar approached the railroad crossing before the rail yard, its bell clanged and a red light pulsed *no*, bleeding along the wet asphalt. He braked, put a foot down. A few cars gunned across, then the crossing arm came down like a clapboard, cutting the action.

A fanfare of horn arrived high, dove low with the train's blast of wind. Then came clattering collateral—rusty car, rusty car, rusty car—each the same as the last, rattling and rumbling thunderous, monotonous, each car's distinctive graffiti even somehow tantamount. Up close, the train's mechanics were anatomical. Edgar saw the train as a surgeon

sees a person: animal in its shoddy strength, at once fragile and resil-
ient—sometimes withstanding gunfire, other times derailed by a simple
slip, bump, clot, or cut.

Coming back to himself, the thought shot through Edgar that he
was watching the troupe's train leaving without him. He had to remind
himself that their cars were parked in the rail yard, weren't departing for
a few more hours. To confirm, he deepened his focus on the passing
train, concentrating on the gaps between cars. In this way, he could see
through it, vanish all its heavy metal. On the other side was the troupe's
sleeper car and, in its lit window, a shadow—perhaps Ava's hair—ani-
mated as if by zoetrope.

The train's coming continued inevitable, relentless, car after car lending Edgar a taste of the infinite. And just when he'd surrendered to the
waiting, the last car passed, the crossing arms lifted, and the bell fell
silent, reminding him that all things must end.

Night Travel

The train sounded, and it sounded sullen. It howled, hovering a note—no—its note not note but chord: several together that make something other, as do words, lovers, as does a cast of actors.

In the observation car, Ava was calculating. She was working it out. Everything was relative.

$$\gamma = \frac{1}{\sqrt{1 - \frac{v^2}{c^2}}}$$

Her favorite part about physics was checking the back of the book. When her answer matched, the stars aligned, even if only for a moment. She would know she'd seen it all: the v and the c, how heavy, far, or fast. When it didn't, she went back to the question, tried to find where she'd gone wrong.

Missing one now, Ava thought of Ben. They'd been a mistake. She thought they'd been moving through life together, but maybe it was only because they'd been on the same trains, in the same plays.

She leaned back in the chesterfield. Its stuffing had worn thin; she could feel the springs. A sometime screech of wheels on rails flared. Did Edgar make it easier to let go of Ben? It wasn't safe to straddle, each foot in one of two canoes.

Ava looked to the open vestibule doors at the observation car's start. She could see through to the sleeper car's rough bucks and bounces along the track. How flimsy the car ahead seemed—her sleeping place, her comfort. It rattled and tossed, but when she was within it, she felt steady, safe. And here on her lap, her pencil lay sedate against the page, though she knew her car must be tossing too. She must be.

It was one thing to peer into a possible future, to see ahead, another to be inside one looking out. Step into the swell, and she'd find sea legs. Ava completed the problem and, this time, had a match. She lit it.

At precisely midnight, Edgar entered the bar car, working his way through the crowded room and passing Chantal and Fallon, who sat at a booth behind martini glasses spotlit by a pendant light. Fallon was sleek without her heavy furs, and Chantal had the gloss of a fresh coat of paint. Her lips glistened.

Art was mixing several cocktails at once, but his face lit up when Edgar slid onto the only empty bar stool. He shook out the last of a shaker across three coupe glasses with his left hand and shook Edgar's with his other. "Negroni coming right up, boss."

Art set the triptych of glassware before a suited businessman, tucked the man's cash in his apron pocket, and spun a black cocktail napkin in Edgar's direction. When it stopped, it held, like a shadow, the place of the forthcoming drink. While Art righted an empty lowball glass and selected bottles from the backbar, Edgar worried the napkin, twirling it on the bar's dark mahogany.

"Something on your mind tonight?" Art asked, playing the part of bartender.

"Nothing more than usual," Edgar muttered.

Art lifted the bottle of gin high over a stirring glass, lengthening and shortening the line of liquor it drew in the air. He measured the pour in seconds and, when its time was up, cut the line with a snap of his wrist. "It looks more something than nothing. What's a bartender good for if you can't tell him your troubles?"

Edgar continued fussing with the napkin, and Art tsked. He added ice to the stirring glass and twirled the liquid with a long spoon. "Only a woman could trouble a man that much."

Edgar's fingers stilled. "What do you know about Ava?"

Art poured the mixture into the glass. "Ava, huh? I knew you were a man of ambition, like me. As I always say, 'Anybody will do for you, but not for me. I must have somebody.'" He laughed.

"Forget it." Edgar began swiveling away on the stool, but Art stopped him.

"What I can tell you about Ava is what I know to be true of every woman: if you know you want to go for it sometime, that sometime should be now. Come out fighting." Art carved a garnish from an orange and replaced it in the large bowl of citrus on the bar. The corner of his mouth tightened with amusement. "Of course, that's the same advice I'd give someone headed to prison."

"Love *is* a prison, isn't it? It locks you in."

"Sure," Art said, setting the drink in front of Edgar. "But it's liberating too, right?"

"Making a move's not the trouble," Edgar said, changing tack. "Or not most of it. The trouble is trusting."

"Ah," said Art as he nodded to a patron standing behind Edgar. He pulled a bottle opener out of his apron pocket, levered the cap off a beer. "What I always say is this: 'If you trust, you will be disappointed occasionally, but if you mistrust, you will be miserable all the time.'"

Edgar slid some cash onto the bar and held up his glass. "I'll drink to that."

Art nodded, turning to a man who'd just taken a newly freed-up seat at the bar, and Edgar carried his drink to Fallon and Chantal's booth.

"About the next play," Chantal was saying to Fallon, looking past her and blowing a kiss to the man at the bar. "How is anyone going to see my star potential if you stick me under an old-lady wig? Why can't I play the bartender?"

"Aunt Isodora is a far meatier role."

"Meatier?" Chantal huffed.

"You're not convincing as a man, Chantal, not with that *beautiful, feminine* figure. I'm much more convincing."

"You would be more convincing to me if you were one, you know."

Edgar swished his Negroni, clinking its large ice cube against the glass as he tried to spin it. The scenery passed.

"Can't you just rewrite it?" asked Chantal. "You're rewriting other stuff."

"Cutting the teenage Lola and making Aunt Isodora Nora's aunt was the quickest fix. This way, you're free to play the aunt, and I can play bartender, Will's old role. We'll come up with a better fix later on."

"But when? We're putting on five-part plays with four people. How long can this go on? Are you ever going to replace Ben?"

"This tour is about experimentation, about developing hits, shows that will make us money. Adding another person will hardly accomplish that. I'm writing the new plays for four, mostly. Besides, I keep thinking Edgar might—"

"I won't," Edgar said. "Not if it involves more than sets or lighting."

Will, arriving, sat in the booth. "Edgar might or might not what?"

"Ruin us all." Chantal motioned to Art for another drink.

"Now, now," said Fallon. "I have just the thing to cheer you up." She reached inside her jacket's inner pocket, pulled out three envelopes, and held one out to each of them.

"Doesn't feel like much," Chantal said, taking hers. She opened its flap and thumbed through the bills.

Fallon lifted her drink, watching the rim to keep it from spilling. "I expected we'd be doing better."

"The shows were half empty," said Will, straightening his blue button-up's collar.

Fallon swallowed. "More like half full, but yes, I noticed," she said through her teeth.

Art approached the table with Chantal's cosmo. "For-the-gor-geous-Miss-Weixler." Each syllable was spoken as though it were part of the Gettysburg Address. He set down the drink, bowed his head.

Chantal lifted her hand to her breast and toyed with the end of a blond lock of hair. "Oh, Art. You know just how to tend to a lady, don't you?"

Fallon rolled her eyes. "A lady? Let's not be hasty." She turned to Art. "You shouldn't go on like that. It goes straight to her head."

"It's my job. As I always say, 'Tact is the ability to describe others as they see themselves.'"

"I'd rather not be a lady, actually. I'd rather go do that." She tossed her head in the direction of the man at the bar and hooked her martini glass in the talon of her first two fingers. Then she turned back to Edgar. "Unless you—?"

Edgar shook his head.

"Then wish me luck." Chantal made a beeline for the bar.

The man, noticing her trajectory, took a deep, flustered drink from his pint glass. When he set it down, Edgar saw that he had one hell of a nose.

"My god," Fallon said. "Are you seeing this?"

Edgar nodded.

"It's enormous! It's beautiful. It starts beaky, noble, and bowed, and ends in that comical, blushing, British bulb. It's a clash of cultures, Britannia defending itself from the Romans. What a nose! It lends him such—gravitas. It's a nose worthy of a character, someone with depth."

Without taking her eyes from the man, Fallon felt inside her jacket for her notebook, her pencil.

Rising like Aphrodite from a sea of discarded clothing, Ava stood from the edge of her bed and stepped into a long aquamarine dress. Her bony shoulders caught the straps. Half-turning to inspect herself in the full-length mirror, she shuddered with a chill. She needed something more. Something warm and worn to wear.

A fur would do, a fox stole. The occasion called for it, after all. She slipped on silver heels and left her compartment for the baggage car. In its farthest corner was a trunk. The lid, warped by water damage, would no longer quite close. She lifted it by its cracked leather strap and slid her arm into the dark. As she raked her fingers through the mink hats, sable muffs, and rabbit capelets, some of them faux, she checked her lipstick in the tarnished mirror leaned against the wall, pressing her lips in a taut line to spread the color. Her hand stopped on fox, grasped it by the tail.

A sharp sting stung the meat beneath her thumb. Ava's mouth in the mirror bowed O as she yanked her hand from the trunk. Four punctures filled with red. The color spread.

Ava lifted the lid of the trunk to look inside, and the fox welled up, spilled over its edge, a drop of blood running.

Straddling the leg of her makeshift desk, Fallon scried, conj(ect)ured.

DRAMATIS PERSONAE
The modus operandi for nondescript JAMES JAMES is playing the part of private eye playing the part of passerby. His beige trench coat and hat are pulp detective de rigueur. His neat false mustache marks him everyman (circa '34).

JAMES knows how a private eye acts, and he acts out it all. The glass door to his office bears his name. Behind it, he smokes with his feet up, slugs bourbon from a paper cup. He gazes through the slits of the blinds, sweats in shirtsleeves, unwraps a sandwich from the deli across the street. When a client comes in, she's trouble on endless legs. She's got a face he wouldn't mind slapping a kiss on.

JAMES tails and tattles. He squeals. He's a rat for hire who knows his role and plays it to a tee.

Act One, Scene One
JAMES takes a seat in the first-class car, a treat. Rule one is to never break

character. He is Reginald Ainsworth, a jaunty British chap on holiday, an
unattached gentleman out to see the world. He hopes he won't have to speak.

JAMES peers over his splayed newspaper. His quarry, CLAUDETTE
REX, is receding down the aisle toward the dining car. As she passes, each
man perks up, all their sightlines converging on the vanishing point of the skirt
stretched taut across her ass.

Fallon worked with the text of the play, joining and rending, destroying
and creating. In writing it, she felt a fullness, somehow, and the piece felt
different beneath her pencil: behind each word was pressure, as though
it could become something.

When the train slowed to a stop at one of the small stations along
its route, Fallon stretched, rose from her director's chair. She left her
compartment, padded down the corridor to the sleeper car's small
bathroom and undressed, carpeting the four square feet of yellowed
linoleum with her wilted tux and tank top.

In the narrow shower stall, there was barely enough room to lift
an arm. Fallon scrubbed her cheeks and forehead, her elbows pressed
tightly to her sides, then turned into the spray. She'd removed the blue
lines from her face with a wipe after the play but hadn't properly washed.
It felt good to rinse away the sweat and stress of performance.

The train's horn sounded in warning, and Fallon had just enough
time to brace her elbows against the shower stall's glass before the train
jolted. Her feet slid a few inches across its plastic floor. Though she was
fairly sure it wasn't possible to fall in such a tight space, this rationale
didn't translate to her body. The thrum of it brought something to
mind.

The water running, Fallon reached a dripping arm from behind
the plastic curtain to grasp one of Chantal's eyebrow pencils from the
toothbrush cup on the edge of the sink. She removed its cap and leaned
out of the spray to write on the mirror, just in case she didn't remember
back at her desk.

The trunk is loaded. The players take a breath. They're ready to leave,
ready to love.

But once she'd dried and dressed and returned to her compartment,
the line was still with her. She sat back at her desk, copied it into her

notebook, and worked it in. When she set down her pen, what she'd written fell into position.

Claudette Rex was dressed as though she'd stepped from the pages of a noir. As she neared the dining-car door, James James folded his newspaper, causing a commotion that made no one but him glance about. He slid to the edge of his seat, waiting for the right time to follow.

Claudette had the Midas touch: her hands turned up gold. A young mother was carrying a baby down the aisle, and James watched Claudette press herself against the seats to let them pass. As they did, she brushed against the woman's arm, as if by accident. At the same time, she unclasped the gold necklace around her neck, slipped it into her pocket. The baby on the woman's hip saw all.

By the luggage racks near the end of the car, an old woman was struggling to place her suitcase on the topmost shelf, the only remaining space. Claudette, as she passed, slipped a hand into the purse hanging at the woman's side and came up with a gold silk scarf. Soon it and she would be gone.

On his way to the private cars, a man in a blue button-up shirt, tan corduroy trousers, and dusty Chucks held the door to the dining car for Claudette. She bumped into him, said excuse me, and put a hand on his back, tossing him a smile. Her eyes lingered on his as she slipped his honey-colored wallet out of his back pocket.

James stood, but just as Claudette reached the threshold of the vestibule, the conductor entered. His uniform was almost that of a policeman's. A whistle hung from his neck. "You should apologize when you bump into someone, Miss Rex," he said. He took her by the arm. "Let's see what you've got up your sleeve today."

Claudette batted her lashes. "Any excuse to see some skin, huh?"

Both her small hands were cuffed in one of his, and she struggled to wrest a wrist free as he pushed her sleeves up to her elbows. The second one rose like a curtain to reveal a wide gold bracelet wedged just below her elbow. When the conductor slid it down her arm, it left behind its phantom traced in pressure.

"Well, lookee there, lucky lady. You just won yourself a ticket downtown."

Claudette balked. "I didn't steal it. It's mine."

"Well sure, it's yours *now*," the conductor said. "But it had to have come from somewhere, and I somehow doubt that was a store. Let's go." He pushed her down the narrow aisle in front of him as the other passengers stared.

"I'm telling you, it's mine!"

~

Without thinking, Will broke through the thickness of his witnessing, projecting his voice. Lines he'd memorized from a high school play came to him, provided a way into the scene.

"Is it illegal nowadays to accept a gift? I agree she deserves something much better, but I'm the one who should be arrested for that crime, not her." He laughed a theatrical laugh.

The conductor stopped and turned.

Will gave a charming smile. "I thought something shiny might keep her close to me, but not close enough, it seems."

Claudette didn't miss a beat. She knew the part. "Bay-bee!" she exclaimed. "I'm so glad you're here!" She draped about Will's neck.

He extended his hand to the conductor. "Will Connaught, lead actor in The Troupe Adores." It was the first time he'd said his new title aloud.

The conductor's face lit up. "Say, my wife and I went to see your play last night! You were one of the scientists, right?"

"Caught me red handed!" He presented his hands as if for cuffs.

"We loved it! Even shed a tear or two." He elbowed Will. "We're no strangers to theater, you know. We played leads in our high school productions, years back. Considered making a career of it."

"So glad we could brighten your evening," Will said. "Can I offer you complimentary tickets for the next time we're in town?"

The conductor noted his audience of passengers. "Oh, I shouldn't. I'm on duty."

"Come, now. We're always glad to have appreciative theatergoers such as yourself in the audience: people with *taste*." Will patted his back right pocket for his wallet, but it wasn't there. He patted his back left pocket, then his front right and left. It wasn't in those places either. When he returned to his back right, however, it had reappeared. Will worried he was losing his mind, but he had to stay in the scene. He shook it off, retrieved two ticket vouchers from his wallet, and tucked them into the conductor's breast pocket with a wink.

The man smiled and clapped his hand into Will's, leaning in conspiratorially as they shook. For a second, he became serious.

"I'd be careful with this one, sir. You have no idea who she is."

"That's exactly what I find so attractive! It's the *getting to know her* that interests me, if you know what I mean."

At this, Claudette, her arm linked in Will's, pushed him firmly through the vestibule and into the dining car, where they took a table. He couldn't stop watching—without looking directly at, of course—her blouse's first button. It was perilously low and loose in its buttonhole. Along her deep neckline, Will sensed more than saw a shade of lace.

"Thanks." When Claudette spoke, she leaned slightly forward, and the blouse's neckline gaped. "That was close."

"Happy to help." Will felt her hand in his lap. He blushed, but then, under the table, she passed him something cold and heavy. When he looked up, her eyes were ready for his.

"I need help with something else too."

Will slowly pulled the item higher on his lap, barely out from under the hem of the white tablecloth. It was the wide gold bracelet the conductor had revealed on Claudette's arm. Its hinge was open, and at the clasp was a carving of two-faced Janus. When it shut, the faces joined at the hair—one forward, the other back.

"Is this stolen?" Will asked.

Claudette looked out the window at an ellipsis of townhouses. "Of course it is."

Will rubbed his thumb across the bracelet, over the tangles of hair where the heads met.

"Well—" she qualified. "Sort of."

He looked up.

"It *was* mine. My mother gave it to me when I was a girl, but I accidentally left it behind at my ex's when I left him. He wouldn't return it. The fucker's feelings were hurt, and he was trying to hurt mine. I had to break into his place to get it back."

"What kind of help do you need?"

"If I get caught again with stolen property—and I'm sure he's reported it—I'm going to be put away for a while."

"Put away?"

"You know, the big house up the river with the chair?"

Keeping his eyes on Claudette, Will drew his elbow back, trying to make the movement nonchalant, and felt again for his wallet in his back right pocket. It was still there under the corduroy.

"Don't flatter yourself," Claudette said.

A man in a trench coat passed their table and sat at the one behind them, back-to-back with Will. To prevent him overhearing, Will lowered his voice and leaned farther across the table toward Claudette. "What would helping you involve?"

"I need you to transport the bracelet for me. You're in that theater troupe, right? I can meet up with you a few towns down the tracks. Where will you be on the seventeenth?" Claudette placed her hand on his knee beneath the table.

"Paris."

"Fancy."

"Paris, South Dakota."

"Ah."

Will raised a hand to his mouth, bit off a torn cuticle on his thumb. "Meet me backstage opening night. I'll have it for you."

She squeezed his hand and looked into his eyes for the first time.

A waiter approached. "Can I start you two off with a cocktail, a glass of wine?"

"Oh no. I'm fine," Claudette said. The train was slowing into the next station. "This is me." She paused to give Will one more long look, then fighting the train's deceleration, she stood from the table and jerked her way down the aisle to the vestibule at the end of the car. Seconds later, Will watched her saunter past on the platform below.

James rushed to tell. He rushed to tell Frank Mitzi, thick-fingered regional pawnshop king. Mitzi wouldn't let Claudette get away with it, wouldn't let her get away. He didn't care how things came, but that they came to him. He looked the other way.

James told about the cop. He told about the stop. He told about the actor and the hand. He told about the arm. He told about the charm. He told about the bracelet and the plan.

Mitzi closed a fist. Things came and went all the time, bought and hocked, he said. He said he'd see those faces again. Both of them.

The troupe had come and gone, all except Ava. Edgar was still in the bar car, partly to see if she'd turn up and partly to drown his disappointment that she hadn't in Campari.

"So tell me, Art," he slurred from his usual stool. "Every train we hitch to has the same bar car, which"—he rushed the word to stop Art from speaking—"isn't so odd, except for the fact you're always working it. How is it possible? I can't seem to—"

The sound of travel roared across the virtually empty car as the door to the vestibule opened. Enter Ava-va-va-voom.

"Well, well, well," Art said as she approached. "You're gorgeous as ever. Maybe more so."

Edgar only dared look peripherally. He caught, from the corner of his eye, a blur of aquamarine, a sfumato of hair. Ava hopped onto the stool beside his. Her arms and shoulders were exposed, her hand bandaged. Its stark white served as a clasp for the stole she held closed about her throat.

"Can I get you a drink?" Art asked.

"I think I'd better," she said.

"What'll it be? I've got that Barolo you like and a nice Carignan I've been wanting you to try."

"I think I'm done with red wine for a while." She tipped her chin at Edgar's glass. "I'll have one of those."

Art's eyebrows rose. "You're full of surprises tonight, pretty lady." He pulled several bottles from the backbar. "Another for you?" he asked Edgar.

"What do *you* think?" Edgar replied lightly.

They watched Art pour and stir and pour and slide the glasses toward them. "Cheers," Art said. "As I always say, 'Things may come to those who wait, but only the things left by those who hustle.'" He gave them a wink and left for the other end of the bar, where he busied himself washing glasses.

The tray of matchbooks was on the bar before them, and Ava took one. She pulled a cigarette from her purse and tapped its filter on the bar's mahogany a few times before striking a match and leaning into the flame. As she exhaled, she lifted her eyes to Edgar's. "Now that you're an actor—" she said. "I have an exercise for you."

"I'm not, though."

"You are too, whether you like it or not. You're a natural. It's what made me notice you."

"You've noticed, have you?" Edgar could finally look. A haze of smoke hung about her, enlarging her hair's aura.

"I have, but you need more practice, more control."

"Then it's a shame I'm off the clock."

"Humor me. Besides, you can't turn acting off. Right now, I'm playing Ava, and you're playing Edgar."

"You're giving me too much credit, or maybe not enough."

"You are, whether you want to admit it or not," Ava said.

There were a few beats of silence, then Edgar surrendered. "What's the exercise?"

Ava swiveled on her stool to face him full on. "We switch parts. You play me, and I play you."

"I should warn you: I've never been much of a player." He smirked. She rolled her eyes. "Somehow that doesn't surprise me."

"You still want to try this?"

"It isn't such a bad thing, not to be a player. Ready?"

"As I'll ever be."

She flattened her smile, slumped on her stool, and stared broodingly at the backbar, fingering the lip of her glass with her bandaged hand.

EDGAR

Hey.

Getting the gist of the exercise, Edgar sat straighter on his stool, crossed one leg tightly over the other, and tapped his foot nervously. He took the cigarette from Ava's hand, looked away, and exhaled a long drag as he turned back. He spoke in falsetto, but flatly, dryly.

AVA

Oh. It's you.

EDGAR

Did I mention I'm an artist?

AVA

No, I don't think so. That's fascinating. So sexy.

EDGAR

It's true. I want to explore all mediums. I'm *really* devoted to my art.

Ava drank the rest of her Negroni in one long take. The ice clattered in the glass when her chin hit its apex. It clattered again when glass hit mahogany. Then she leaned slowly toward Edgar, landing on his lips. Her mouth was still cold, tinged bitter from the drink. It was like taking a sip.

"Are you still me? Or are you *you* now?" Edgar asked when she pulled back.

She took his hand.

EDGAR
Wanna come back to my compartment?

The train picked up steam. In its locomotive, the conductor squinted down track, looked to the last thing lit where the train's light bled into darkness. However far he could see, he'd be there soon enough, then beyond it. He blinked to refocus, remain vigilant, though in his gut he knew if he pulled the brakes right—now—it would take hundreds of yards to stop, roughly eighteen seconds, an end point somewhere out there in the dark, far beyond the reach of the light.

But stopping was his only defense, only offense. The inertia of the train's weight roared down the line, coming and coming, like a life, like love or death, inevitable. Sometimes he would feel an inkling, a premonition of something on the track, out there in the dark, and reach for the brake, hover his hand over the lever, his stomach turning unsure.

The train entered the tunnel.

They were in his narrow bed. Ava's head rested on Edgar's chest, which said: *A-va, A-va*. No matter how closely she pressed against him, he felt too far. The hull of his body kept her from him. Like one capsized, she could only cling, only sink.

She ran her hand up and down his seabed, diving from his bottom rib to the soft continental slope of his stomach, then back up into the shallows, beaching her fingers. They caught just where a boat would have run aground. There she hit a ridge: a scar over his heart.

Their voices hovered above a whisper, mindful of the others asleep—yawn, yawn, and yonder—in adjoining compartments.

Edgar lifted her bandaged hand to his lips. "Caught you red handed."

Ava sucked in a breath. "What?"

Edgar laughed. "What happened here?"

"What about *your* scar? You first."

"No, you."

"I went first last time, in the bar car." She smiled.

"You were being me. Technically, I did."

She sighed. "Fox bite."

"The fox?"

She nodded. "I grabbed for something I shouldn't have."

"I beg to differ."

"Then it was worth it." She motioned toward his scar. "Now you."

"Burn from a scalding pot, years ago."

"From cooking?"

He shrugged.

The corner of Ava's mouth lifted. "It needs a better story. Let's say it's from a pirate, out at sea, a pirate's cutlass."

He laughed. "This little *cut lass* right here, wielding her blade."

Ava felt a stab at the thought of the prop knife she'd wielded against his kiss, but she fortified her walls, which still stood strong around her smoldering hotbed. She drew her fingertip like a blade across the raised and rosy flesh of his scar.

Edgar stopped her bandaged hand in his and pinned it between his warm palm and the cool white sheet. "Scars there are rare. It's instinct to protect it," he said, then lifted her chin so her eyes rose to his. "Promise you'll never lie to me."

Ava ran her finger over the ridge again, the scar she could have caused. It was a line in the sand, and she kissed it. She crossed it.

MILAN, NEBRASKA

February 13

One dark eye peeked around a tied-back curtain at the edge of the stage. After a struggle with the weighty drapery, Ava stepped out from behind it. Then Edgar emerged, blinking in the light, a kiss of red lipstick smeared across his mouth.

"Why don't you want them to know?" he asked.

"This is still new. Let's wait until we're sure of it."

"I'm sure." He kissed her again, lifting his hand to where hers lay lightly against his chest. "I love this. You always do this. Ever since that first time."

Ava glanced stage right and stage left, then retracted her hand into the sleeve of her faded black Henley, stretching the cloth to his mouth and wiping off the mark she'd made. "I have to stop putting it on."

Edgar's eyes shifted. "After last night, I know you're not putting *me* on," he teased. He leaned in again, but Ava was focused on removing the red with her sleeve. The cotton caught on his stubble.

"The lipstick, I mean," Ava muttered. "I mean the lipstick."

She walked across the stage to a pile of folding chairs and lifted one, but before she could open it, Edgar took it from her hands, unfolded it with a creak, and motioned for her to sit. He began setting the other chairs in a circle, the last of which he sat in himself. Almost as soon as he had, the others arrived, completing the circuit. Fallon jolted into action.

"The play opens on the Italian countryside, just outside Rome. It's 1913, and Lord Edward Sylvius (played by Will, of course) has discovered the ruins of an ancient Roman village—" She struck something out with her pencil. "Make that *villa*, near a crumbling aqueduct. His new bride, jealous of the time and attention he's spent onsite with a beautiful local girl, ignites his cache of dynamite, destroying both villa and aqueduct and maiming the girl, for whom he'll forsake his new bride."

Chantal stopped rubbing her thigh and knocked on her prosthetic leg. "That would be me!"

"If you're going to flaunt your disability on street corners, we may as well get some use out of it here too," Fallon said. Then she turned to Edgar. "We've never shown the explosion. It happened offstage and was described in dialogue, but now that you're on board, maybe you can make a grand climax of it."

"I've never worked with pyrotechnics before," Edgar said. "But I'm sure I can put something together."

Fallon shook her head. "You're flying too close to the sun, my little Icarus. I'm thinking confetti, something you'd see on election night or New Year's Eve."

"Paper?" Edgar asked. "We want to convey the danger and intensity of the actual explosion, right?"

"Yes, but we can't—"

"Not an actual explosion, sure, but something that shoots up sparks, at least, a little smoke. Let me work on it. I'll do my research, test the thing thoroughly, make sure it's safe. It'll be great. Word will spread, and we'll have people coming from miles around."

Chantal piped up. "It won't do us much good if we blow them all up, will it?"

"We'll already have their money at that point," Fallon said with a wink. "But it might hurt our reviews."

"I doubt pyrotechnics are even legal. Fire in a crowded theater and all that, right?" Chantal said.

"I'm not going to make a bomb." Edgar scowled. "But confetti's not good enough."

Fallon turned to Ava. "You're being awfully quiet. Care to weigh in?"

The group's attention shifted, and Ava found herself in the spotlight. She looked from one face to another. "I'm just—I don't know anything about what might be possible, but if Edgar can come up with some effect that's safe and would also look better than confetti, why not let him try it?"

Chantal snapped her gum. "I love you, Edgar, really," she said, pausing pointedly. "But there is absolutely no way I'm stepping one foot"—Fallon held her tongue—"on a stage with anything remotely resembling actual explosives."

"But the paper will be too—too cute. It's not quite right," Edgar said.

"When it comes to explosions, I prefer cute," Chantal said.

"No one can get hurt," said Fallon. "We literally can't afford to lose one more cast member. Besides, nothing we can do onstage is more terrifying than what an audience can imagine."

Stravinsky's dissonance collided in Fallon's compartment. As she listened, a thrill ran down her spine, and the down on her arms stood in ovation. She scried, conjectured.

CHANTAL twirls in the dark park's grass. She is six.

CROWD
Five. Four. Three. Two. One. Happy New Year!

Fireworks burst. Before her, CHANTAL's mother sits cross-legged on a blanket, swigging gin from a flask. It glints another color each time.

The fireworks unfurl among the stars, draping over the crowd. CHANTAL tips the weight of her head back to watch and feels her throat tighten, like it does when she catches rain on her tongue. Her mother tips back her flask, laughs.

Boom! A close crackle flashes, its volume a farce, then a force throws her, blows her away from her body.

When the world snaps back, it is muffled. CHANTAL's breath rasps against the gasp of those nearby within the larger crowd's laughter. By clearing away, encircling her in a circumference either of protection or abandonment, the crowd places her on a sort of stage. Only her mother comes close, lifts her. CHANTAL is carried a long way, laid on a gurney. The night sky weeps willows of light.

She wakes the next morning drowsy and calm. Her lower leg throbs, but when she looks, it is gone.

Chantal learned the hack from her great-grandmother, who'd used it during the war. For a little flirting, a wink, and seven dollars, she'd picked up a parachute at a military surplus store on the outskirts of town. The troupe's vintage wedding dress was on its last legs, finally too tattered and yellowed to be used. It was time to retire it. Chantal was making a fresh one from clean, light white silk.

She unfurled the chute onstage, the only space large enough. It ballooned, took forever to fall. As she watched, she saw the dress in the fabric, couldn't imagine entrusting it with her life.

The pair of heavy metal scissors she held had been her great-grand-mother's too, the family's only heirloom, surviving five generations of wharf air when everything else had gone lost. Their painted-black handles were chipped—in places, rubbed to raw metal—but the blades had been honed. They shone.

Chantal ran them across the fabric, let their weight make a slit in the silk, light as air. It billowed on the draft her hand pressed forth as she undid the seam a woman had sewn while thinking of a man she'd let down easy.

꙰

With the knuckle of his index finger, Edgar wiped a run of sweat from just inside his eye, careful to avoid getting sawdust in it. The irony wasn't lost on him; he was constructing tumbling ruins.

Outside the baggage car's open fourth wall, stone-painted plywood crumbled erect as if in rewind as he lifted each block, stacked it, slid its smooth face against another's. The way the blocks fit together made him think of Ava, her cheekbone filling the hollow below his shoulder, her fullness everywhere he lacked. In the same way, he fit her.

Edgar slid two more faux stones against each other and was squatting to lift the last when he heard the rail-yard gravel crash. A group of men emerged from around the end of the baggage car. All were large, with muscly shoulders shrugged tight to thick necks, and each wore a different tracksuit with sunglasses. They were a flock of brightly colored ne'er-do-wells.

The leader of their lazy v-formation beat the side of his fist slowly and forebodingly against the car as he walked down its length toward Edgar. Its painted name, Romeo, received an extra punch. The car tolled as the man slowly lowered his hand. Edgar extended his, but it wasn't taken.

"We've got a message for your man, Will," the man said.

"I'll go get him," Edgar said. But before he could step into the baggage car, the man stopped him.

"Tell him our boss knows. He knows, and he wants that two-faced bitch back, and—uh—" The speaker looked to the others. "There was something else."

The rearmost man leaned in with a prompt. "Something about Paris?"

"Oh yeah. Mitzi can't wait to see your man in Paris. Tell him, 'Break a leg.'"

The man smiled—partly with pride for remembering the message, Edgar guessed, and partly with pleasure at the thought of how the breaking would be done. A prop detonator, which Edgar had just finished for this week's play, was standing in the rail yard nearby, and the man pressed down its plunger, blasted open a fist to feign an explosion. Then he walked back into the vee of the group behind him, turning their formation inside out and leading them back around the end of the car. As quickly as they'd come, they were gone.

❧

Ava woke alone. Something was missing.

She thought of Ben, of Edgar, then hit on the fox. For the first night this season, it hadn't come, or if it had, she hadn't noticed. Then she remembered. Last night—after Edgar—it hadn't shown either. She sat up in bed.

❧

February 14

Fallon kicked down her bike's stand and clicked its lock closed around the post of a No Parking sign. The floppy guidebook she took from her pocket had been opened countless times. Its spine read Milan in flaking gold leaf, and its limbs were limp and loose, the edges spotted with foxing. She breathed in the bouquet of its pages.

> As a global fashion capital, Milan houses the headquarters of Italy's most impressive luxury brands, from Armani to Versace. To place yourself at the center of it all, take a saunter through the Via Montenapoleone fashion district, where both the shop windows and shoppers are reminiscent of the most luxurious spreads in *Vogue*. It's like being on a fashion show's front row.

Fallon looked up. On a cross-street near Main Street's strip of shops, the window nearest her was filled with taxidermied ermine, fox, hawk, and otter. They were posed, frozen in the midst of their natural behaviors, forced to act out a hunt or frolic, flight or snarl.

As Fallon continued down the street toward the small grocery at the end of the strip, she saw a figure walking toward her on the wide sidewalk. Soon she could make out a short, older man. He wore a fedora, suspenders, a crisp white shirt, and neatly pressed suit slacks with a sheen to them. As he passed her, he touched a finger to the brim of his hat, said, "*Bonjourno.*"

Fallon wondered what he was doing here, of all places, where she was surprised anyone spoke anything other than English. Even English was debatable. She lengthened her already long strides in the direction of the grocery. There, she selected a few cheeses and a box of Saltines.

When she returned to the private cars, she set to work in the observation car making a cheese plate, steeping tea. The troupe stacked crackers and fogged their cups with cream.

Fallon saw Ava's knuckles brush Edgar's when she reached for a cracker, their thumbs touch when she passed him a teacup. His finger didn't fit within the loop of its handle, and the way he cupped the porcelain in his rough hands made it seem more breakable.

Fallon rubbed her hands together. "I can't wait for tonight's climax. The audience won't see it coming."

"Is it fair, though?" asked Will. He bit into a cracker topped with yellow cheddar, and it crumbled into pieces, some of which he caught beneath his chin.

Fallon's eye fell on him. "What do you mean, fair?"

"I don't know." Will shrugged. "They're coming to enjoy themselves. It feels wrong, somehow, drawing them in to trick them."

"They're paying to be entertained, to be immersed in another world, and we're helping them do that." Fallon shifted her address to the troupe as a whole. "We're simply asking the audience to pull its weight. After all, they have a part to play too."

Somehow, the parachute silk felt heavy. Turning toward the dressing room's cheap mirror, Ava went white. In the distorted reflection, which made her shorter and wider, the dress engulfed her. She was a ghost, or sheeted attic furniture for sale, exchanging owners. Once again, she was a bride.

Will's voice carried through the thin wall. "We dress to suit the weather of most days."

Ava had been dropped like a paratrooper into the midst of marriage. On her wedding day, she'd felt costumed, as though she and Ben were playing the parts of bride and groom. They had laughed, said the vows like lines.

"Dress to suit—dress to suit—"

She hadn't wanted to look at it, but now, in her costume, her marriage felt real. She was a wife, whether or not she would be much longer. She tried to speak the word, couldn't say it in a way that wasn't whisper.

Fallon and Ava waited in the hush of the theater's lobby. It was empty except for a boy uniformed in a maroon pill-box hat and jacket who, with a broom and a dustpan on a long handle, swept ticket stubs, popcorn crumbs, and gum wrappers off the garishly patterned carpet. Because the theater now featured more movies than performances, action-film cardboard cutouts populated the corners of the room and concessions were being sold—a concession to profits that Fallon could understand. She worried, though, whether the snacking would prove distracting.

In a khaki safari suit, heavily padded about the middle, and a pith helmet, Fallon pressed an ear against the double doors that led to the theater proper, covering the other to mute the purl of the soft-drink machine. Her nose, buried deep within a bushy red mustache, itched, and she lifted a hand now and then to scratch it. On hearing her cue, she swung open one of the double doors and flipped down its stop with her toe. Ava followed suit with the other. Then a spotlight lit the end of the theater's aisle before them, and arms linked, they stepped together into the heat of it. Ava could feel Edgar's eyes behind the brightness, seeing through her wedding gown.

The sparse audience creaked in their seats, craned their necks. Chantal had dressed Ava's dark hair in an updo, and without a wig, she felt naked. She felt herself. The volume of the music lowered in deference to the dialogue, and she rose on her toes to stage-whisper into Fallon's ear.

BEATRICE
I'm not sure I can go through with this.

Fallon let out a deep, open laugh and patted Ava's hand.

DALLOWAY
Your father isn't here, God rest his soul, but if I may, I'll dispense with a bit of fatherly advice. Lord Sylvius is a great man, a man with a good position and a good deal of money. He'll make you very happy. Every bride gets cold feet. Besides, it's too late to turn back. All your guests have arrived.

The audience was indicated with a sweep of Fallon's hand, and in the catwalk, Edgar flipped a switch, lighting the house. There was a murmuring. Then the bridal march began, and Fallon started walking Ava down the aisle.

At first, each member of the audience looked to see what the others would do, but as soon as a few stood, everyone hustled to their feet. Programs slipped from laps, and theater seats flipped closed as the house rose, playing the role of guests.

Onstage at the end of the aisle, Will waited in a beard and a safari suit of his own. When Fallon and Ava reached him, Fallon stepped behind them to play officiant, marrying them in a brief ceremony that concluded with her urging Will to kiss the bride. Will leaned forward and obliged.

Above the detonator's raised plunger, which begged to be pressed, the spotlight wavered.

❧

Will was aroused from sleep by a dream. He lay in bed, staring at the ceiling, thinking of Claudette—her hand's brief alighting on his thigh when she passed him the bracelet, the curve of her breasts filling her blouse to full sail. His wind gusted.

He'd see her in the next town, where she'd likely watch his performance. He pictured her mouth, its spit-shine and softness, he thought. He thought, and the thought made it harder.

❧

February 15
THE MIDWEST CHORUS | THEATER REVIEW
The Aqueduct of Sylvius
The Troupe Adores
The Gesture Theater
Milan, Nebraska
Remaining performance: tonight at 8 p.m.

Many of The Globe Theater's more than one million annual visitors may not realize it, but they're not seeing the same stage Shakespeare set foot on. The London site is a recreation of the original Globe, which was located about 750 feet east. In fact, even the "original" wasn't. It owes a debt to The Theater, England's first permanent such structure (itself no doubt an improvement on countless pro-genitors, harking back to the earliest amphitheater).

The Theater's twenty-one-year lease stipulated that the theater company owned the building and the landlord owned the land beneath. When the lease was up, the landlord made plans to tear the theater down. Legal squabbles ensued, until he left for his country house at Christmas. Then, over the course of one night, the company dismantled the theater they considered rightly theirs, carrying away its timbers and leaving nothing but bald foundation. The following spring, those materials were used to build a new theater on the other side of the Thames: The Globe.

This, surprisingly, is not even the most exciting act in the building's history. Fourteen years later, a cannon shot used for effect during a performance of *Henry VIII* set The Globe's thatched roof on fire, burning the place to the ground. No injuries were reported, save a man whose breeches were extinguished with a bottle of ale. The place was rebuilt the next year.

We bring all this up for two reasons, the first being that we, like that man, never imagined that by attending a performance—on a Tuesday night, no less—we'd be taking our lives in our hands (or, rather, handing them over to someone else, someone who'd dangle them for a bit of fiction). For a cheap thrill, Fallon Finn-Dorset has shattered the sacred and delicate pact between entertainer and audience: namely, that no matter what troubles or dangers we bear witness to onstage, we remain safe and safely anonymous in the dark. That is the comfort and covenant of theater.

On opening night, to our horror and disgust, Ms. Finn-Dorset brought down that wall. At the play's climax, there was a confetti explosion, a powder puff of smoke and, propelled by this blast, the eponymous aqueduct's stone column toppled forward across the first few rows of seating. There were screams, curses, then—just before crashing down—the stones were caught by a wire and hung suspended, swinging above the heads of the audience. We need hardly tell you that this nearly caused heart attacks. One woman fainted, a man wet himself, and many (even at the back of the house) left in disgust before the play's end.

We also bring up The Globe because, like Shakespeare treading the same boards of a theater reinvented time and again, The Troupe

Adores have grown too accustomed to traveling back and forth (and back and forth, and back and forth) over the same old tracks. All season, their plays have been preoccupied with what has come before and, with the exception of *St. St.*, have been a parade of the days of yore. Yawn.

Please, Ms. Finn-Dorset, present your modern audience with something *au courant*!

☙

Ava made the most of the morning sun, enjoying time she'd expected to be bitter. If she didn't know better, she would have suspected herself as its source. No matter how hard she tried to contain it, a warmth within her leaked out, like the border of light around a closed door on a dark hall. She unbuttoned her cardigan and lay on the green wooden roof of the observation car.

There was a cloud overhead in the shape of a tree, maybe the very tree Ava had seen on her way back from the theater the night before. The unseasonable weather had fooled it into blooming, but the evening chill must have made it drop the endeavor: the ground beneath was felted in white-blossom faux snow. She'd gone out of her way to step through the petals.

But Ava had come here to work. Rolling over, she slid her script closer. Before she could read a word, though, the car creaked with the weight of a climber, and a dark head of hair crowned the ladder. Ava smiled in anticipation of Edgar's arrival. Then she got it.

"What the fuck was that?" Edgar said, even before his head was above the roofline.

Ava sat up, glanced over the edge of the car. "Please. Lower your voice."

"Why did you kiss Will that way? With your hand on his chest?" he asked at the same volume, stepping toward her.

Ava could feel his heat where the roof once touched. "Did I? I can't remember. It must just be habit."

"That was a *real* kiss. I thought you were actors. You didn't rehearse it that way."

"We never rehearse kisses," she said. "It's awkward. And the kiss wasn't actually real."

"*Actually*, it was."

"It was an actual kiss, but it wasn't a real one."

"I could see the way you were looking at him, even from the catwalk."

Ava glanced over the edge of the car again. "Edgar, please," she said. "What if someone hears you?"

"What if they do?" he said, standing over her. "Tell me the truth. Are you with him? Is that why you don't want to tell anyone about us?"

Ava shrugged. "We've been doing this a long time."

Edgar's eyes widened.

"Acting. We've been *acting* together for quite a while. And kissing is part of the job. Sometimes I kiss Fallon too, depending on our roles. I don't think about it when I kiss Will, and he doesn't either."

"Oh, he thinks about it," Edgar muttered. "I can guarantee that." He looked off into the rail yard, then back at her. "What about Ben? Did you kiss him too?"

Ava's mouth felt dry. "I did," she said. "But, Edgar—all of us live together in such close quarters; there's hardly any privacy. I want to make sure of what we have before telling the others. No sense making announcements when we're not even sure, right?"

"I know what I have. Or I *thought* I did."

"Edgar, you hardly know—"

He interrupted. "I won't be part of a lie."

"We're not." Ava scooted closer to him, took his hand, and pulled him down to squat beside her. "We're just not saying anything."

"That old argument? Now we're lying to ourselves too?"

"I don't see it that way. It's our right to privacy, this being none of their business. All we have to do is act professional in front of them, just for now."

"Act, huh?"

Edgar's hands came up, reached for Ava's face. She flinched, but he tucked a baroque curl behind her ear, stabbed his hand into the depth of her cardigan's pocket, and pulled out her pack of cigarettes. She watched him remove a cigarette with his teeth, then light it and exhale deeply. Ava could taste the smoke.

"If we don't keep this a secret, I can't do it," she said.

"For how long?"

"Through the end of the tour. If this is still working then, everyone can know."

Edgar rocked back from his heels to sit beside her. "If they ask me directly, I'll tell them the truth."

Ava lifted the cigarette from Edgar's lips, took a drag. "Then we'll have to be careful."

Edgar traced her shadow on the roof with the toe of his boot. Her rogue tendril of hair had blown free again. Its silhouette flailed in the wind.

☙

On the sidewalk before the town's busiest strip of shops, Chantal and Will waited to go on. Chantal had costumed them as respectable preppies, both in khakis and pastel polo shirts. Her hair was tied back in a bouncy ponytail, the ends neatly curled.

"Almost ready? I think we actually drummed up a little business last time," she said.

"Just a minute." Will fumbled in his pocket and drew out a slip of paper, reading, "Every word and phrase—word and phrase—he speaks is true—is true." He leaned over the street, splashing vomit into a pothole puddle, then spat and wiped his mouth with the back of his hand.

"Know your lines?" Chantal asked.

"Hold on. One more, one more. These coins—" He coughed. "These coins will be needed to pay—needed to pay his debt—pay his debt. Duh. Okay, I'm as ready as I'll ever be."

The pair clasped hands and ambled along the shopfronts toward the bandstand in the center of town. It was a touch after five, and the area bustled with people heading home from work, running errands, and picking up dinner. Many carried jackets over their arms; the spring-seeming sun was all anyone was talking about.

When Will and Chantal reached the bandstand, they climbed its first few steps. Then, falling slightly behind her, Will dropped gallantly onto one knee, which paunched his waist over his belt. Chantal turned to him.

WOMAN

Wait. What? What are you—

Will reached deep into the front pocket of his khakis, tilting to tug something caught where the fabric creased. He pulled out a ring box and held it aloft, tried to open it on the hinged side, then rotated it in his hands, opened it, and presented it grandly to Chantal, whose mouth gaped open at nearly the same angle.

WOMAN

Oh—oh my god! Oh my god!

She lifted trembling hands to her face, covered her mouth, then threw her head back and laughed, eyes wet with tears. A sea of people formed before the bandstand. Elbows poked, fingers pointed, heads motioned others to take notice. Will smiled at Chantal and held out a hand to her. As she took it, turning her face from him to laugh now and then, he spoke loudly enough for the entire square to hear.

MAN

Baby, from the first time I saw you in that movie-theater box office, right when I leaned down and said into the hole in the glass, 'One for *Need for Speed 3*,' I knew you were the woman for me. And now—now that we've shared our lives for the past seven years, I can't imagine it without you. Will you spend the rest of your life with me? Will you make me the luckiest man on Earth and be my wife?

The crowd sighed, twittered. Passersby clotted with the crowd like a forming scab.

WOMAN

Oh, babes. Yes, of course I'll marry you! I love you so much!

Will swept his eyes across the crowd.

MAN

She said yes!

Will pushed the ring onto Chantal's finger, or at least to the first knuckle, where it stuck, then he spun her around onto his knee and kissed her. She lifted a pointed foot to the crowd's applause. The scene complete, Will and Chantal stood, grasped hands, and took a bow, holding their heads low for a few beats before rising.

Chantal addressed the crowd from her diaphragm. "If you enjoyed this performance, come see The Troupe Adores perform *The Aqueduct of Sylvius* tonight at The Gesture. The show starts at eight, and tickets are only twenty-five dollars."

"If you like love stories, you'll love this play!" said Will, holding up a fan of tickets.

"Enjoy a little romance at the best show in town," Chantal said. "Don't be shy. That's right. Get your tickets here!"

Looks were exchanged, faces fell. Disappointment spread throughout the crowd. Grumbles were smiled through by the players as if they weren't heard.

At the farthest edge of the crowd, a bicycle took off, powered by tuxedoed legs.

❧

This time, the audience knew what was coming; they'd come for it.

A detonation box stood center stage, its plunger cocked. Will, in safari gear, gestured at the backdrop, whereon was painted, among Tuscan hills, the site of a ruined villa. The rest of the cast huddled to hear—Fallon and Ava in matching khaki, and Chantal in a long black wig, kerchief, loose peasant blouse, and skirt. Will's monologue, though, flew past them, out into the dark of the house.

SYLVIUS

Today, we blast into the grand hall of the ancient villa. Who knows what treasures have lain there in the dark, waiting centuries for us to unearth?

He swept his arm toward the arch of Edgar's aqueduct above them.

SYLVIUS

For look what we have in plain sight! This incredible piece of engineering! This work of art! It has been here both for those who deserved and understood it and those who didn't, in rain and snow, in war and peace, for lovers and assassins, for babies and dying men. Through all this it has stood. And because it is immortal, let it be a reminder to us, then, that we will someday die.

Yes, we will die, like the men who designed the aqueducts, those who built it, the granddaughters who nursed them in their old age, and the great-great-grandsons of those women, who passed along this road beneath these arches and remembered a time of greatness. Like them, yes, each of you will die, passing into history. What evidence will be left of your lives to remember you by? Your children, who will curl up and be gone soon after? Their children or children's children, who will recall you but dimly in your drooling, toothless frailty?

Each of us must die, and because we must die, we must live to create something that will outlast our brief time here, something for a kindred spirit generations later to consider and build upon. Only in that way can civilization move forward. Live! *Live*, knowing always that you will die, most likely sooner than you'd like, maybe even today!

With these words, Will stepped behind the detonation box. He saluted the group, who returned it. Then he pressed the plunger.

In the wings, Edgar pressed a switch.

There was a boom. Confetti flew, and the stones toppled, but with the audience expectant, the danger was reduced to novelty. They laughed and applauded as the column's stones swung suspended just above their heads. A powder puff of gray smoke settled.

The playwright paged through her notebook.

> *BUD MONCRIEFF sits in his rickety director's chair in the front row of the high school drama room.*

> MONCRIEFF
> (*Raising, then lowering, one wiry eyebrow*) Hello! Earth to Will! What's your character's struggle right now?

> WILL
> (*Scuffling his Chucks on the classroom's makeshift stage*) Um.

> *The class titters.*

> MONCRIEFF
> (*Mockingly*) Um, um, um. He's in love!

> WILL
> That isn't a struggle, though, right? She loves him back.

MONCRIEFF

Isn't a struggle? If love isn't a struggle, I don't know what is, *especially* when reciprocated! The more you love, the more you worry about how to keep it, struggle to have your love returned. When you love, you can lose. There's more opportunity for pain! There's risk. There's danger!

Right now, all I see from you is love, and that's (*singing*) *booor-innng*. Show the struggle. It can be something small: how he hesitates before he tells her something disappointing, how he still opens the door for her after all these years of marriage. The little struggles add up to the big stuff.

The bell rings, signaling the end of drama class. Students flutter-shut their scripts, and the scrape and thump and rustle of bags being repacked orchestrates the universal music of class endings. The stage's dull-black ramp groans hollow with footfalls. Only when the noise climaxes does MONCRIEFF creak back in his chair, perch a threadbare elbow on its sagging cloth armrest, and cross his legs, revealing flaccid, graying black socks and loafers so worn they wear like gloves, the outline of each toe clearly visible. With his unkempt eyebrows raised, as if incredulously, he peers over his reading glasses and proclaims after the fleeing teens.

MONCRIEFF

Remember, you're all going to die! You think you're young and strong and invincible. You think you have forever. But every one of you will die, maybe today!

A fly buzzed near Fallon's ear. She swatted, stopped mid-stage on her way out of the theater. The silence had presence. The empty house seemed to be watching.

Another buzz drew her eye to the sky of Edgar's backdrop. There, a black spot punctuated the blue. Fallon crept closer, held up her hand and—slap—nailed it. Then there was another buzz.

Beneath her slowly lifted palm, the fly was still intact. She ran a finger over its flatness, shook her head.

Ever since Edgar came on, Fallon would reach a hand into an alcove and have it rebuffed by the wall. She'd try to pick up a card and find it painted on the tabletop. For a second, she'd blink, let her brain catch up as she tried to re-see. She was starting to question everything.

❧

Scrubbed of makeup, Ava exited the theater through a tight backstage hallway piled high with park benches and birdcages, a coiled stairway on rollers, and a cannon that would never be fired. From her path, she lifted a tumbled ass-head mask that must have dressed a Bottom, then—fox—startled, her heart like a bird crashing about in a house.

Hearing no flight-scuffle or flee, she, wincing, lifted the mask again by an ear. There was indeed a fox beneath, but taxidermied. Like the one in the cars, it wasn't quite there but for its teeth.

Night Travel

The somehow hollow train horn's chord blanketed the night, under which a few lonely souls lay awake, hearing it as if howled from their own heart's hurt, as though they and the train were the only two stars in the dark.

❧

A whistle issued. Lying on her back in bed, Ava pictured the little steam-cloud forming above Fallon's kettle in the observation car. As she did, the thought of Ben floated over her.

She stretched a hand toward her marble-topped nightstand. Looping her finger through the strap of her purse, she dragged it onto the bed and across the comforter, opened its zippered pocket, and pulled out a crumpled and folded sticky note, yellow as though with age. It was penciled with a phone number. Her hand shook, wavering, waving the paper like a surrender flag.

She lifted her phone, dialed, and held it to her ear.

❧

At her makeshift desk, the playwright wrote.

The phone rings, and BEN answers.

                              BEN
Hello?

                              AVA
Hey.

                              BEN
Who is this?

                              AVA
(*With surprise and exasperation*) Who is this? It's me!

BEN

Oh. Hey. You sounded different.

Fallon dropped her pen and tore a clump of pages from her notebook. "God"—rip—"dammit." She didn't know where she was going with the scene, why she kept raising, razing, raising the troupe's imagined pasts, but she knew she liked the blankness, that like a character's, it could be filled with anything at all. The trouble was, this scene was nothing. She crumpled the pages and tossed them in the small waste-paper basket, then lifted her teacup to her lips, but the too-hot water scalded her tongue. She rolled its roughness against the smooth roof of her mouth.

Somehow Fallon's folly with the last play had transformed into a strength, but the unpredictability unsettled her. In theory, she could control the words on the page, the look of the stage settings, how the actors performed the plays, even the audience's reactions. But it never turned out that way. She found herself writing things she hadn't set out to; the actors forgot lines, made additions, dropped props; and the audience lost attention when they should cry, laughed when they should fear.

Most importantly, she couldn't control the troupe's reviews. Based on the latest, next week's play was all wrong. She'd been working on another drama set in the past; the very thing the critic had asked to be spared. Who would care about the likes of Frank Mitzi? Or Claudette Rex or James James? What she needed was something modern, with higher stakes: a sexy espionage. She'd start over, keeping the trench coats, upping the villain. The detective would become an intelligence agent; the pickpocket, his partner in every sense of the word.

Fallon would woo her audience yet. As the train lurched its first, she thought again about the man she'd seen on the street in Milan. She touched pen to paper—scried, conj(ect)ured.

There was a place for everything. Just inside the baggage car, Edgar reconstructed the fallen aqueduct. He stacked the boulder shells in their dark corner and tucked his detonator beside them. Only the heavy trunk remained out of place, but due to its width and weight, he couldn't lift it alone. He peered inside, looking for ballast to jettison, but the thing held only furs; its weight was in its wood and hardware.

Grabbing one of its brass handles, Edgar dragged the trunk to a spot near where it went, which was barred off by a stack of long planks on the plywood floor. Their ends were piled high with other items he'd have to move to slide the trunk in place, and there was nowhere else for it to go without blocking a walkway. Edgar rasped his stubble, realized he should have asked for the stagehand's help while he'd had him there unloading the theater's van. Now he'd have to wait until Fallon or Will came through on their way to the bar car, after they'd changed back into themselves.

Edgar moved on, packing glasses in newspaper and returning each to its slot in a cardboard box. He had just closed the flaps when the door marked Private opened, and a short, stocky man peered in. His thick gray hair was bright against his olive skin, and he moved with a sort of power, a youthful elan. But for that, he reminded Edgar of his grandfather. He was what Edgar had always wished his grandfather to be.

"Can I help you with something?" Edgar asked.

The man questioned the car with a gesture. "*Boobity boppity?*"

Edgar recognized Italian, though he hadn't learned to speak much more than basic phrases. He took a stab. "This is a private car—uh—*macchina privato?*"

The man's face fell. "Aha! *Scuse, scuse.*" His voice dipthonged with each syllable of apology.

"That's okay. *Non problemo.*"

The man started to leave, but Edgar called to stop him. "*Una momento! Una momento!*"

The door opened, and the man leaned back in.

"Can you help me move this? Uh—*assist—assistenza?*"

By way of translation, Edgar pantomimed lifting the trunk, a language they both spoke. The man's face lit, and he re-entered the car. Edgar held out his hand, gave his full name. The man's palms were rough with callouses.

"Cosentino! Ah, *Italiano! Siciliano!* Boobity boppity. Boobity. Boo bippiti boo!"

Edgar shook his head. "Ah, *scuse. Italiano, si,* but *non parlo.*"

The man wagged a scolding index finger in front of his smile, gave his name, and gestured toward the trunk.

"I'm usually okay alone—uh—*solo,* but that's a heavy one." Edgar mimed the lifting of something heavy, then back pain.

"*Prego, prego.*" The man nodded.

With effort, the two took up the trunk's brass handles, lifted it over the stacked planks, and set it in its slot along the wall. Before they had fully straightened to standing, the man gestured at the gape in the lid, tried pushing it closed, but Edgar shook his head, pointed to the water damage.

"Aha," the man said knowingly.

In the observation car, a flash of red. Fox skidded to a halt on the tabletop, plucked the smallest peach from the nest of a basket, pivoted, and leapt to the floor. Pausing cautious in shadows, it skulked down the corridor at a trot to the baggage car, the peach in its teeth like the flesh of a ripe, young animal, tender to the tooth.

The fur trunk's lid gaped a slit, a way in. Fox took it, pushed its nose in and slid skull and shoulder blades under, hoisting the lid a little, then dropped down into the dark. It curled against a fox tail on the bottom, devouring—all chin drippings and wet chest—and the peach was gone. Only the pit remained.

Fox stood on its hind legs, stretched its front paws up to the lid's gape. It scrabbled with its hind legs on the trunk's wall, trying to push itself up, but the stole Ava had taken out earlier left not quite enough to climb on. Fox panted. It leapt at the opening, hung on the rim for a second with its front paws' claws, then fell back into the dark. The lid was too heavy without leverage.

In the chair at the end of the observation car, Ava waited. She waited, but again there wasn't a ring. She lowered the phone from her ear, looked at its screen. There was half a bar of signal here, between towns. She couldn't reach Ben, not now.

The future was unseen behind her, the past before. Looking out the back of the train, she watched the ground they'd already covered reel out and let time pile up behind her as she was pushed through it faster than felt natural. The speed beat her back. She was a current break, a bear facing downstream in whitewater.

The physics book was in her lap, open to the chapter on Doppler Effect.

Because blue light has a higher frequency than red, the spectral lines of an approaching astronomical light source exhibit a blueshift, and those of a receding astronomical light exhibit a redshift.

$$f_o = \frac{v+v_o}{v+v_s} f_s$$

Ben, then, was red. Ava saw it whenever she thought of him. His light was far off and growing fainter, and he hadn't even glanced back with a call. She clenched her jaw. He was the red of fury, of the blood she wanted to beat from him. He was the red of passion, the wine he expounded on, the color of her heart, which he still had some hold on. He was the red of leaving.

And if Ben was red, Edgar was blue, a bruise. His light kept coming, relentless. He was something to assuage her ache, someone moody to feel blue against, someone to purple the pain. And now, alone, Ava wanted to feel wanted, wanted her heart-hurt forgotten.

She'd arrived at the answer, but it was wrong. She erased what she'd written, brushing the rubber shavings off the page with a shhh, shhh, shhh.

The last smears of beard glue were never easy to remove. Will turned off the faucet of the sleeper-car bathroom's pedestal sink and let his chin drip as he blindly groped for a towel. Drying his face, he put his glasses back on, then slicked down the dampened first few waves of his hair. It was time to head to the bar car, but at the thought, his stomach lurched. It wasn't that he didn't want to meet up with the others; it was something else. His stage fright was bleeding beyond theater. He drew a slip of paper from his pocket, where he'd stashed a few for emergency use.

"The theft of the pearl pin—" he whispered to himself. "The theft of the pearl pin—pearl pin—was kept secret—secret." He heaved into the toilet.

The bracelet was burning in his pocket. He felt it through the corduroy covering his thigh, but that was the safest place to keep it. He pursed his lips and screwed them far left to gnaw the inside of his cheek, shifted the kiss far right to bite the other side.

There was a rap on the bathroom's accordion door. "You ready to go?" Fallon asked.

Will released the suction on his inner cheek. He struggled to open the door, which stuck in its track, then he stepped out into the car's narrow corridor.

Fallon walked past him to Chantal's compartment and knocked on its accordion door. "Come along to slaughter, my little lamb. I have a treat for us on the way to the bar car."

Chantal emerged, removing earbuds, and followed. They passed Ava's empty compartment, crossing the vestibule to the baggage car. On opening its door, Fallon started to say something, then stopped, paused. Her height blocked Will's view ahead.

"I have something planned, if you'd care to join us," she finally said. Her voice was different, but Will wasn't sure how. When she continued forward, Will saw she'd been speaking to Ava and Edgar, who stood together behind the scarred worktable.

When everyone had filed into the car and encircled the table, Fallon reached beneath it and pulled out a pewter champagne bucket. She lifted a bottle from its ice bath and, with its dripping base pressed against a growing wet spot on her white tank top, removed the foil from its neck. The bottle was stopped with a cap instead of a cork and cage, and Fallon set its metal teeth against the edge of the worktable and slammed her hand upon it. The cap flew off with a pop. She poured five flutes full and held the last aloft, gilding the bubbles in the sharp light from the overhead bulb. The rest of the troupe followed suit.

"Fornication!" Fallon proclaimed.

Will saw Edgar and Ava's glances collide, glance off.

Fallon repeated the phrase, emphasizing each syllable and laughing. "For. An. Oc-ca-sion such as this one, a toast is in order! Tonight's show was great, thanks to every single"—her eyes met Ava's—"one of you. May all our pain be sham pain!" She reached inside her jacket, pulled a stack of white envelopes from its inner pocket, and handed them out.

Will lifted the flap of his, thumbed the bills within. "Hear, hear!" he exclaimed.

"There, there. We didn't do *that* well." Chantal laughed, leaning Will's head upon her shoulder in mock consolation. "But the champagne's a good idea. We have something else to celebrate. Will and I are engaged!"

Will saw Ava and Edgar's glances dance once more and looked nervously at Fallon, who grunted.

"I saw your little stunt," she said. "And I wasn't amused. I was planning on talking to you about it later."

"Why not now?" Chantal taunted. "It deals with the troupe's success, so everyone should hear."

"Wait—what happened?" Ava asked.

"I was riding through town this afternoon, when I saw a crowd gathered by the bandstand," Fallon began. "I, of course, went over—as you know, I'm always interested in entertainment that appeals to the people—and who did I see but Will and Chantal playing out a *pretend* proposal."

"Why are you using that word? Like what we did was so dirty?" Chantal asked. "How is it any different from what you do?"

"I write lines, create characters, and incorporate themes and symbolism. You slapped together an ad to sell tickets."

"And we sold some—you should be thanking us! Right, Will?"

He looked at the ground.

"I suppose you did," Fallon countered. "A few. But at what cost?" She finished the contents of her flute. "Look, this is my troupe; it's my reputation on the line. I told you before, people don't like being tricked."

"They love being tricked! It's why they come to our shows. Besides, you were literally tricking them with this play, until the review came out and spoiled the surprise."

"There's a difference between knowingly engaging with a fiction and being tricked on the street. People don't like it, especially when the reveal is disappointing."

"You were mad because we acted out something horrible, so we acted out something happy, and now you're mad about that too. You asked us to help promote the troupe, and we spent a lot of our personal time doing that, and yet you're still not satisfied. You're never—"

Will was flooded with relief and gratitude as Edgar stepped in. "To that point, can't we just be pleased about this win? We finally have reason to celebrate—right, Fallon?"

"I suppose."

Edgar motioned to Chantal and Will. "And you won't try any of these stunts again without running them past Fallon first, right?"

"Oh, absolutely not. Never," Will said as Chantal, massaging her thigh, looked ceilingward.

"Let's celebrate, then." Edgar held his flute aloft. "To our continued success—and more importantly, to two of our very own finding love!"

"Now that, I can cheer," Ava said, clinking her glass against Fallon's, then Chantal's and Will's, dispelling the cloud in the room. When she reached her glass toward Edgar's, they met not at all, then too roughly.

☙

As the troupe filed out of the baggage car on their way to the bar car, Ava signaled Edgar to stay behind. "'To two of our very own finding love?' That was risky."

He smiled. "I'm starting to like living dangerously."

"Speaking of which, did she see us?"

"Who?"

"Fallon. I think she walked in on us kissing when she led the others into the car."

Edgar answered with another kiss, firm but giving, so unlike that weak, wet kiss of Will's Ava had been enduring for days. It sent a flurry of heat up her chest, as though someone blazed the flame in a hot air balloon. Similarly, it was dizzying.

Edgar looked at her in the lamplight of the baggage car, and Ava wondered what he saw. When she thought of him now, she overlaid him on an imagined future husband she'd had as a girl. The man had been faceless, with a suggestion of dark hair and stubble and a sense of intensity. When she married light-haired, playful Ben, she'd had to dismiss this, but here was Edgar, the kind of man she'd always wanted but assumed she couldn't win. She kept thinking he'd wake up one day and see her for who she was.

Which brought her back to the question. "Really, though. Did she?"

Edgar shrugged. "If she did, she would have said something, right?"

Ava shook her head. "You don't know Fallon. I think we'd broken away by the time the door opened, but—"

"Who cares if she did? Forget it," Edgar said, wafting away the smoke of her hair as he drew his hand to her cheek. "What's the worst that could happen?"

☙

The kiss had reminded her of the other, the one with the trick knife. Fallon wet her index finger on the tip of her tongue, continued flipping forward and back through her notebook. The rest of the troupe was chatting in a booth at the far end of the bar car, but she had gone straight to the bar.

"If you're looking for a martini, I think I found one for you," Art said, lifting a bottle high as he poured gin into the aluminum shaker.

Fallon grumbled a hmph.

As he began shaking the drink, he called across the car to the rest of the troupe. "The usuals this evening?"

They nodded.

"Except—" Ava paused poised as she waited for the noise of ice-violence to end. "A Negroni for me, please."

Fallon shot a look at Chantal, but she didn't notice. Her full attention was on Will as she slapped a hand on his corduroyed thigh.

"Actually, Art—Will and I had better keep drinking champagne, and lots of it," she said, shifting over to sit in Will's lap. "We got engaged this afternoon."

Art raised his eyebrows. He popped open a bottle of sparkling wine and held it out to Chantal with two glasses, but she took only the bottle, lifting it to her lips for a long swallow and then tipping it to Will's. Will drank as best he could as the stuff trickled down his chin, then shrugged, sheepish, as Chantal ran her fingers through his (until then) neatly parted hair.

"You all are full of surprises, that's for sure," Art said. "As I always say, 'Marriage is neither heaven nor hell. It is simply purgatory.'"

Ava laughed, a touch too loudly.

Ava waited for the others to fall asleep, waited for Edgar, dipping the flute glasses one by one into the warm, soapy water in her compartment's sink and rubbing them with a sponge. As she picked up the last, there was a racket in the corridor. Will and Chantal were returning from the bar car, shushing each other between giggles, stumbling, and bumping into the corridor's walls. No wonder. The two had celebrated their fake engagement with enthusiasm all evening, declaring toast after toast and growing increasingly handsy. By the time Ava left, Chantal had the entire bar car singing along to "Chapel of Love."

Still holding the wet glass, Ava peeked out through the gap where her broken accordion door wouldn't quite close. Chantal had Will pinned against the door to her compartment, and they were making out furiously. As Chantal pulled her shirt over her head, Will stared at her breasts, which were cantilevered in a red-lace bra. Chantal cupped his hand over one of them, then the actors fairly fell back into her compartment.

Ava resumed wiping the flute with the sponge. The scene had been surprising, at least when it came to Will's behavior, but if she could so easily witness it, how likely was it that Fallon or one of the others had witnessed her and Edgar, maybe even earlier that night?

As the thought roiled up, a shard of glass broke off in her hand. Ava's too-rough cheers with Edgar must have caused a hairline crack. The water blushed.

঵

At her mirrored desk, Fallon scried, conjectured.

> *There are lies told to bolster, for braggadocio. Lies of language: wordplay or vagueness, with or without qualm. There are life-changing lies and those that don't matter. Lies of betrayal or kindness. Or convenience, to make one's life easier. There's the right-in-the-eye lie, the bald-faced and pie-bald. Lies half and whole, regretted or caught. Lies to fit in or stand out. There's the foundational lie and the supplements told to uphold it. Lies confessed, left unsaid, or forgotten. Some printed in newspapers or taken to graves. Or made by gesture: a nod of agreement, so easy to tell.*
>
> *EDGAR hates them all. But now he has one of his own. He's a liar.*

The train was braking, sounding. Fallon stood from her director's chair and lifted a corner of red velvet curtain to peer out the window. Ahead, a sea of animals: cattle.

She managed to get one slipper on before abandoning the other and jogging out of her compartment and down the corridor's close-napped carpet to the vestibule's steep stairs. As she swung the door open to the cool night air, the train shuddered. It was moving slowly through a tide of cowhide. Gathered alongside the tracks, the lowing animals roiled below her.

The horn held a long blast, then blasted again for punctuation, and the train stopped. Fallon stood on the stairs in her silk pajamas, feeling the dark eyes and the night breeze, her bare sole cold on the rough metal.

Paris, South Dakota

February 16

Edgar lifted Ava's hand from his heart, his scar. He slipped out of her bed without waking her, stretched his thin tee over his head and shoulders, and stepped into his jeans. To hold the accordion door closed, he'd wedged one of his boots in its track, and he struggled to free it. Then, carrying the pair, he left Ava's room. Behind him, her door gaped.

In his compartment, Edgar slid a small canvas out from under his bed. He mixed a few colors of paint on the palette atop his nightstand and touched a brush to it, then to Ava's cheek. He'd assembled her portrait from parts—wrist and clavicle, lash and lobe—taken from the photo he'd snapped at the bar in Lisbon. In it, a cloud of cigarette smoke doubled the dark cloud of her hair, and her eyes weren't yet composed for the camera. He'd caught the tail end of a thought in them. There was a ghostly orb of light over her right shoulder, where the camera's flash must have reflected off a sign on the wall behind her.

As the morning's first bird sang, Edgar sat back on the bed to study his work. He shaped a highlight along the edge of one of Ava's curls, touched another to the corner of her mouth. Dipping a brush into the black, Edgar added a fly on the canvas, on Ava's neck. He was finished. He rubbed the brush with a rag daubed in turpentine, then squatted beside the bed, lifted the navy blanket draping it, and slid the portrait beneath. There, the back of his hand brushed a leather roll, weighty and well worn.

Edgar pulled out the roll and set it atop the bed, untied the thong that secured it, and unfurled it with a few bats of his hand, releasing its scent of hide, smoke, and cologne. Within were column-like pockets for five knives. Identical handles repeated down the line.

When Edgar's grandfather passed, the knives had passed to him. Like the leather roll, Edgar had seemed a fitting place to put them. He remembered his grandfather alone at the side of the house, sleeves rolled, scoring the evening with hits against a weathered target until it was too dark to see, sometimes later.

Edgar pulled the first knife from its slot.

❧

Fallon stood before the Eiffel Tower. In the blurry morning light, it reminded her of train tracks. She almost felt she was in France, except the tower's rails peaked barely above the lowest branches of the nearby trees. She turned with a sneer, cracked her beaten guidebook.

> Ah, Paris, the City of Light. The very air trembles with romance. Those who come here alone can't help but fall in love, and those in love fall deeper. What better place to do it (ahem) than within sight of *La Tour Eiffel*, that most upstanding landmark of the modern age?

The scent of freshly brewed coffee and buttery pastries wafted on the wind, and Fallon scanned the strip of shops that made up Main Street. The town had capitalized on its namesake. Under a red-white-and-blue-blocked awning was a bakery labeled *Boulangerie* in wide gold lettering. Fallon released her grip, let the book unwind, and leaned her bike against a mailbox.

Before the tiny bakery's door could be pushed fully open, it banged into something, knocking out a wave of bready scent. Its glass was cloudy with condensation, and when Fallon peered around it, she saw that the door had collided with a table at which Ava sat. There was cappuccino foam on her upper lip, and she was dressed as Edgar in a worn white tee and faded black jeans. She'd added a dark scarf for warmth and, in the spirit of the place, a beret.

Fallon couldn't look the other way. She threw her head back, lifted her hands. "Can we stop pretending I don't know what's going on?"

Ava's cup rattled in its saucer. "What do you mean? What's going on?"

"Ava, I'm a professional observer. Whatever you and Edgar are doing with or to each other is fine by me. Just don't insult me any longer by pretending I don't notice." She looked over Ava to the bakery's counter.

"Fine. We've been seeing each other."

"Yes, and surely everyone else has been *seeing* you too." Fallon scanned the menu board.

"They have?" A blush bloomed up Ava's neck. "They know?"

"I don't know for sure, but I don't know how they couldn't."

"You won't tell them, will you? I want to be sure what we have is real—before we make it official."

"Right." Fallon pushed past her toward the counter. "And as you discover these ontological truths, by all means do share."

Ava spoke behind her. "Please don't say anything to Edgar about Ben. He doesn't know, and if he found out, he'd be very hurt."

"I wouldn't dream of meddling." Fallon pivoted on her heel. "But I'm interested to see how you'll pull this off, quite frankly. How will you keep this from the others, if they somehow don't already know? And what's your course of action long-term? Edgar's bound to find out about Ben eventually, and from what we've seen of his moods, I doubt he'll take it well."

Ava looked down at her cup, stirred her coffee.

"It's quite a plot," Fallon continued. "I can't wait to see how it ends." With that, she turned back to the counter and ordered, pronouncing the ar in *croissant* as a wah. On her way out, she hummed the first few bars of Tchaikovsky's "Swan Lake" over the crinkle of the white paper bag in her hand.

❦

Boxed Fox scratch-scuffled in a trunk filled with furs.
　Tchaikovsky

Tchaikovsky Rachmaninoff
　　　Shostakovich Tchaikovsky Rimsky-Korsakov
　　Scriabin

Prokofiev Rachmaninoff Arensky
　　　　Ustvolskaya Ustvolskaya　　　Shaposhnikov
　　Stravinsky
　Glinka

❦

Edgar stood knee-deep in the weeds at the edge of the rail yard, twenty feet from a beech, holding one of his five knives in one hand, the other four in the other. He felt battle-bruised. Love had done this.

He threw the knife with all the might he could muster, which wasn't much this morning. It skimmed the bark of the tree and flew past it, landing blade-up in the mud.

It was fine, Ava's propensity to lie. Society was built on the stuff. *Nice to meet you. I'm doing well, thank you. We should do this again soon.* In Ava he had someone honestly dishonest, dishonestly honest—an artist. There was nothing to confess; it was her profession, like his own little lies, his trompe l'oeil, he thought for the thousandth time. Besides, even if she lied to others, he knew she'd never lie to him.

Edgar zipped his hoodie, threw the hood over his head. The sun was bright and warm, but the trees shivered in a cold wind that continually changed direction. Supporting the knife's handle on his left wrist, Edgar carefully placed the fingers of his right hand atop the darkened marks of patina on its blade. He eyed the beech trunk, aimed, feigned a throw, then threw. As the metal left his hand, adrenaline thrilled Edgar's finger-tips, but the flat of the blade slapped flaccidly against the tree, and the knife ricocheted into the grass.

A laugh on a gust turned him. Fallon was riding toward him up the hill, thrusting her bike steeply side to side as she pedaled. There was another fit of wind, and her laugh was taken, blown back. She was a film out of sync with its sound.

Edgar worked another knife from the bunch. He threw, and it missed the tree entirely, skipping once along the ground. When Fallon was a few strides away, she hopped off the moving bike in one swift motion and dropped it to the ground in a cloud of dust. Her laugh rose, and she brushed her hands on her tuxedo pants. The wind blustered behind her, lifting her short blond hair into a halo.

"What do you have there?"

Edgar offered up the two-knife bouquet. She considered, selecting one the way she'd pick a tarot card from a fortune-teller's fan.

"There are marks where your fingers should go," Edgar said, point-ing them out on the blade.

Fallon matched her fingers to the shadows and lifted the knife, weighing it in her hand. Its handle hung heavy, bending back her wrist. She took a step forward and threw. The blade pierced beech bark, stuck, then drooped slowly with the weight of its handle and dropped to the ground.

"Almost," she said. "Hand me the other."

Ava sighed, relaxed farther into the chair at the end of the observation car. She'd told. She'd told Fallon. She could point out to Edgar she'd told. It would be some small concession, buy her another two weeks. That was all she needed to make the end of the season. From there—away from the rest of the troupe and at a halt, letting the world rush past her—she could think about what to do next. All she knew was that if Edgar found out about Ben, she'd lose everything she had left.

Will lunged a stab at Fallon with a length of metal pipe, but she parried his blow with her own, then swiped at his head. He stepped back, yielding her one more foot of the observation car's Persian rug.

"I thought this was where I was supposed to start overpowering your character: Asp, the villain," he said, keeping his pipe between himself and hers.

"It was," she said. "But a little improvising here and there keeps it from looking so choreographed."

Will thrust. "Tell me about Agent Ford."

"I've told you, Will"—Fallon drove him back a few more steps—"everything you need to know is in the script."

"But how can I play him without knowing where he's coming from? His fears and passions? What his childhood was like?"

"Make up whatever you want. It doesn't matter."

"It does, if you want an authentic performance."

Fallon stopped, lowered her pipe. "Do you feel like you know me, Will?"

Will dropped his arm by his side, shrugged. "I know you pretty well, sure. We've been working together for years. We travel together, live together."

"Do you know what my fears are? My passions? Do you know what my childhood was like?"

"Sort of, but—"

"Exactly." Fallon put her hands on her hips. "What do you really know about your average acquaintance, or even friends or family members? You know where they're from, that they love cats, maybe, or chocolate. You know how they tend to act, how to push their buttons, and the story of that big, emotional thing that affected their life. Is that knowing someone?" She continued without waiting for Will's response. "Hasn't anyone ever surprised you? You're only privy to what they'll tell you, show you. The rest you fill in yourself."

Fallon settled back into her fencing stance, lifted her pipe. "You can never truly know another. You can only know yourself, and many don't even know that much." She thrust. "The audience will see who they want to see up there, Will. If it makes you feel better to make up a backstory, make up whatever you want. But don't fool yourself into thinking it matters."

"It matters to me. I'm trying to *be* this person, not be his friend."

"Then make him up the way the rest of us do, the way we make ourselves."

Will wiped his brow with his forearm and tried to settle back into his stance, but Edgar entered. He collapsed on the chesterfield and let his eyes roam absentmindedly to the landscape hung on the window glass.

"Have either of you seen Ava? I mean—" He came back to himself. "I thought everyone would be in here."

"Christ," Fallon said, knocking away the tip of Will's pipe with hers. "Pull yourself together."

Will looked from her to Edgar and back questioningly, and Edgar rasped his stubble.

"I forgot to tell you," he said to Will. "Someone came by for you the other day. They wanted me to give you a message."

Will stopped mid-strike. "A woman?"

"A woman?" Fallon echoed incredulously.

"A group of men, rough types," Edgar answered.

"What did they say?" Will lowered his pipe. Taking advantage of the vulnerability, Fallon jousted forward to stab him with hers. He hardly noticed.

"They said something about a two-faced bitch? And that they'd see you here, in Paris? Oh yeah, and to break a leg. Do you know what it's about?"

Will could feel his face grow hot, but he fought back the flush. He placed his hand in his pocket nonchalantly, touching the bracelet's carved faces while keeping his own equally expressionless. A bead of sweat was forming at his temple, but he willed it away. It was some of his finest work.

"I—I have no idea. Probably just some old friends."

"*You* used to hang with 'rough types'?" Fallon asked, shooting him a look.

"It's just the kind of joke my drama-school buddies would pull," Will countered as Chantal came into the car.

"There is such a weird vibe in here," she said. Then she smiled and held up a scolding finger. "You were just talking about me, weren't you?"

Seeing her, Will could hardly look. He felt his palms sweat, his mouth dry. He wasn't sure what he'd been thinking the night before. He'd never considered Chantal anything more than a coworker or possibly a friend, but he'd been daydreaming so much about Claudette lately, he had to admit he was a little sexually revved up. Then with the fake engagement and the celebration and all the wine and that red bra, things had spiraled out of control.

The thing was, besides the blond hair, Chantal looked a lot like Claudette—sweet Claudette, who would be meeting him in this very town, a beautiful woman who entrusted him with her most precious possession. It was as though he'd cheated on her. Had he? What if she found out?

Will's stomach lurched. He dropped the pipe and fled from the observation car, pushing Chantal and Edgar aside as he made for the bathroom in the sleeper car.

❧

The troupe stood on a bare plywood stage in a gap-planked barn, its walls striped by slant morning light. Every now and then, a wisp of hay floated down from the stocked loft.

Fallon addressed the troupe. "In this scene, Asp—who I'll be playing—is on a dock, loading his luggage into a speedboat. He's got Agent Rachel Starbuck tied up, and he's taking her with him." She brushed a bit of lint from her tux's lapel. "Will, you're going to come up behind him—me—to try to stop him. I'll grab a pipe from the dock, you'll grab another, then we'll fence. Chantal, when we start fighting, keep clear, okay?" She clapped. "Let's give it a go."

Chantal held her hands behind her back to feign being tied up and started in on the part of Agent Starbuck. All the usual nonsense was gone from her voice.

STARBUCK

Where are you taking me?

Fallon replied in a Texas drawl.

ASP

You'll find out soon enough.

STARBUCK

You won't get away with this. The agency is probably closing in on you as we—

Chantal dropped character. All the nonsense was back. "This isn't working for me."

"You're Agent Rachel Starbuck," Fallon said. "She's been taken—"

"I understand what's going on. I'm just not feeling it. Why would Agent Starbuck just give in like that? Why would she go with this guy without a fight?"

"She's being held hostage."

Chantal sighed. "I see this character as someone who makes her own destiny, someone with balls. She became an agent for a reason. What if, while Agent Ford is fighting Asp, instead of playing damsel, Starbuck breaks free and pulls a gun out of the trunk? She could turn it on both men, tell them she was never on either of their sides, that she's actually a triple agent, then flee alone in the boat." Fallon tried to break in, but Chantal talked over her. "And another thing: why would she go with Agent Ford? He's not even handsome. No offense, Will. *You'll* be handsome underneath that awful rubber nose, of course."

Will still couldn't look at her. He nodded. "No offense taken."

Fallon rolled her script into a baton. "The nose is part of the plot. And she's going with him because he's her partner. She's on his side, remember? Besides—" Fallon slapped the paper tube against her thigh. "What you're proposing doesn't even make sense. How would she know there was a gun in the trunk?"

"She could have seen Asp pack it," Chantal fired back.

"Then why doesn't he grab it himself? Why pack it in the trunk in the first place?"

Chantal paused. "Those are actually good questions. Why doesn't the villain have a gun? Why are two spies fighting with pipes?"

"They found them on the dock," Fallon blustered. "Why does anyone do anything? Lord knows."

Will was starting to sweat. "If we change this scene, it will ripple through the entire script, and I already have my part memorized."

Fallon joined him near the wall. "He's right. You can't just throw in something new on a whim without having it ricochet throughout the rest of the story. We make this change, then a few more, and before we know it, the entire play has to be rewritten, re-rehearsed, and re-memorized."

"Though, maybe Chantal has a point," said Will. "Why wouldn't my character have a gun? Why wouldn't they have a gunfight?"

Edgar called down from the catwalk. "Because it's more expensive."

"Is it? How?" asked Chantal.

Ava spoke up. She was accustomed to solving problems. "We can have Asp hold Starbuck at gunpoint, instead of tying her up. Then Will—Agent Ford—comes up from behind with a gun. Asp turns to face him, and Ford pulls the trigger point-blank, but he's out of bullets. When Asp hears the click of the gun, he's relieved but distracted for a second, and in that second, Ford kicks the gun out of his hands. They look around for weapons, grab some nearby pipes, and start fighting with them. Asp knocks Ford out. He loads Ford and Starbuck into the speedboat, but just as he's about to get in himself, my character—Agent Kate Harrow—shows up, holds him at gunpoint, and rescues her colleagues. Will that work for everyone?" Her fingers itched for the scratch of a penciled check mark.

Chantal set her paper coffee cup on the edge of the stage. "Of course you've made yourself the hero. What about my character also getting a gun out of the trunk?"

Everyone groaned.

"There can't be a third gun," Fallon snapped. "I've humored you enough this morning. You have your role, and I have mine. I'm the playwright."

"And the director, and the owner, and the manager, and an actor. Every role is yours," said Chantal.

"That means every problem's mine too. I'd be happy to trade places with you."

"But if there was a third—"

"A third gun is too *easy*, Chantal. You of all people should understand that."

Fallon saw Chantal's hurt look toward Will, who for some reason wouldn't meet her gaze, and knew she shouldn't have said it, as clever as it had been. But instead of apologizing, she slipped back into the robe of character, reset the scene.

Will shuddered. He lay the script on his lap, wrapped the woolen throw tighter about his shoulders and, looking up at the blank bank of windows, came back to the observation car.

Fallon had delivered the new scripts just after dinner, and Will had posted up on the tapestried sofa to memorize the new blocking and lines. An end table held his half-full or, tonight, half-empty coffee cup. He'd been at it for hours, and his mind felt overstuffed. There was so much more work to do before tomorrow's performance, before morning rehearsal, even. But first, he needed a break.

Earlier that evening, the troupe had gone to a French restaurant for dinner, one far too romantic, with candlelight and huge leather menus they'd held up like walls between them. He'd taken care not to end up seated beside Chantal, but when he tried to wedge between Ava and Edgar, Edgar had shouldered him to a seat directly across from Chantal, which may have been worse. The thought of her now made him think guiltily of Claudette and, in turn, the threat he'd received. He screwed his mouth to one side and chewed the skin inside his round cheek.

To distract himself, Will picked up his phone, surfed his way to a performance of *King Lear* by The Rude Mechanicals, and tapped on the arrow to play it. The video unspooled, and Ben entered as the character of Edgar, leading a blind and elderly Earl of Gloucester.

GLOUCESTER
When shall we come to the top of that same hill?

EDGAR
You do climb up it now: look, how we labor.

Ben continued leading the old man across the flat stage.

GLOUCESTER
Methinks the ground is even.

EDGAR
Horrible steep. Hark, do you hear the sea?

GLOUCESTER
No, truly.

Will tapped pause. He'd always loved the scene, how the character, Edgar, asked the blinded Gloucester to imagine the landscape the way the playwright asked the audience to populate the bare stage. Then there was Gloucester's doubt. He would not be led blindly.

Will couldn't be sure he was as convincing onstage, couldn't under-stand why an audience would believe him or why they played along. His performances were a paper moon compared to Ben's.

He thought about tomorrow's opening and, despite his worries about Mitzi, felt a tingle of excitement. Claudette would be there. Maybe she'd show up before curtain, ask to be admitted backstage. Or maybe when he entered the first scene, he'd see her in the front row, her beautiful eyes trained gratefully, adoringly on him. She'd wait for him by the back-stage door. He'd hold out his arm to her, give an almost imperceptible bow, say, "Good evening, my dear. Care to accompany me to dinner?"

Oh god no. He'd say, "I've been thinking about you all week."

Or, "Oh, hey. The girl from the dining car, right?"

Or maybe, "Can I buy you a drink?"

Or better, "Will you join me for a nightcap?"

So much hinged on the performance. Will refined and edited his lines and hers for the meeting, mouthing all the ways the scene could go—her part so unpredictable—until he drifted off to sleep.

Paris had been perfect. That afternoon, Ava and Edgar had strolled arm-in-arm past the Eiffel Tower, split a baguette in the park, kissed along the river. The cars' public spaces had been feeling uncomfortably close, but in town after town, the two grew closer. Each night, they lay awake in the wee hours, whispering in the dark. Though the door to Ava's compartment wouldn't quite close, they could no more leave than if they'd been locked in together.

Edgar considered this in the baggage car as he sanded a headboard lain like a tabletop over two sawhorses. The door to the sleeper car rat-tled, and Ava slipped in, shut it behind her. She was beautiful in rose-col-ored sweatpants and a loose, nipple-tented tee shirt. Her small breasts bounced with each step, and her hair looped a disheveled sketch about her face. Watching her come nearer, Edgar tried to slow his breathing.

"A bed should never be work," Ava said.

"A woodworker once told me," he whispered, not quite getting enough oxygen. "That every good piece of carpentry should be built"— he inhaled—"strong enough"—he inhaled—"to fuck on."

Ava laughed by way of exhale. Her breath was hot on his neck. "Well, we are in Paris."

Edgar took her hand, fine-boned as a bird, sat on the headboard, and lifted her lightly to straddle his lap. Behind him, on the wall thick with scenery, hung a canvas painted with the inside of a hotel room. It had been pulled for this week's play.

"You're something out of a dream," he said, threading his fingers through hers. "This just doesn't seem real, with no one else knowing."

Her glance moved past him. "Fallon knows," she said.

Edgar caught his breath. "You told her?"

"I did, but I don't want to tell the others, not until the end of the season. I like keeping you to myself, having our own little world within these crowded cars. Can't we stay here in dreamland, just until the end of the season?"

The pressure of Edgar's hand on hers increased. "But I want to tell everyone. We should tell the others too. I want to tell everyone, starting with you, that I—love you."

The words floated there in the air, suspended, and there was a feeling in Ava's chest of both pain and pleasure, as though a lioness were devouring a gazelle.

She didn't know what to say, what she *could* say, so she slipped her hand out of his and kissed him, made the kiss count for answer.

In the trunk, two black eyes watched and paced, burning to be released. Fox panted, scrabbled. Something wild, it clawed and gnawed, heard the troupe, in sleep, stirring in bed, each in their separate compartments, every body within its own box.

Fox pawed the trunk's wooden sides, circled in the dark. In the dark of its body, its soul circled too.

After what seemed like days, dawn reddened the glint of baggage car Fox saw if it rose on its hind legs, and it yawned, curled its tail around it like a stole, and slipped asleep. It dreamt it crossed a field of snow, following a dotted line of rabbit tracks, trotting its own over.

The playwright wrote.

It began with Adam and the naming of animals, but one name was never enough. Ever since, we've been thinking up more. We've added surnames, pet names, classifications in Latin.

Take *Equus caballus*: a racehorse, one name for the barn and another in print, stretching its neck across the forms. Call it thoroughbred, call it colt or boy or champ or fucker. Each one a work of trompe l'oeil, standing in.

Some names are doubled, even within themselves. A-va. The name has fang. The v pivots. Spun, it seems the same whichever way it lands, but it isn't. The ah vs. the ey. It's a two-faced card, a coin.

The fox had a flip side too. It was called *Vulpes vulpes*, but each of its same names wasn't. It was subtle. The fox wild and not-wild both. It couldn't be trusted. It held added hazard.

Like you, honey.

࿇

February 17

"I say *forest*," Fallon said. "And I take you there."

The troupe was gathered over breakfast in the observation car. It was a potluck, of sorts, with each contributing an item. Gripping a steaming pot of water with an oven mitt, Fallon dipped in a slotted spoon and gently laid a poached egg onto each players' plated piece of toast. She went from end table to ottoman to pouf like an island-hopping explorer.

"Or *seaside* or *home*," she said. "*Graveyard. Antarctica. London*, 1600 or 2099. I have only to name a place to create it, make you create it for me. A bed suggests a bedroom; a pair of shackles, a dungeon. They'll see the rest. We need only a hint. Your version"—she met Chantal's eyes—"may not be mine, may not be his." She gestured toward Will. "But that's not necessarily a problem. It's just the nature of reality, isn't it—each of us seeing things differently?"

Edgar had brought coffee. Crunching into a bite of toast, he reached toward the end table on his right to refill Ava's cup, leaving just the right amount of room for her cream.

"The viewer bears half the work," Fallon said. "In that sense, you can't have art without one. You can't act without an audience."

"Sure you can. People fool themselves all the time." Chantal reached for the salt and peppered her egg with it.

Fallon sat on the chesterfield and leaned over the gray velvet pouf her plate was balanced on. "But then they're their own audience, aren't they?"

"What about people who write poems they show no one?" countered Chantal.

"Is that art?" Fallon asked, setting down the pot of water. She set a fist to her hip bone and lifted a teacup and saucer with her other hand. "If a tree falls in a forest—"

Edgar reclined in the wingback, raising its front legs off the floor. A boot on the mahogany-paneled wall kept him tilted.

"What about the sets? Aren't they crucial?" He shook his head. "If the sets aren't even needed, why am I here?"

"Now there's a question," Fallon said. "We don't need the sets, but having them adds to the spectacle. The more elaborate, the better. That way, an audience feels it's getting its money's worth. It lends a definite *je ne sais quoi.*"

"A what?" Chantal asked.

"We're magicians," Fallon continued. "With a word, we can make a forest in the minds of others, spend an evening in the twelfth or twenty-fifth century, bring back the dead, create someone and become them."

"But none of it's real," Edgar said.

Fallon fired back like she'd been waiting for someone to say it. "But it's true. That's what matters."

After that afternoon's rehearsal and before their first performance, the cast, save Edgar, returned to the observation car and splayed themselves across the upholstery like a sprayed deck of cards. There was not quite enough time to start another chapter, begin a new game. Listless, they listed against cushions, ran lines in their heads.

The white wingspan of her notebook open, Fallon watched Ava from the corner of her eye. She watched Edgar through the window, throwing his five knives at the beech, then retrieving them, fore and aft in the high grass. Hit. Hit. Hit. Hit. Hit.

Without Edgar, Ava was a machine missing a part. Together, they hummed with tension. When one shifted, the other adjusted. Even the slightest cough would garner a furrow of concern. If their eyes met, they lingered a beat too long, and in that meeting stretched between them a joke, a question, a chastisement, a lifetime of love.

Hit. Hit. Hit. Hit. Hit.

Fallon, like a lightning bolt, bolted upright. The others looked up in half-interest. A finger trailed off a window-fog drawing, a woolen pill picked from a throw was dropped, an orbiting quarter stilled on the knuckle it circled.

Fallon had been watching all season, but she hadn't seen it before. Could Ava and Edgar be the perfect fodder for her hit play?

The barn's drafty group dressing room was separated from the stage by a burlap curtain. Will, wearing a blond wig and a grotesque prosthetic nose, drew a slip of paper from the hat.

"See—see the cat—see the cat glaring at the scared—scared mouse." A hand in the hat. A rustle of paper. "The quick fox"—his tempo tripled—"quick fox, quick fox, quick fox. The quick fox jumped on the sleeping cat."

Will chewed the inside of his lip. His stomach surged. Hot saliva flooded his mouth, and he bolted to unbolt the door, then fled across a narrow strip of grass to the porta-potty outside the barn. He yanked open its light plastic door, ripped off his wig and prosthetic nose, and vomited into the pool of other people's piss and shit. The contents of his stomach splashed into the blueish liquid, churning up a range of smells, chemical and organic. This set a second wave of nausea in motion. He retched again, then spun around to take a few deep breaths of fresh, country air. Light from within escaped the dark barn-theater, making each gap in its slats visible. Through them, Will could see the rest of the cast changing.

Earlier that evening, once the hum of arriving audience had grown to a decent pitch, Will had walked onstage, pulled back the burlap curtain that sagged over a strung string, and peeked out. Rows of hay bales were being used as seating. Many of them were full, and much of the front row was filled with young men—an anomaly compared to most of the troupe's performances. Under careful side-parts and thin necks, they wore baggy white button-up shirts with wide black ties and black suit slacks. The man on the bale closest Will had met his gaze, his face expressionless. If Will didn't know better, he'd have said they were part of a church group, but they had to be the men Edgar mentioned. He'd seen no sign of Claudette.

Will felt the weight of the bracelet in his breast pocket. The lump of its faces sat atop his soft stomach, and its metal pressed against his chest. He wiped the corner of his mouth on his sleeve and had just turned to head back into the barn when a white-suited, bald-capped Fallon blocked him.

"What are you doing?" she asked, gesturing at his wiglessness, his prostheticlessness. "It's almost time to go on!"

Will groaned. "Do I have to wear all this nonsense? I can barely breathe in the nose, and the wig is hot."

"Nonsense?" Fallon stopped, turned Will to her. "You know it's crucial to the plot. Let's get Chantal to re-glue you. Put your wig back on."

"I don't feel well. I don't know if I can go on tonight."

"We go through this every time, Will. You'll be fine. Your nerves always vanish once we're underway." With her left foot, she stepped on the right heel of her lizard-skin cowboy boot, pulled out her foot, and squatted, adjusting the stuffing in the boot's toe before stepping back into it.

"But this is—"

"We finally have a decent house, for some reason," she said, setting the wig back on his head. "Let's clinch this."

Will followed Fallon back into the barn. He sat still as Chantal reaffixed his nose, then he removed his glasses and took his place behind the curtain, but as the play got underway, all his attention rested on the men in the front row, who reflected it back. His pulse was pounding in his neck. He made an effort to sit up in the bed onstage but was pulled back down by the weight of Ava's lazy arm on his bare chest.

AGENT HARROW
Stay, Mike. It's early.

Having nowhere else to go, Will burrowed into character. He tried it on, trimming and hemming as a tailor would a suit, letting the seams out here then gathering them there, shifting the material until it was suitable, fitting, ready to pin.

AGENT FORD
Asp will be meeting the Russians today. If we play our cards right, we'll finally be able to retrieve the stolen microchip.

What lines—a perfect fit! For a few seconds, Will was gone. Someone else was speaking from his body, using his voice. Some person-on-paper inhaled, lived for as many words as that breath could produce. His part in it was nothing but lung.

AGENT HARROW

Promise me you'll be careful?

AGENT FORD

I'll be only as careful as you will, my dear. And I know you too
well to think you'll stay safely away.

AGENT HARROW

Please. I need you.

Will turned his round face from hers.

AGENT FORD

I warned you about getting attached.

Ava stifled a sob. It wasn't theatrical, and it wasn't hers. It was the near-
tears of a woman in love—worried and hurt—a moment of belief. The
actors became audience along with the rest of the house, and for all its
falsehood, the play became something.

AGENT FORD

I'll meet you at the bazaar tomorrow. Noon. Near the parrot
stalls. Don't be late.

Will placed his hand on the headboard and leaned to kiss the reclining
Ava, but the front row caught his eye in periphery, and the blurry wall
of wide shoulders knocked him from character. He paused a second,
lost, then headed quickly for the door stage left, stopping just before
he exited.

AGENT FORD

And, uh, dress, uh—um. Wear something hot.

Something woke Fox. It froze amidst the furs. Through the gap beneath
the trunk's warped lid, it saw two black legs approaching, foxlike in
black slacks.

Fox gathered its muscles, coiled in the corner, and kept its eyes on
the light. It was ready to strike. The lid lifted slightly, and a human hand

slipped something in. The object dropped heavy through the layers of fur hats, stoles, and muffs.

Fox had just worked up the courage to sniff it, when four more legs came closer—thicker, these. The trunk was lifted, swung between voices. For several seconds, Fox was at sea, sailing its captor's conversation, then the trunk was set down with a knock. So was Fox.

Soon a growl started, the growling of a hundred humans. In the dark, Fox snarled back.

A speedboat waited at the end of the dock, which was raised above the stage's sea of plywood waves. Will slunk down it, stalking Fallon, who in her bald cap and white suit held a gun to Chantal's head. The burn of the front row's eyes on Will's back rose the blood to his cheeks, but he stepped out from behind a stack of packing crates, pointed his pistol, and delivered his lines.

AGENT FORD
I'm afraid you'll have to change your travel plans, Asp.

Fallon turned, swinging the barrel of the gun toward Will, but he pulled the trigger first. A puny click indicated he was out of bullets. The men in the front row groaned. At the click, Fallon flinched, and in her spot of feigned shock, Will kicked the gun from her hand. A pile of pipes lay between Asp's trunk and a stack of shipping crates. Fallon grabbed one, felled Will with a blow to the shoulder. Chantal grabbed a second pipe and slid it to him. He stood, still rubbing his shoulder, and began dueling Fallon. Will's nerves gave him heightened senses, helping him foresee her thrusts, parry sooner, jab faster. Fallon seemed to be actually fighting.

Amid the commotion, Chantal took a few slow steps back to the trunk, then shouted over the battle-clatter.

AGENT STARBUCK
I couldn't have planned this better if I'd tried, boys!

The line wasn't in the script. Fallon and Will whipped their heads toward Chantal mid-thrust, glaring daggers. Will's eyes drifted to the line of men, who were scarier without the certainty of the next line. For a second, he thought he caught sight of Claudette at the back of the barn, but it was hard to tell without his glasses. Then Chantal lifted the trunk's lid and—in a blink—bolted claw, fang, and fur.

The audience gasped. Will leapt from the animal's path, landing half on the edge of the dock, half off. He hung for a moment, becoming aware, too late, of his fate. As he fell onto the rows of plywood waves, his elbow crashed into the side of the moored speedboat, bursting the papier-mâché, and his ankle flashed a bright light of pain that bleached, for a second, his vision. The fox was a swipe of red stage right.

The burlap curtain swept closed. Fallon stepped out before its swinging skirt, still in costume. The discussion buzz faded.

"Is there a doctor in the house?" she asked.

A man stood from the back bale. "I'm a vet," he called. "Large animal. That work?"

Every pair of eyes swept the house for another option, but there wasn't one. Fallon shrugged, and the man made his way forward. Heads craned. Fallon drew their attention to her through sheer volume.

"Ladies and gentlemen, as you have just witnessed, an unfortunate accident has taken place. Will Connaught, playing the part of Agent Ford, has fallen." Fallon's sentence was just ending when inspiration struck. "Unconscious," she added. "In a crushing blow to the adage, the show *can't* go on. Please accept my apologies, and thank you all for coming."

She bowed deeply, then slipped behind the curtain, where Will lay, limbs akimbo, between two wooden waves, as though swimming. He was awash in the rest of the cast.

Fallon crouched beside him. "Are you okay, my little tossed die?" she asked, removing her bald cap.

Will turned toward her but kept his eyes on his foot. "I think my ankle's broken," he groaned. "Why'd you tell them I was unconscious?"

"The play didn't go as planned, but that doesn't mean we can't make a show of it." She rapped a knuckle on the plywood stage. "They paid for one, didn't they?"

February 18
THE MIDWEST CHORUS | THEATER REVIEW
The Slip
The Troupe Adores
The Fox Theater
Paris, South Dakota
Remaining performances: tonight at 8 p.m., tomorrow at 3 p.m.

It was Eve's fault, the Fall, and in this case, we blame Fallon Finn-Dorset. Needless to say, the performance fell short.

It's a story old as time: a man and a woman get tripped up, fall head over heels, but lo and behold, they're opposites—one devious and the other gullible, one straightlaced and one fun. The fact is, however, opposites don't attract.

Study after study catches us choosing partners with similar facial proportions, ages, upbringings, attitudes, education, and beliefs to our own. We're more likely to select someone with a similar sounding name, even if it's just the first letter (thus the Donnas and Donnys, Seths and Bethanys, Aarons and Karens). How better to recreate ourselves in offspring and live on? Indeed, what we want in a mate is ourselves, or else, someone we wish we were, brave enough to taste the apple.

In other words, Adam wasn't innocent. What he loved in Eve was himself. The temptation lay within.

But the self changes. Experience evolves our thinking. Each day we love, we drift too. The danger is looking up to find ourselves miles off course, with a mate who's someone other.

The thing is, we could have sworn it was a fox.

Will winced as Chantal gingerly rolled the cuff of his corduroys above his injured ankle. The night before, the vet had declared it sprained. He'd even driven the troupe back to the private cars after the performance and, with Edgar, served as a crutch to get Will safely inside and onto the observation car's tapestried sofa. Will wasn't sure what they would have done, had the vet not been there.

Like a movie nurse, Chantal daubed the minor scrapes on Will's ankle with an iodine-soaked cotton ball. There was nothing to do but succumb.

"Aren't you supposed to do that right away, *before* the scabs form?" he asked.

She shrugged, then restacked several of the car's mismatched throw pillows on the other end of the sofa and lifted Will's foot onto them.

She smiled. "If you need *anything* else, just whistle." Leaning forward, she wiggled her shoulders, swinging her heavy breasts from side to side in burlesque.

Will looked away, and she turned for the door, stopping at the threshold.

"You know how to do that, don't you?" she said in a breathy, velvety voice. "You just put your lips together—and blow." She blew a long, high whistle.

Will forced himself to remember Claudette. He wondered whether he'd missed her, whether the men had scared her off. He struggled to sit up. "Did anyone ask for me? After the show?"

"I almost forgot," Chantal said. "This guy stopped me on my way out of the theater—shaved head, muscles—" Her eyes went dreamy. "I mean, that's no surprise. It happens all the time, but he had a message for you from your friend, Mitzi?"

Will lowered his chin in acknowledgement, and Chantal, wincing and rubbing her left thigh, continued. "He said he was sorry he missed you and that Mitzi himself will be at the closing performance in Lyon, unless he hears from you before then. He'll meet you backstage, but Mitzi"—she raised her fingers in air quotes, hooking them with each syllable—"don't like to travel." She screwed the cap back onto the iodine bottle. "Does that mean anything to you?"

Will paled, stammered. "It's just an old pal who keeps threatening to surprise me at a show."

Nausea lifted his shoulders, which Chantal took for a shrug. Long after she left for her compartment, Will lay worrying his thumb over the bracelet's faces.

In her compartment, Fallon scried, conjectured.

A teenaged CHANTAL loves showing off for boys.

BOY 1

(*Splitting firewood with an ax*) It takes a man to deliver the splitting stroke!

CHANTAL

Don't kid yourself. Us girls know exactly what to do with wood.

BOY 2

I dare you to give it a try.

CHANTAL

The ax? Or the wood?

The BOYS snort, punch each other's shoulders.

BOY 1

Split that one there, if you know so much. You've seen it done.

CHANTAL

I have indeed.

CHANTAL sets a piece of wood atop the stump serving as chopping block, lifts the ax over her head with effort, and lets its weight drop. The blade glances off the edge of the wood and ricochets, hitting below her knee and splitting her leg with ease. She steps backward, off her left leg, which—timber—falls to the ground. The BOYS scatter.

When Chantal entered the vestibule and closed the door to the observation car behind her, Fallon, a fury in black, gripped her by the wrist.

"You went off script," Fallon chided. "And look what's happened. We're already without one actor, but without Will, we're finished."

"The audience loved it," said Chantal.

"They loved it when Will fell. They couldn't care less about your last-minute addition, and now it's ruined us."

"Which wouldn't have been possible without me. Admit it: I made the play better."

"You made it worse. So much worse. Don't you see what you've done? What'll we do without Will?"

"He's just being a baby. He'll be back on that ankle in no time."

"That's perfect, because it's exactly how much time we have left to make something of this goddamned tour."

Chantal rolled her eyes.

"I can stand in for a man in a character role, but we need an actual man to play lead. Who will play the male parts now?"

Chantal drew her eyes up Fallon's height. "Edgar?"

Standing on his bed, which he'd dragged against the door to his compartment, Edgar slid the thick art book closer across the bedding with a socked foot. The spread displayed Michelangelo's *Creation of Adam*. Edgar was copying it onto the wall, which was filled with color.

Only the right side, God's, was there. He rode on a cushion of angels, a red cloth in the shape of a brain behind them, and His arm extended nearly to the edge of the doorframe, straining to touch an unseen Adam's hand. On the wall, just beyond the reach of God's outstretched finger, was an old-fashioned push-button light switch.

There was a knock on the accordion door, and Edgar called to come in. The door folded back to reveal Fallon, two paper cups in her hands.

"Oh," she muttered, taking in Edgar's superior position and seeing the way barred by the bed.

"Yeah?" he grunted.

"I know it's nearly noon, but I brought you a coffee." Fallon held up the paper cup, and Edgar took it, shifting his paintbrush to his left hand, which held a palette. "What are you up to?" She kicked off her tuxedo slippers and stepped up onto the mattress, sinking to her ankles in the bedding, then turned to look at the wall. "My goodness, my little putto. This is tremendous."

Edgar took a swallow of coffee, then set it on the compartment's small counter. Holding up a finger to Fallon, he stepped off the bed through the doorway. He reached for the light switch with Adam's lax hand, pressed it to turn off the light, then turned it back on again. All the while, God strained. Fallon laughed. She hopped off the bed beside Edgar and reached for the switch, becoming Adam herself. The room darkened and lit.

"You're so talented—your painting, your photography, and let's not forget your acting, either. Your swan was incredible."

Edgar rasped his stubble, took the paintbrush again in his right hand, and resumed painting. "I'd actually love to forget my acting. And I'd love for you to forget it too."

"Now, Edgar. I know you want the troupe to succeed." Fallon cloyed her voice. "But you see, with Will injured, we have no choice but to cancel the last two performances of *The Slip*. This season, we're already down one actor after losing Ben, and I'm afraid we can't continue with this play without at least one more man."

"Why can't *you* play it? You play men all the time."

"The structure of this play is the issue. Both of the male parts appear in the same scene, so—"

"What about putting on a different play for the last two performances? I could get out one of the previous sets, whip something together."

"That's tough, you know? I can't expect the actors to perform without at least a couple of rehearsals."

"We have plenty of time today. We were going to rehearse anyway."

"Edgar, if you don't help us out by playing this part—"

"If the others can't be expected to take on a new role at such short notice, then I can't either. Besides, I told you, I'm not an actor."

"Surely you've picked up most of Will's lines during rehearsals, or the gist of them anyway."

Edgar continued painting. He jammed his brush into a daub of green paint on the palette then slashed the shape of the gauzy fabric under God on the wall.

The sweetness dropped from Fallon's voice. "If you don't help, I'm going to cancel the other two performances. You don't want that, do you? You'd be letting everyone down."

Edgar shook his head. "Sorry. I can't."

"Can't say I didn't try," Fallon said, slapping a hand on the doorframe. "And can't say I won't try again." She leaned into the room to reach for the switch one last time, but paused, peered closer at the wall.

"I found the fly in this one," she said, reaching out a finger, but there was a buzzing, and it lifted, left.

Night Travel

February 19

Click clack, click clack, click clack, click clack, click clack. The train, it ran iambic, counting time. With speed, the lovers traveled farther between ticks, grew closer between talks, so that by some phenomenon, time dilated, and the night of travel seemed to sometimes last a week. The distances decreased. They felt they'd known each other for forever. Therein lay the danger.

It had been strange, getting two nights off due to the cancelled shows. When Edgar entered the baggage car, the dust-covered CD player was blasting Prince, and Chantal was hard at work on a stool behind the table. Its battered surface was dressed for evening, spread with silver sequins. One of her hands was up the crotch of a showgirl costume sitting in her lap. She sang along to the song's chorus, nodding her head at each syllable: *lit-tle red cor-vette*. Edgar retreated a step, knocked loudly on the doorframe.

As if she'd been doing something illicit, Chantal jumped, swapped postures. She yanked her hand from the costume and stretched it up to one of the shelves behind her. A click stopped the music. The same hand worked to fluff her hair as she addressed Edgar.

"I've been meaning to get to a few costume repairs," she said. "And I figured there's no better time than while Fallon's furious with me. It might help my case if she sees me working when she passes through on her way to the bar car." As she spoke, she massaged her thigh absentmindedly.

Edgar sequined the length of his index finger by pressing it firmly on the tabletop.

"We're not going to the bar car tonight," he said, examining his work.

"What?" Chantal stopped sewing. "That'll be a first."

"We're bringing drinks back to the observation car, so we can be with Will."

"I know one girl who's not getting lucky, in that case."

Edgar brushed the sequins from his finger. "I have something for you."

"I *am* getting lucky?"

"Yes and no."

He gestured for her to stand and, when she did, grabbed her stool and walked past her, setting it down in front of the tarnished, full-length mirror.

"Please," he said, motioning to the paint-spattered seat.

Chantal sat, looking in the mirror, then sat up a little straighter and tugged slyly at the bottom of her shirt, exposing a touch more cleavage.

Edgar swept his eyes to her face. "We're going to rewrite your brain." He knelt, took her right foot from the stool's rung, and removed her tennis shoe, placing her bare foot on the floor.

"I feel like Cinderella," Chantal twittered. "Except you're taking the shoe *off*—even better."

Edgar lifted the mirror from where it leaned against a rack of costumes and set it between her knees.

"And still better," Chantal said.

He leaned the mirror against her left thigh and placed a hand on her prosthetic leg. "Now look into the mirror," he directed. "If you look at the reflection and ignore the frame, it should look like you have a left foot."

Chantal nodded, wiggled her toes.

"Now keep watching the foot in the mirror, and start to stretch it," Edgar continued. "Good. Spread your right toes, lengthen your arch, watch, and convince yourself you're seeing your left foot stretching. Feel it release."

"Oh my god. Seriously?" Chantal whined. "I've done some crazy acting exercises and some *very* interesting things with mirrors, but—"

"Treat it like acting, then. You're a woman with two legs, opening and closing your left foot."

Chantal obliged. "Does this actually work?"

"It's supposed to. It fools the mind into giving up the phantom-limb pain. When you see the foot opening and stretching, your brain can't account for it being cramped, so the pain goes away. The more you practice, the better the phantom should feel."

"Where'd you learn this?" She kept her eyes on her lifting toes in the mirror.

Edgar rocked back from kneeling to squatting. "From an article a few years back, about how the mind and eye work together to create your reality."

"I knew you were a nerd, but seriously?"

Edgar shrugged. "It seemed applicable to my work."

Their faces were close together, and Edgar felt Chantal come closer. Just before her lips brushed his, he rocked back on his heels. His hands flew up as he lost his balance, fell.

"You know I'm not interested," he said, righting himself and brushing the dust from his jeans. "I made that clear before."

"But why not? Everyone else is."

Edgar felt the confession, the declaration, rising to his throat as he thought of Ava, but then, thinking of Ava, he swallowed it. "Let's leave it at that."

Chantal sighed. "Someday I'll get you to notice me. Just wait."

Fallon shut the door to the private cars behind her, crossed the vestibule, and entered a public sleeper car. As she passed a roomette with an open door, a voice within called to her.

"Who goes there?"

A few steps farther, she heard, in a louder voice of doom, "I *said*, 'Who goes there?'"

Fallon backed up and peered in. Two berths were unfolded on the wall, taking up most of the compartment. On the upper bed was a birdcage, occupied by a smallish green parrot.

"Hello," it said, its tone intimate, maybe even a little sheepish.

"Well, hi," Fallon replied. "Aren't you clever?"

The parrot blinked, cocked its head to one side, the better to see her. "I love you," it said.

"And I you, my little pillow," Fallon answered. "Are you traveling alone?"

The bird turned slowly, maneuvering its feet on the perch with care. With its back to her, it side-stepped down the length of the rod, climbed down the cage's metal bars by gripping them in its beak and feet, and came forward to the cage's door, where it paced rapidly back and forth.

"I love you," it repeated. "I love you. I love you."

When Fallon reached the bar car, it was bustling. Art was hustling to make drinks and clear empty glasses, and the passengers were drinking them nearly as fast as he could shake them. Fallon was no exception. As soon as Art set the martini before her on the mahogany bar, where she'd elbowed a narrow place, she belted it. A cloudy, cone-shaped swig of gin was all that remained. Its brine reminded her of tears, and unlike her usual first drink on a travel night, it didn't feel celebratory or well-earned.

The past two days had been rough. They'd been wasted. Without Edgar on board to play a part, Fallon had to cancel the last two performances of *The Slip* and refund the rest of the weekend's tickets. She was tired—of fighting for survival, of working so hard to prove art was worth something. The feeling was a burned-out fatigue, a fuzziness in her brain and dry irritation in her eyes. In the evenings, she'd sigh, and could feel a deep ache in her lungs, as though they were tired of breathing.

Fallon drained the last of her gin and raised the martini glass to flag Art's attention. He was at the opposite end of the bar, chatting with a patron who could have been Fallon's see-saw partner, had the bar a fulcrum. Art nodded at her without breaking his conversation. She watched him flip over his shaker, reach for the gin on the backbar.

Had Fallon first written about Art before or after she'd met him? She couldn't remember, but *there* was an actor. Art was a servant, through and through. He was selfless: a nobody, in that he was anyone you wanted him to be, a mirror reflecting each customer. He laughed with those who cracked jokes, chatted with those who needed company, listened to those who needed to unload. For customers who didn't want to see him, Art was invisible. He was sharp nods and quick movements for those who barked orders. He set himself to the tip dangling before him, doing whatever it took to move it from their pocket to his. There was no Art to it, nothing under the Arthur Conan-Doyle or the Abraham Lincoln. He'd only taken on Honest Abe because that's who people wanted him to be, who they told him he was. To Fallon, Art would present a consistent face, but watching carefully, she'd catch him playing different parts for others.

Art garnished the drink and broke off his anecdote to deliver Fallon's glass. "You okay tonight?" he asked her quietly when she didn't flash him her usual smile.

"Just peachy. Just peachy. Thanks for this," she said, lifting the fresh martini. "I'll also need a Negroni—make that two—and a cosmo and a beer—a lager. We're having our drinks in the observation car tonight—a quiet night in, to lick our wounds."

"That bad, huh?" Art shook the drink. "All I can offer is, 'Be sure you put your feet in the right place, then stand firm.'"

"But what is the right place, Art?" Fallon asked. "What says the champion of the people? What do the people want?"

"Everybody likes a compliment; that's for sure." He touched a long, knobby finger to his upper lip. "But seriously, I'd say they want magic. Something bigger than themselves, unwieldy, some transformation or manifestation. It can't hurt, at any rate. As I always say, 'Always bear in mind that your own resolution to succeed is more important than any other.'"

"Indeed," Fallon said, but the roar of laughter from a nearby table drowned her out.

The troupe may not have been meeting in the bar car, but Chantal still wanted attention. She entered the observation car, hoping the others could smell her fancy, new shampoo. She checked the belt of her ter-rycloth robe, removed the towel wrapped around her head, and rubbed her wet hair with it. Fallon was sipping gin on the chesterfield, Will was lying on the tapestried sofa, and Ava and Edgar were on opposite ends of the car. Chantal scooped the cosmo from a wooden tray on one of the end tables. Despite his rejection earlier—mostly because of it—she slipped into the wingback closest to Edgar.

Fallon cleared her throat. "We're nearing the end of the season, but we're no closer to the hit we need to continue touring this spring. I thought I'd take the question to the people, so to speak. You tell me: what do the people want?"

Chantal flourished her cosmo, pinky aloft. "They want what we all want: love."

Will nodded. "But more than love, really: trouble in love. They want someone to get into trouble but, more so, out of it."

"Exactly," Ava added. "Someone improved. That's what we all want, right?"

Chantal yawned.

Ava fussed with a corner of her cocktail napkin. "Of course, there's also sex and scandal and murder and gossip."

"Better leave those to me," Chantal said.

Ava rolled her eyes. "What I'm saying is, people want drama."

Edgar chimed in. "They want something honest."

"You talkin' to me?" asked Chantal, trying to catch his eye. "You talkin' to me? 'Cause I don't see anyone else here."

Will twisted on the sofa to look at her. "You talkin' to me?" he echoed.

"You're missing something, with your lip," Chantal said. "More like this, like, 'You talkin' to me?'"

Will lifted one side of his upper lip. "You—You talkin'?"

Chantal's eyes stabbed at Edgar's. "Who the fuck do you think you're talkin' to, huh?" Then dulled. "Edgar, let's hear yours."

Edgar scooted deeper into a slouch over his sketchpad, crossed a boot over his thigh, and took a swallow of Negroni.

Will jumped in on him. "Oh, come on. Hit me with it!"

"I wish I could, believe me," Edgar grumbled, hunkering lower over the paper and pencil.

"What's that? You talkin' to me?" Will resumed.

"Who the fuck do you think you're talkin' to?" added Chantal. "Come on, Edgar!" She stood and moved nearer his chair, gesturing aggressively. She was pointing, poking. "Huh? Huh? Who the fuck do you think you're talkin' to? I don't see anyone else here."

Exploding into motion, Edgar jumped to his feet and slammed his sketchbook shut. He made for the door to the observation platform, growling over his shoulder, "Stop bothering me with your fucking games. I'm not an actor. I live in the real world."

"What's his problem?" Will asked.

"You heard him," Chantal said, bending to pick up Edgar's pencil from the rug.

But Fallon had stopped listening. Edgar was unpredictable, like an animal. It was compelling. Trouble in love, she thought, scandal, magic, something honest. The stars became constellation. The hit hit her. She would try to write it.

Ba dum, ba dum, ba dum, ba dum, ba dum. Blanketed by the open physics textbook and notebook in her lap, Ava sat in bed under the light of a single lamp, reading the chapter on thermal expansion. The train beat on across the miles, and her heart beat on too, making the long trip from Ben to Edgar.

That rhythm was created by distance. Each rail of the track was gapped, each strip of steel one segment of a dotted line, something separate. Space was left between each piece to allow for the temperature-induced swelling and shrinking of the metal. In sunshine and ice, the rails would change, would breathe, inhaling and exhaling throughout the day and year. When the steel wheels hit the gaps, it beat the train to life: ba dum, ba dum.

This distance between spans protected against breakage, preserved the integrity of the metal. And in the same way, the distance Ava kept between her and Edgar, that small cushion, was keeping them from conflagration. Her walls still stood about her burned-out city, but her gates were aflame. She wanted to give herself over fully, be Edgar's, but doing so, telling him everything, would be their end. She knew as soon as she gave in, it would be over. She refocused on the problem at hand.

$$\alpha_L = \frac{1}{L}\frac{dL}{dT}$$

☙

Ankle elevated on a pedestal of pillows at the end of the tapestried sofa, Will panted a few times, abs afire, then inhaled and lifted his torso, holding it and his breath as he attempted to shift a few of the pillows behind him. They shifted, slipped against each other. He rested again for a second, then in one clean motion, rose higher while yanking one from his lumbar back to the top of the stack. Settling his head onto it, he tapped the arrow on his phone's screen and resumed The Rude Mechanicals' performance of *Henry IV, Part I.*

Will couldn't stop himself repeatedly watching each scene available online, as if Ben was rehearsing for him in perfectly identical runthroughs. As he watched, he felt his stomach churn, his mouth dry. Enter Ben, and he'd retch, dry heave. He watched perfect Ben punctuate each perfectly delivered, perfectly articulated line with the perfect gesture and facial expression. He looked deep into Ben's eyes during close-ups, searching for an iota of Ben, but there was none. The man disappeared into each role. If one said they'd seen Ben's Hamlet, they'd seen nothing more.

Upon the word *fox*, Will started, pressed pause, struggled to sit up. He dragged the dot on the timeline a few seconds back, then tapped play again.

...like the fox,
Who, ne'er so tame, so cherish'd and lock'd up,
Will have a wild trick of his ancestors.

Fallon leaned nearer the mirror of her makeshift desk, and her reflection leaned in conspiratorially. She looked into her eyes and saw herself behind them, as if in costume, her skin's slight slackening showing wear where before there was none. An impression was setting in on either side of her mouth, the beginnings of parentheses. Some nights now, it seemed everything she said was an aside.

The cancellation of the last two performances in Paris had caused the troupe to drop into the red. They'd crossed into loss. With four plays left, two old and two new, it was time to rally, come up with a showstopper. But all Fallon wanted was to stop the show.

Up next was a repertoire favorite, a love story, but she'd rather create some destruction, make something new—something black and sleek, better suited to her mood: a panther of a play to bite and scratch, escape the grasp of audience. If they wanted nothing from her, that's exactly what she'd give them. She opened the thesaurus on her desk. This one would be for her.

The train came to a stop beneath an area light that shone through the compartment's window onto the mirrored desk and, from there, glinted directly into Fallon's eyes, as though someone shipwrecked was sending a signal. Wincing, she slid a bookmark over the spot of bright, and the resulting shadow tied itself across her eyes like a bandit's mask.

Fallon would steal the show. If the start of art was the blank canvas, the end of it was the black canvas. Nothing was possible beyond it. She dashed off a list of words into her black-jacketed notebook, closed it. She'd drag the house as far as it could go.

The red velvet curtains in Edgar's compartment were closed, but one curtain ring was missing. Where the fabric sagged, an eye of early morning light peeked in, creating a camera obscura that projected an upside-down film of the passing landscape onto the opposite wall, where God strained.

Watching, Ava lay against Edgar's blacksmith shop of a body. He radiated heat; someone was stoking his stoves. Her right ear was pressed against his scar, and she could hear his heart chuffing blood—onward, ever onward—trusting his veins to direct it where needed.

In her other ear, Ava heard the train engine powering them across the country, onward to town after town through the last stop of the season, the last place she was sure he'd be hers. She was a passenger in all this, one who boarded and, beyond, bore no onus for the when or where of arrival. For how could she tell him about Ben? Each day she didn't made the prospect that much more difficult.

"Has this happened before?" Ava asked, nodding toward the projection.

"Only when everything's perfect," Edgar said. He rolled her onto her back, so he lay in the crook of her arm, and twisted a tendril of her hair tightly around his finger until the tip of it purpled. "Let's go somewhere together, when the tour ends, get away from this place, this cage."

Ava nodded a halfhearted nod.

"I love you," he said, and kissed her. Then, eyes on hers, he waited.

Ava couldn't speak. She wasn't sure.

"We're on our way to Rome, you know," he said. "It's the last place I lived and the last place I ever wanted to be again." He rasped his stubble. "I swore I'd never go back."

"But you're not." Ava soothed a hand through his dark hair.

He pushed it away. "Aren't I?"

Looking at her again, Edgar saw almost everything. It made Ava's heart catch in her throat. It battered her burning gates. She looked back at the projection of the landscape on the wall, watched a flock of birds drop from the sky of a field into a sea of blue sky.

Rome, North Dakota

February 20

"Fuck the schedule," said Fallon. She leaned forward in one of the observation car's armchairs, a mismatched teacup and saucer in her hand. "We're going off book. We're bumping *Let Them Eat Cake*."

Will sat up on the tapestried couch and took a gulp of his coffee. The steam fogged his glasses, and he worried to himself as he waited for the lenses to clear. *Two new plays in a row?* As it was, the season's schedule was madness, but somehow knowing what was coming kept Will grounded. The repertoire favorites between the new plays also gave the cast a bit of a break. He could imagine how nervous he'd be now if he hadn't been saved by his ankle.

"But you can't!" Chantal whined.

"Are you talking to me?" Fallon asked, emphasizing each syllable.

"'Cause I don't see anyone else here," Chantal muttered on cue before shaking it off.

Will didn't dare chime in.

"The shepherdess is my best role!" Chantal continued. "I look fire in the costume, and I—"

"I can," Fallon interrupted. "And I have."

In the seat farthest from Will, Ava piped up. "But don't we need the favorites to supplement the new plays? Can we drop this one without drifting into the red?"

Fallon snorted. "We're well within it already. Can't you smell the blood?"

"Then we need this play more than ever. It sells."

Fallon cracked the teacup and saucer onto the end table beside her chair. "I don't know what else to do without Ben, without Will."

"Men, men, men," Chantal said. "Can't live with them—"

"But we could live without them, if we—" Ava said.

"We can't perform with an all-female cast." Fallon shook her head. "They won't go for that gimmick out here. This isn't Brooklyn."

Will glanced nervously at Ava, but she didn't flinch.

Fallon grinned. "We have you, Edgar. You could solve all our problems."

Edgar shook his head. "I'm not an actor." He took a few long swallows from his travel mug.

"We could work with you, minimize some of the parts," Will said. "Just until I'm back on my feet, as it were."

Chantal piped up. "You were wonderful as the swan. No one could take their eyes off you." She batted her lashes.

"That's exactly why I don't want to do it. I told you: I don't like performing. You hired me to build sets. That's why I'm here."

"There won't *be* any sets to build before long," Chantal said.

"What about Art?" Edgar huffed.

"That's not a bad idea," Fallon said, crossing her ankle on her knee.

"It's not a good idea either," countered Chantal. "Think he can play anyone other than himself?"

Will scratched the back of his head. "You mean Lincoln?"

"Same difference," Chantal said.

"Isn't that what we're all doing?" Fallon said. "Playing ourselves? Besides, my little deerstalkers, there's nothing to solve." She waved dismissively. "I've written something new."

Ava set down her coffee. "But there's not enough time to learn it by tonight!"

"It's a one-woman show. You'll need only help me with the set and costume."

"So let me get this straight," Chantal said. "An all-female cast is too avant garde for you—"

"Not for me. Never for me," Fallon reminded. "For *them*."

"But a one-woman show is fine? How am I supposed to get discovered if I'm not onstage?"

"That's a good question, a wonderful thing to consider next time you think about going off-script."

"As soon as this tour's over, I'll be packing for LA—somewhere they appreciate actresses." Chantal crossed her arms over her chest.

"Right. Well, you're mine for at least the next two weeks, anyway. Lucky me."

"Fallon, please," Ava cut in. "Let's do *Cake*. We can cut the scenes with more than three characters and take a few roles each. We could even do the quick changes onstage. The audience will love it. Do it for me? As a favor?"

"A favor? Should *you* be asking *me* for a favor right now?"

Ava leaned back in her seat. "Why are you so hell bent on failure?"

Fallon swept her hands from one end of the car to another. "This is all mine. I made all of it, including you. No one's going to tell me how to run it. You're all lucky to have jobs as full-time artists, and you know that."

"I thought a job paid," Chantal muttered.

"Let's rally, bring ourselves back into the black," Ava said. "Give us the chance, at least."

"An excellent segue," said Fallon, rising from her chair. "It's time to get to work."

The cast groaned, stretched, dawdled, and rose reluctantly from the upholsteries, leaving their teacups and mugs on the end tables.

Only Will remained. When he heard the others crashing away through the rail yard's gray gravel, he removed the Janus bracelet from his pocket, looked it face to face to face. He chewed his inner lip. Claudette hadn't shown in Paris like they'd agreed. But those men had. He hoped they hadn't found her, hoped she was okay, hoped she hadn't forgotten him, but more than anything, he hoped she'd forgive him for sleeping with Chantal.

Will sat up on the sofa, gently lowered his injured foot from the pedestal of pillows, and stood, adding gradual weight. The ankle held. He shifted more, and it held. But just before all his weight was on it, before he could take a proper step, it stabbed. He was healing faster than he'd expected. Or the sprain hadn't been that bad. He'd be back onstage in no time, back in the crosshairs of those thugs. His cheek chewing redoubled.

Quick footsteps approached the observation car from the vestibule, and Will dove back onto the sofa, swung his leg up on its pedestal, threw over the throw.

Chantal stepped through the doorframe. "I've been meaning to ask you: want to promote the performance with me in town tomorrow? I know it's a shitty show and all, but it can't hurt. And I have a new idea."

Will gestured to his ankle. "I can't. I can't go anywhere."

Chantal scowled.

"Yeah. Well." She toed the threadbare rug. "I asked Edgar to come back for us with the van, give us a lift to the theater. Want to come with? If you're good, I'll sit on your lap."

At the thought of leaving the private cars, Will's stomach turned. "I—" he started, then leaned over the side of the couch. There was just enough time to grab a magazine on the floor beneath him before vomiting onto it.

Chantal wrinkled her nose. "There's no need to be rude."

On his wooden crutches, Will fled the observation car, hobbling down the sleeper car's corridor and through the bathroom's accordion door. He closed it behind him, then leaned the crutches against the narrow shower stall. With barely a limp, he stepped up to the sink and, letting the water run, rummaged in his pocket for a crumpled slip of paper.

"The soft cushion—the soft cushion broke—broke—the man's fall," he read in a whisper. What if it had? His stomach flipped as he felt the fall again, saw the wall of men in the theater's front row, shoulder to shoulder. Will spun and dove for the toilet, clattering over the crutches, and spattered the white porcelain with sick.

There was a knock at the door. "You know you're not going onstage, right?" Chantal asked.

Will spat into the toilet, flushed, and yelled over the rush of water, "Ready in a minute!" But he wondered if he ever would be. Deep down, he knew he wasn't lucky. He'd never catch a break, not from a gangster nor a girl, not even of a leg when he needed it most.

February 21

This was war, and Fallon was readying in the backstage dressing room. Nearly every inch of her was covered in black fabric. She wore her tuxedo pants with a black silk shirt buttoned as high as it would go. Black gloves covered her hands; black socks and tux slippers, her feet. With a brush, Chantal added a few last daubs of black eyeshadow, filling Fallon's eye sockets completely.

When Fallon had arrived on Main Street earlier that evening, scanning the street numbers on the buildings for 563, 563, 563, she thought she'd been mistaken. Number 563 wasn't The Midnight Theater; it was (according to the bold brown seventies font on the yellow stucco building) John Wayne Elementary. Fallon wondered for a second if she'd transposed the numbers, then rapped on one of the double glass doors the faster to find out.

Before long, a woman approached from the depths of the building. Her blurred yellow shape had gathered form as it neared, reminding Fallon of a koi rising to the surface of a murky pond. After unlocking the doors and pushing one open, the woman confirmed, "Yes, The Midnight's what the teachers named the stage in the cafeteria. They took a vote."

The woman had led Fallon through darkness and solid double doors into the "theater" proper. A risen stage stood at one end of a large elementary school cafeteria. Its walls and linoleum were a yellowish off-white, so Fallon hadn't been able to tell if the color was intentional or a product of age and neglect. At that early hour, the long lunch tables were tented in half and rolled to the room's edges. The faint smell of steamed broccoli issued from an adjoining kitchen, mixing with the odor of bleach. It was the most depressing room she'd been in for a while, but she thought it might be for the best.

Fallon struggled from a child-sized plastic chair built for someone less than half her stature. She removed her black velvet cloak from a crotch-height hook (which belonged, according to purple marker on masking tape, to Averie), spun it over her shoulder like a matador's cape, and pulled the hood over her head. She was ready.

Onstage, Fallon played DARKNESS. She was pitch, ebony, jet, raven, soot, obsidian, onyx, ink. The stage, too, was cloaked in it. She sat onstage on a black stool. That was all. This was it.

Her skin and teeth were the only white. Her eyes, the only brightness. She looked out into the dark of the audience at nothing, at everything, absorbing the light. The score was silence. At long intervals, a bell rung, knocking from her a well-articulated word.

Bell.

DARKNESS

Dark.

Bell.

DARKNESS

Dim.

Bell.

                    DARKNESS
   Cloudy.

Bell.

                    DARKNESS
   Murky.

Bell.

                    DARKNESS
   Vague.

A quartet of creaking seats began to tune.

Bell.

                    DARKNESS
   Opaque.

Bell.

                    DARKNESS
   Tenebrous.

A hiss emitted from whispers.

Bell.

                    DARKNESS
   Obscure.

Like iron filings drawn to magnet, a smattering of couples stood, sidled toward the aisles.

Bell.

DARKNESS

Obfuscous.

The clip of heels echoed.

Bell.

DARKNESS

Gloomy.

After eight more minutes of the same, the tap of the trickling audience wrenched left, and the rows of seating began to flood. Those making their way down the aisles watched the stage with their minds in the lobby. Those still seated watched as one watches the rain from inside a shop, hoping for a break in which to make a dash for it.

Bell.

DARKNESS

Somber.

The cafeteria doors flapped open and closed.

Bell.

DARKNESS

Drab.

Even the last, at last, giving up.

Bell.

DARKNESS

Dull.

The show went on for forty-five minutes. When it was over, there was only one person in the audience besides Ava, Will, and Chantal: a man in the back row. He was at the cusp of middle age, scruffily bearded, wearing a faded, moth-eaten sweater over pleated khakis. When Fallon stood and made a slight bow to him to indicate the end of the piece, he removed his glasses and, folding them, placed them in his shirt pocket, then switched off the light on the tip of his pen, click-retracted its tip, and flipped the cover of his notebook closed.

On his way out, he looked back over his shoulder, as though making sure she was finished.

As soon as the backstage door slammed shut behind him, Edgar regretted staying so late at the theater. He'd been dawdling, using up the evening so he wouldn't have to think, hoping Ava would return, but by the time he left, Rome was in full swing.

It was far more Romelike at night. The streets were crowded with couples on their way to or from dinner, and the patios of Italian restaurants pushed out into the cobblestone streets, each piping through its sound system either a well-known aria, a Frank Sinatra song, or "That's Amore" into the candle-dotted dark. Edgar felt the wail of a headache starting up from a long way off. He'd sworn he'd never come back.

Thinking about Rome and its heartache brought Ava to mind. She didn't love him, or at least hadn't said so yet. He hoped he hadn't frightened her away. Some people were funny. They wouldn't say how they felt until they were sure, as if love was a mystery, a misery not to be trusted. Edgar had always declared his feelings. This had brought him a lot of pain.

As a couple walked past him, arm in arm, the man's shoulder bumped Edgar's, which bumped his hip into a table. Its candle's wax splashed over its flame, dampening the romance for a young couple who unclasped their hands across the white tablecloth, now stained with red wine, and frowned at him.

To make it clear that the bump hadn't been his fault, Edgar yelled back over his shoulder. "Hey! Asshole! Watch where you're fucking going!"

He continued up the street, but now every couple at every table watched him, mouths moving with what he was certain wasn't pasta. He pretended not to notice, but every time he tried to tune out the onlookers, he found himself back in Rome, barraged with memories. Even the most painful were cheapened copies of actual experiences, like this place.

Edgar never needed a Negroni more, and the one consolation of finding himself in Rome again was that he might be able to get one outside the bar car. Beside a place called Pizza Navona, there was a bar called The Trevi. Inside, straw-wrapped chianti bottles held candles on each tabletop, fake grapevines complete with fake grapes wrapped the low, rustic ceiling beams, and the bartenders and servers wore red-and-white-striped shirts. A man with a thick mustache was playing "That's Amore" on accordion.

"*Buena sera*," greeted the bartender in a flat American accent.

Edgar slid onto a stool and, in his triggered state, flinched at the Italian. "Shit. Sorry. *Buena sera*." He said the phrase quickly, as though it burned his tongue. "I don't suppose I could get a Negroni?"

The bartender dried his hands on a towel and slung it over his shoulder. "What's in it?"

Rome was so Romelike! Walking the candle-lit, cobblestone streets, Fallon sighed. Café tables flanked the road, wafting out into the dark as if carried along on the aria-thick wind. Couples strolled past her with their fingers entwined. She'd just finished dinner al fresco: pasta and *vino* and tiramisu. Tonight was about love. She opened her guidebook, which must have once belonged to a library. Its yellowing plastic cover crinkled.

> Behold the Roman Forum (or *Forum Romanum*, when in Rome)! For centuries, this was the hub to which all roads led. It was central to every Roman's life, the site of the market, elections, processions, speeches, criminal trials, and gladiatorial matches. The oldest and most important buildings in the city were here, and that meant Rome's most important men were too. As you walk among the ruins, imagine the place as it was: the buildings tall and majestic, the square alive with energy and pomp.

Darkness fell across the page, and Fallon stopped, looked up. She had walked to the end of Main Street, past the last of the streetlights, and here, just beyond the last café, stood (but barely, among its rubble) one wall of a disintegrating brick building on a dilapidated lot. Kismet. The ruins were even more ruined than she'd imagined. She skimmed down the page.

> As you can imagine, the Forum was home to many historic events,

including the assassination of the emperor Galba in 69 A.D. When
one of his earliest supporters, Otho, was hailed emperor by a group
of rebels, Galba, too ill to walk, directed his troop of guards to carry
him on a litter to meet the group. According to Plutarch, when the
rebels (rather predictably, we must say) pulled their swords on Galba,
he offered them his neck and said, "Strike, if it be for the good of
the Romans!"

"Strike, if it be for the good of the Romans," Fallon repeated to herself.
She turned on her heel and headed back toward the strip of nightlife,
choosing the most atmospheric bar. As soon as she opened the door,
the candlelight and wafting accordion music gave her goosebumps. She
shimmied into its grapevine-covered dimness in thrall.

Fallon felt like a tourist. And a little vacation was just what she needed
after such a rough show, especially because until Will's fall, she'd felt the
troupe had been making headway. She slid into a booth near the door,
but when she lifted her hand to signal the staff, she was surprised to
see a familiar head of dark hair at the bar. Fallon opened her notebook,
clicked the end of her pen to expose its tip.

The playwright wrote.

*From the way EDGAR slumps on his barstool, anyone can see he's had a few
too many. Several women are seated there expressly for that reason.*

*A mustachioed SINGER, spying the chance to play matchmaker, steps
forward. He readies his hands on his accordion, fills it and his lungs with air,
and releases the first O of "O Sole Mio."*

*It strikes EDGAR like a blow to the face. He takes hands to the sides of
his head, looks down into his whiskey, moans, "No."*

*The accordionist heads straight for him, and the women perched nearby pick
up their giggling. The SINGER shows no mercy, leaning closer, releasing note
after note, blow after blow. EDGAR waves him away, but the man only smiles
knowingly, winks.*

*EDGAR lets the note build behind him for as long as he can stand it, then
stands.*

EDGAR
Stay away from me with that thing.

*The music falters, then continues in a musical interlude that the man speaks over
in a fake Italian accent.*

SINGER

Rome is a beautiful place for love, no? (*He looks pointedly at the ladies, then back at EDGAR.*)

EDGAR

No. No love.

SINGER

(*Raising his accordion*) I give you experience *Italiano*!

EDGAR

(*Shaking his head*) I've had it already.

SINGER

Enjoy, yes? (*He finishes the interlude, takes a deep breath, and launches into the next verse.*)

EDGAR

I said, I've had it!

He shoves the accordion, lending inertia to its weight. The SINGER hangs in the air off balance for a second before toppling backward to a soundtrack of scrambled notes.

The place goes silent, and now EDGAR has an audience. He turns to the bar, finishes his whiskey in one knock, steps over the singer, and walks out the door.

Edgar awoke sweating. He threw off his navy blanket and sat up on the edge of the bed. He had to have Ava. He stood, steadied himself, and on the way out of his compartment, reached halfheartedly for God's hand, missing the switch.

Edgar entered the light of the corridor and moved past the others' rooms, concentrating on being quiet. When he pulled open Ava's accordion door, a blade of light struck her blanketed shape, and a streak of red fled the room, brushing Edgar's leg.

He stepped into the dark, fumbling to close the door behind him, stripped off his clothes, and rambled into the bed. Though it was warm under the covers, Ava's feet were icy as a corpse. Even her bottom was cold. Edgar wrapped her feet in his, pressed his heat against the length of her. She sighed in her sleep and settled her hips back into him, her wet little sex petting his hardness. Then she sighed again. "Bennn."

❧

February 22
THE MIDWEST CHORUS | THEATER REVIEW
Untitled, or Panther Under New Moon
The Troupe Adores
The Midnight Theater
Rome, North Dakota
Remaining performance: tonight at 8 p.m.

"Dark and deep it was, so clouded that though I probed with my sight to the bottom, there was nothing there." –Dante, *The Inferno*

❧

Fallon wrote in pencil on the newsprint, in the empty space just under the review.

And the light shineth in darkness, and the darkness comprehended it not.

She cracked an egg on a ceramic bowl's thick lip, leaving a wound just wide enough for gravity to labor the slippery yolk through. It was death dressed as birth, or death's birth, birth's death. Whichever, it reminded her of a soul leaving the body.

The egg hissed onto the pan. Fallon's spatula was still in her compartment's small sink, dirty from last night's dinner, and she rinsed it quickly. Holding it at the ready as the egg whites whitened, a drop of water fell from it onto the buttered pan, intensifying the hissing. She watched the drop's diameter shrink to nothing as it evaporated. Another drop fell onto the pan, and she watched again, though this one, when gone, left a froth-spot in the butter. A blip.

It put her in mind of a life, from God's point of view, one flash in the pan, nothing more than a second of disappearing. She flipped the egg. But then some of us leave a mark, like that second drop: a conspicuous absence, tenuous evidence of our once-was. That had to be her. It would be.

❧

Hit. Hit. Hit. Hit. Hit.

Edgar walked the seven paces to the tree, pulled the blades from their wounds. He was getting better, but his heart felt pummeled. He couldn't shake it. When Ava said "Ben," had she meant it? Was something sleep-said likelier to be false or true?

She must have slept with Ben.

Edgar told himself that everyone had history. That this took place before him. That he'd had loves before too, everyone did, but it didn't stick.

As he paced back to his throwing spot, Edgar saw Ava hop off the edge of the open fourth wall of the baggage car. He rushed over, motioning for her to follow him around the end of the car.

"Did you sleep with that Ben Sterling character?" he asked, knuckles white on the knives.

Ava took a step back. "Where is this coming from?"

"I need to know if you slept with Ben."

"I was going to tell you," she started.

"Is that why you don't want the others to know about us?"

Ava nodded. "Yes, but—"

Edgar broke in. "Do you fuck every man who joins the troupe?"

"Of course not."

"Have you fucked Will?"

"I don't think anyone has ever 'fucked' Will." She took a step toward him. "And, Edgar—you know that's not me. Somewhere inside of all this"—she gestured at his agitation—"you know."

"Tell me one thing. Did you love him?"

"Will?"

"No. Ben."

Ava's eyes scanned Edgar's face for a few long seconds. "I've worked with them for so long. I love them both," she said, shrugging, in a tone that made nothing of it.

Edgar had thrown five questions, all he had, and was empty handed. All five had stuck, but none hit their mark. Before he could respond, Ava leaned toward him and breathed a kiss onto his cheek. Then she quickly disappeared around the corner of the car, leaving him, once again, alone.

It was nearly time. Will lay on the tapestried sofa, his foot propped on the pedestal of pillows. His stomach churned. The others had left the observation car to gather their things; it was almost time to head to the theater to watch the final performance. Hands trembling, one eye on the open doorway to the vestibule, he fumbled in his pocket, pushing past the stolen bracelet to draw a slip of paper. He mumbled quickly through the sentence.

"The black trunk fell from the landing—black trunk fell." Vomit rose to the back of Will's throat, but he swallowed it. "You might warn me next time," he muttered.

Stretching his torso longer along the sofa to better parse his pocket's folds, he fumbled another mangled slip of paper from the sweaty clump inside. "A thick coat of black paint covered all—covered all."

There weren't many in the audience that night, but those there knew that the difference between the scene and the seen was belief. It was simply a matter of trust.

Edgar, in the catwalk, couldn't shake a tickle of déjà vu, which went deeper than the repetition of the play. For a long time, he'd been floating along on the sensation, until even the déjà vu became déjà vu. Whenever he was sure it was winding down, another current would catch him, as though it had all been written beforehand. He didn't like the feeling of being carried on the current of a script.

Every thirty seconds, he rang the bell for another of Fallon's black words.

She had to put an end to it. Ava sat on the edge of her bed and unzipped the compartment in her purse's lining. The crumpled sticky note's penciled phone number had faded. It felt like forever since Ben had placed it in her hand, walked out the door.

Then Ava did it. She dialed it. Her pulse raced.

A woman with a nasal New Jersey accent answered. "Rude Mechanicals, box office."

Ava tried to speak, but something stuck in her throat. "Ben Sterling, please," she croaked.

"He's preparing for a performance right now. May I ask who's calling? Are you a member of the press? A fan?"

"I'm his—" Ava faltered.

"You're his?"

"No. Well, sort of? Just tell him it's over. He'll know who it is."

Ava hung up. She exhaled. She was free. She was free to tell Edgar she loved him, to tell everyone, if their love lasted the season. Because it was easy to get swept up on the road, spending every day and night with the same few people, she still wanted to wait before any announcements. In the cars, one tended to cling, forget practicalities. It was how she'd fallen for Ben. Ava fell onto the mattress with relief, causing a scrabbling, a scratching beneath.

That night, in Edgar's bed, Ava played her best self, improvised a heart without hurt. She watched him watching her lift and lower herself and, to come closer, pictured herself as he saw her, as an audience would.

A few thick strands of Ava's dark hair calligraphed Edgar's bare chest, something illegible but for one tendril forming, with his scar, an x. He placed the bones of his palms over the round caps of her shoulders and, with only their skin between them, guided her off him and onto her back. Soon Ava could feel the wave approaching from a long way off, raising the surf. She braced for the crash, and when it happened, released, letting the undercurrents tug her this way and that. When the wave receded, it took with it everything shrouded in depth, anything that could do harm. What was left was a rock pool starred with anemones. They glittered in the shallow water, displayed as though in a case, and Ava buoyed with joy. Despite all that had happened, she had this. She had Edgar.

The joy of the thought made her laugh. It started quietly, not much above a sigh. And from there, Ava's laughter expanded, took hold. Edgar smiled, chimed in. Burying his face in her neck, he laughed as she shuddered under him. She could hardly catch her breath. Then the feeling sank. It pulled her under.

Her next laugh was half-sob, then whole sob, then a whole note holding. Edgar, face still pressed to Ava's neck, kept laughing, which made her cry harder, tears hot and heavy. When the wetness on her cheeks reached his, he jerked back his face to search hers. His smile dropped as he watched her try to force one and, with his thumbs, wiped away her tears. Ava slid out from under him.

In the sleeper car's small bathroom, she sat on the toilet, leaning over her lap, and sobbed silently into her knees, shuddering exhalations until her lungs burned for air. Then she'd gasp and shudder again. But the weight of the sadness was somehow exquisite. To feel it was a relief, something Edgar had given her.

Fox snarled terrible. Behind the tapestried sofa, it crouched over a pair of Ava's panties it had dragged from under Edgar's bed. Fox gnawed, shredded, threaded its canines with lace torn in the vvvvv, its machinery of teeth.

Alone in his bed, Edgar dreamt of Ava. She stood outside in the sleeper car's narrow corridor, playing with the accordion door. She shut it, teased it open a slit, and slid one long, bare leg through the gap. Then she pulled the leg out and shut the door again, opening it a second later to reveal herself in another pose.

The door closed. It opened on Ava, head thrown back and back of hand to forehead. The door closed. It opened on Ava, both hands framing her face at the chin. She smiled, batted her eyes. The door closed. It opened on Ava in a Bond-girl pose, her index fingers forming the barrel of a gun. The door closed. It opened.

Ava gave Edgar a low bow, then spoke with put-on gravity and a thick Russian accent.

AVA

Voila! And now, forrrr my final illusion of the eve-nink, I vill attempt the eem-possible: utter vanishment. One—

She partially closed the door on each count, then opened it fully again.

AVA

Two—

She winked.

AVA

Three!

She yanked the door closed, and the latch slapped the catch but didn't stick. Just as the accordion door bounced back open, Edgar awoke in his bed, in precisely the position he'd been in in his dream. He blinked. The doorway gaped blank. She was gone.

Only the brightest planet persisted dimly above the wash of the rail yard's flood lights, under which, within the sleeper car, Fallon was at work in her tight compartment, at her makeshift desk, inside a circle of lamplight. The world closed to the white page beneath her pen like a silent film's iris out, a pupil reacting to brightness.

Fallon squinted. She was a magpie in her black, her jacket framing her tank top's white breast. At the edge of the mirrored desk, her tuxedoed torsos dovetailed like a playing-card king. She touched her pencil where they met, crossed out a sentence. Usually, if she lacked for a line, she looked deep into the darkness behind her reflection, a seer scrying in a black glass for what would be, and listened. It was writing, but it felt more like writing it down. This play, however, was different. It was partly what had been.

The playwright wrote, "A Hit," and waited for the rest to follow, but all she could hear—somehow, though it was winter—were crickets.

NIGHT TRAVEL

The train followed docile, led by the leash of its track. But beneath, between the rails, its underbelly clanged with dragging chains, shivered with loose screws. It rumbled and grumbled, sparked and thrashed, devouring mile after mile. Where it went it went with will, with hunger. It fed on distance.

❧

The train had hardly left the station before Ava started for the dining car to pick up something special for Edgar, something sweet. She went from car to car, fox-trot box-stepping to pass others in the narrow aisles. After two passenger cars, a sleeper car, and the bar car, she entered, from its cool vestibule, some sort of retail car lined with shops.

Here Ava lingered, dreaming her way from window to window. A women's clothing shop neighbored a barber shop advertising shaves and haircuts. Next came a café with a mural that lent the impression its patrons were dining alfresco. A small bookstore followed, stocked mostly with magazines, then a flower shop. The last stall was a pawnshop. Ava stopped. The urge to give something more to Edgar struck her, a hock on a lark. She'd give up her ring.

Inside, a round, middle-aged man with patchy gray stubble was leaning back in his stool behind the counter, nearly asleep. Seeing Ava, he perked up.

"Good evening, miss. How can I help you?"

Ava unzipped her purse's most private pocket, angling the bag toward herself to block its contents from view. She removed her wedding ring and zipped the pocket closed. "How much could you give me for this?"

She placed the ring on the counter, and the clerk picked it up. He rubbed the face of its sapphire on his cuff, held it to the light, then squinted at it through a jeweler's loupe.

"I could do fifty."

"Is that all? It's precious. Genuine sapphire, genuine gold."

The clerk shook his head, lowered the loupe from his eye. "The stone's manmade. It has bubbles, from where the material was heated. See?" He held out the loupe.

Ava took it but didn't look. "And the gold?"

"It's twelve karats, but even so, I can't sell this ring for more than about eighty-five dollars. If I'm to make something off it, fifty is all I can do." He slid the ring toward her across the glass countertop, but Ava pushed it back toward him.

"I'll take it," Ava said. "Leave it, I mean. I'll take the fifty."

"It's pretty. You sure you don't want to keep wearing it?"

"Very."

A lightness flounced Ava's steps from the shop. There was no going back. Ben's leaving had ripped the picture of her future from its frame, but Edgar had filled it again, painted in a portrait of life after love, love after life, love upon love for a lifetime. How lifelike it was.

The playwright paged through her notebook.

FRANK MITZI, 5'2" thick-fingered regional pawnshop king, means business. His fists glint with rings. His chest, back, and forearms are furred, each finger bearing the same sparse dark hairs combed over his head.

He has a front, you see, and it's more than a store. What you need to know before you step in is: what's his is his, and what's yours is his too, when you're running short. MITZI knows what goes around comes around.

From the desk in the glass-walled office at the back of his pawnshop, MITZI sees two COPS enter the store. Two HENCHMEN in tracksuits sit in the chairs facing him. They turn around to see what he's looking at, start snorting like pigs.

HENCHMAN 1

I smell bacon.

MITZI ignores them. He leans back in his chair, kicks his feet up on the desktop, and watches the COPS cross several gaps in his office's vertical blinds as they make their way to the shop's front counter. When they address the CLERK, he tosses his head toward the back of the store, toward MITZI. The COPS make a beeline.

HENCHMAN 2

What is it, boss? Whatcha done now?

The HENCHMEN grin at each other, and MITZI growls.

MITZI

Keep quiet. Let me handle this. (*He drops his feet to the floor, sits up straight, smooths the sparse hairs over the top of his head with a hirsute hand. The COPS enter the office, bumping the vertical blinds, which collide in clicks and clacks. MITZI stands.*) Good afternoon, officers. To what do I owe this pleasure?

GOOD COP

We were in the neighborhood, thought we'd stop by.

MITZI

(*To his HENCHMEN*) Why don't you boys go have a smoke, eh?

The men don't budge. MITZI furrows his brow, and a line grows there, across his forehead, as though it's one more hair.

MITZI

Go on. Scram.

The HENCHMEN rise reluctantly from between the chairs' metal armrests, looking the COPS up and down, brushing shoulders with them on their way out of the small office. The COPS hold their ground, maintain eye contact. MITZI holds out a hand full of rings, offering the seats, but the COPS don't take them.

MITZI

How? (*His voice gives out, and he coughs, clears his throat.*) How can I help you?

GOOD COP

The Johnson County sheriff's office called this morning to report a rash of burglaries. We want to know if you've had any suspicious activity here.

MITZI

Suspicious?

GOOD COP

More pawns than usual, people coming in with a lot of items, repeat pawners, that sort of thing.

MITZI

(*Taking a white handkerchief from the pocket of his tracksuit, daubing his face, and returning the cloth to his pocket*) Nothing recently, officers. You know how I am. I always let you boys know right away when I see something fishy. (*He smiles, but it's more like rictus.*)

BAD COP

Sure you haven't seen anything? I imagine you can see a lot, from in here. (*He sweeps an arm toward the view of the front counter.*) It won't be good for you if we find out later that you have.

MITZI

I'm sure. I'm sure. But like I said, I'll let you know right away if I do, officer.

BAD COP

(*Putting a fist on the desktop, leaning over it toward MITZI, and speaking through gritted teeth*) I hope you do. The chief isn't ever going to be as flexible again as he was last fall. You lucked out then, but now it's a lot less trouble for us to have you locked up. Right, Marcus?

GOOD COP

(*Patting BAD COP on the shoulder*) Now, now, Mr. Mitzi has told us he will, and we have no reason to doubt him.

BAD COP

(*Growling*) Come on, Schmidt, let's grab a donut. I'm buying.

Gear tinkling from their belts like windchimes, the COPS hoist the waistbands of their pants, adjust the angles of their nightsticks, and tuck their thumbs into the bands of their hip holsters.

MITZI

Thanks for stopping by, officers. Like I said, I'll talk to my staff and have everyone keep their eyes open. (*As he watches the COPS walk out of the shop, the vertical blinds slice his view of the sales floor the way the bars of a jail cell would.*)

"Finishing the next play?" Art set the martini on the mahogany bar before Fallon, and the thin layer of ice on its surface nearly sloshed over the rim, kissing the lip but remaining contained, somehow, through surface tension.

Fallon closed her notebook. "Re-reading something I wrote earlier tonight, but it's all wrong." She rapped her pencil's eraser on the page a few times. "I gave up on this one, but now I'm toying with it again because I'm not sure what else to do. I think I have a great idea for a play, my hit play, but I fear I'm developing a whisper of a conscience. Would I be a terrible person if I played out someone else's moment onstage?"

"Onstage, they're all your moments, and as I always say, 'It has been my experience that folks who have no vices have very few virtues.' What kind of a moment, exactly?"

"I'm not usually queasy about plundering, but this was a private moment, involving people close to me. One that's founded a sort of fledgling happiness." She grimaced. "It would feel like telling a secret, but only those involved would know where it came from. To everyone else, it'd be fiction."

Art furrowed his brow.

Fallon continued, "With a climax so strangely beautiful, so beautifully strange, this play could be great. It could save us."

Behind her, Will and Chantal had taken the last open booth in the far corner of the bar car. Chantal was already flirting with three men, who were motioning to Art for a round of shots. Art let his weary eyes rest on Fallon's a second before flip-setting four shot glasses onto a round black tray.

Fallon searched his face with concern. "Have you been working?"

Art sighed, poured Jägermeister down the line of glasses. "I'm going on seventy now—far longer than Lincoln lasted—and it's getting harder and harder to play him. I'm dying my hair and beard and taking anything that comes along: furniture-store grand openings, President's Day car dealership sales, high school lectures, whatever. But it isn't enough." He gestured with the bottle. "At least *this* is a role that literally always needs filling, but I'm getting too old for it too. My body isn't holding up well anymore over the course of a shift."

"We could use you," Fallon said. "We really could, and for much more than Lincoln. I'm sure other troupes could too. Why don't you shave the beard, drop the persona? You'd make a great farmer or artist, a statesman, a king or a doctor, maybe even a professor."

Art rested the bottle on the bar, and Fallon reached out, placed her hand over his where it gripped the glass. She smiled. "What do you want to be when you grow up?"

Art shrugged. "It doesn't matter what I want to be. This is what I am. I can't change." He screwed the aluminum cap back on the Jäger.

"But, Art—sure you can. You can be anything you set your mind to. You could be so much more."

He lifted the tray of shots to his shoulder. "Maybe, but it wouldn't be me."

Art headed out from behind the bar toward the booth of men, and Fallon slid off her stool and beelined to Chantal and Will. "Can one of you run to get Ava and Edgar?" she asked them. "We're coming up on the end of the tour, and I'd like to discuss the last two new plays."

Chantal gasped sarcastically, hand to clavicle. "Our god deigns to speak with us lowly mortals about—about creation?"

Edgar lay on Ava's bed, watching her dress. She was always dressing and undressing: for the day, for performance, for unwinding, and for bed. Now she undressed and dressed for the bar car, dressed and undressed and dressed, unsure of what to wear. When she settled on a long red dress and moved to the mirror, Edgar undressed her again in his mind, dressed her in the negligee she'd maybe put on later, watched her take it off.

Ava saw him eye her and redressed him teasingly as she leaned closer to the mirror, compact in hand, and began making herself up to look natural. She worked a mascara wand across her eyelashes, added nude-colored shadow, brushed subtle blush on her cheeks, and finished with a lipstick the exact shade of her lips. Her head was covered in rollers. She unpinned one from the crown, and the dark lock fell to her shoulder, bearing a slightly different curl than usual.

"I have a surprise for you, swan."

Edgar lifted an eyebrow.

"Not that—that'll come later." She pulled a white bakery box from beneath her bed and slid it toward him across the sheets.

He opened it. "Lady fingers?"

"Right," said Ava. "Thought we could use something sweet tonight."

"I could stand for something even sweeter." Edgar looked her up and down. "Are there strawberries or whipped cream, anything we could"—here he lifted both eyebrows—"dress them in?"

"Just the bare fingers, I'm afraid." She waggled her left hand at him, thrilling at the flaunt, though he couldn't know anything was different. She took a cookie from the box, offered him one. He bit.

"All the better undressed, my dear."

Ava leaned over the bed to kiss Edgar, and he rolled on his back, dropped a hand to her hem, and ran it up her leg. When he reached the lace edge of her panties, she stopped him, mumbled into his lips, "We should go. The others will miss us."

"What about what *I'm* missing?" Edgar asked, laughing.

Ava roused him reluctantly from the sheets and led him by the hand into the narrow corridor of the sleeper car and through the baggage car. As they neared the heavy door marked Private, the train bounced, making Ava stumble. She steadied herself on the door handle, then planted her ballerina slipper firmly for leverage. The door creaked open, achingly slow, and the vestibule roared.

At the threshold, the cars' metal edges lifted and fell in alternating bounces, sliding back and forth against each other like tectonic plates, like vertebra. Ava stepped past the open door marked Private and onto the passenger car. Deciding to risk it, she rose on her toes to give Edgar one last kiss before they joined the others. Their lips touched only a second, then her car moved independently, wrenching them apart.

As though drawing back a curtain, Chantal opened the door to the vestibule between the public and private cars and—*voila!*—revealed the end of what must have been a kiss between Ava and Edgar.

Her jaw dropped. Her eyes went wide. Then she smiled, bared her teeth.

Hoping Ava would do the same, Edgar had hung back as the rest of the cast left the bar car for the private cars, but she hadn't met his eye. He was forced to follow.

Fallon and Chantal vanished into their respective sleeper-car compartments, Chantal in the company of a young man wearing flip-flops, surf shorts and, for some reason (indoors and at night), a visor. Ava, then Will in his crutched canter, made for the observation car. Will collapsed on the couch and set his ankle on its pedestal of pillows as gently and resolvedly as a crown on the head of a head of state. Then, pulling his phone from his pocket and putting in his earbuds, he settled in.

Prepared to outlast him and spend the last of his day alone with Ava, Edgar retrieved a pencil nub and small notebook, curved from its place in his back pocket, and sketched. She took her usual seat looking out of the back of the train, only the cumulonimbus of her hair visible.

The physics textbook read $E = mc^2$.

What did it mean, besides genius? Poof! Matter transforms into energy. Ava took heart. Any thing had, latent within, the seed of another, the ability to play another role, given the right conditions. A rock could transform into heat, a star into light. A smoker could quit. A liar could tell the truth. Ben's wife could become Edgar's.

In the beginning, God made *atom*: from the Greek, meaning indivisible, a marriage of particles, a coupling, a pairing off. And like a marriage, an atom's bond could be broken, each particle remade with another. To come together or break up took energy, though, left each a little less. A woman marries, loses her name. A man divorces, loses his house. There's no love or love lost without repercussion.

Ava lifted her eyes to the dark windows reflecting the car's interior. Both Edgar and Will were still behind her, turned away, and she was bookended by the backs of their heads. Her reflection swayed gently with the train's motion between those two planets, one dark, the other lighter.

Then Will shifted the pillows behind his head, and a small rectangle of light from his phone appeared by his wavy brown hair in the black glass. In it floated Ben. His face hovered, mouthing blank verse atop a puffy white cloud of Elizabethan blouse. Ava's breath caught. She felt like an astronaut looking back at Earth, that old home, from the moon. From where she stood now, Ben looked so small, so insignificant.

Ava knew telling Edgar would breed relief or regret, maybe both. It was hard to hold it all in. She wanted to tell, wanted to be understood and loved for what made her her, even the mistakes. Besides, it was only a matter of time before he found out. That had been a close call,

Chantal almost catching their kiss in the vestibule. She wouldn't have been able to stop herself from telling Edgar.

Ben's eyes, in the reflection, glowed green, like a cat's hit by headlights, and Ava, swiveling her chair to see the source, caught a tuft of red disappearing into the dark of the vestibule.

Hours later, Fallon emerged from her compartment in her silk pajama pants and tank top, carrying an empty teacup on its saucer. She padded down the corridor of the sleeper car, traversed the noise of the vestibule to the observation car, and switched on the hot plate to bring the kettle to a boil.

"I'm glad you're still up," Fallon said to Will, the only one left in the car.

"Ava and Edgar were out here for a good while after the bar car, but as soon as she got tired, he did."

Fallon rolled her eyes. "*Heated* is more like it."

"What?"

"Never mind. Honestly, it was a stretch." Fallon plucked two epees from an umbrella stand in the corner and tossed one to Will. He reached out a hand too late, and the thing bounced a few times from tip to hilt on the threadbare rug.

Fallon motioned with hers for him to pick it up. "One bout," she said. "Just until my water boils." She squatted into position, extended her arm, and pointed the tip of the blade at Will in challenge. Removing his earbuds, Will halfheartedly stretched to reach his epee's hilt. He glanced back at his foot on its pedestal of pillows, as though worried it would topple.

"*En garde!*" Fallon said, flourishing her weapon. "*Prêts? Allez!*" Then she came at him. "How's the ankle?"

Will caught her thrust. "I'm still not well enough to go onstage, if that's what you're asking."

"I'll write you the part of an invalid." Her riposte rattled. "A wounded soldier. You'll never need to leave bed."

He evaded her point. "I'm just not ready yet."

"I know you've always had stage fright, Will," Fallon leveled between quickening breaths. "But what's going on? Has it gotten the best of you?"

"It's not that. It's just—"

She made a cut. "It's just that you're terrified of life? Of living? Of being Will Connaught?"

Will sat up, recovered, and disrobed her of her foil. It skittered across the floor. "And you're living as your true self? Dressed in a goddamn costume every day?" He carefully lowered his foot to the floor and used his crutch to stand. "I'll be in my compartment."

Fallon lowered her blade. "If you don't want to act anymore, Will, just tell me. Admit it. I'll be sorry to see you go, but I'll find someone else."

"The truth is, I'm in trouble." Will swiveled around on his planted crutch, hobbled back to the sofa, and dropped onto it. "I met this girl."

Fallon knocked Will's pillows onto the floor and sat beside him. She sucked air through her teeth. "I see."

"Oh no. No. Nothing like that. She's a—she seems to, well, *borrow* things from people."

"She's a thief?"

Will didn't acknowledge the question. "She asked me to carry something for her. She was supposed to meet me so I could give it back, but I must have missed her, and now this guy and his men are after me, or her, or this *something*."

"His men?" Fallon deflated.

Will nodded. "These guys, they seem like they're—not very understanding."

"So give them this something. What do you care?"

Will let his eyes move from Fallon to the dark window. "That's the trouble. The trouble is I do."

"That does complicate things." Fallon rubbed her collarbone. "What do you mean when you say these guys are 'after you'?"

"They threatened to meet me backstage at the closing performance in Lyon." Will covered his face with his hands. "They didn't say exactly what they'd do, but I know it won't be good."

The kettle whistled. Fallon placed a hand on his shoulder. "Don't worry, Will. Let me handle this. I'll think of something."

She rose from the sofa, filled her teacup with steaming water, and made her way back to her sleeper-car compartment, where she slumped into her director's chair and stared down at her face in the mirrored desk. Gravity tugged the skin forward, aging her what she hoped was at least twenty years. Her pompadour was overlong. The crest of it was fallen.

Fallen slid her notebook closer across the desk's cool glass. It was long past time to write her hit about Ava and Edgar, but she was having trouble getting started. The feeling of failure made her think of Art. She rotated the pencil between her fingers. Then Fallon scried, conj(ect)ured.

ARTHUR CONAN-DOYLE doffed his stovepipe hat, removed his white button-up and black pants, and slipped one arm, then another into a flowery red Hawaiian shirt, leaving it unbuttoned. He stepped into a pair of jeans, then made his way to the bathroom, where he took a small pair of scissors to his curtain beard, filling the sink with hair. Letting the water run, he lathered his face with shaving cream, lifted a razor to it, and removed the last vestiges of Lincoln. At last, he was himself.

The words were coming easily now. Fallon could hear them like a stream, babbling. All she had to do was dip in a cup. But not just any words would do. She stalled, pen to page. It was time to stop experimenting, stop lashing out. Her blackout play had overthrown the schedule, and she was running out of tour. To balance the books, she would put on two new plays for the last two stops. Two more shots. The words this time, the characters and plot, they had to be right. The next play had to kill.

Lightning lit up her compartment's dark windows—uncloaking, for a second, the nocturnal landscape passing at a clip. Fallon leaned over her desk like a pianist at keyboard, a puppeteer over marionettes, a chemist over potions, blind to everything but the play, the page.

Another bolt of lightning lit the sky, but she missed it; she was script-omniscient. From outside the play's time, she saw it stretching aft and fore like unwound film—beginning, middle, and end simultaneous—and she had to get it down. She scratched the itch in ink. Even when her right hand cramped, she kept scrawling. Somewhere behind her, in Edgar's room, God reached out His hand.

Lyon, Wisconsin

February 23

When, for the first time, Fallon entered the theater in Lyon, even she felt out of place amid its aging fin de siècle swank. The building was so carefully preserved in its decline, it was like touring a ruin.

In the golden morning light coming through a clerestory window, the dressing room walls were doffing (or donning, depending on perspective) their dark-green wallpaper. Drooping strips hung (or clung) like algae on the walls of an ancient fountain, and a seashell motif on the crown molding—*Molding indeed!* thought Fallon—strengthened this effect, as did the upholstered furniture's urchin-like black tassels, which gripped the moss-colored carpet. A current from the heating vent rippled and bobbed the wallpaper's tatters, but the blowing air hardly qualified as warm. The weather had been hinting at winter the past few days, but the season had finally arrived behind last night's storm. The cold seeped through the walls.

Fallon's goosebumps prickled against the silk lining of her tux despite the stack of scripts, still warm from the photocopier, clutched to her chest. Taking a deep breath, she waded across the thick carpet to the vanity lining the room's long wall and, in the circle of light at each player's spot, dropped a copy of the new script.

Then she, as though she could hardly believe what she'd done, stood rubbing her hands for warmth, the gesture of a villain.

The bed was narrow enough without two bodies. Land-locked on the side against the window, the curtains of which were outlined in light, Chantal turned roughly in the sheets to wake the man whose wide swath of back (and backne) was bared to her. She'd woken from a dream to this: no dream at all.

The man was a blur but for an impression of his general type. She'd been distracted last night, hadn't been able to enjoy her performance or his, remembered faking a come to urge on his own, so she could put an end to what turned out to be a disappointing evening. It was time for him to go.

Chantal coughed loudly, turned, and turned again in her straitjacket of sheets, careful to bump the man each time. Her thoughts shot again to Edgar, Ava, the kiss she thought she caught the end of. That Edgar could withstand her advances made sense, if he was fucking Ava. Chantal doubted any man could remain celibate in the bosom of such opportunity.

The man in her bed stirred, and Chantal yawned loudly, stretched. Rolling over, he smiled. His eyebrows were unruly and his jaw too strong for the rest of his face, but there was something about it she liked, even in the light of day. She should have enjoyed herself more last night, would have, if she'd been able to focus.

The man tossed off the sheet, sat up at the edge of the bed, and stuck a foot in the leg of his boxers, dragging them closer. When he stood to pull them on, Chantal turned her face to the window, thought of Edgar. Why not her? Why *her*? Edgar didn't know Ava was married, but in teaching Chantal the mirror trick for her foot, he had helped her—something no one had ever done. He was a good person, and she'd be doing a good thing by telling him. Now she could help him, tell the truth, maybe reap the reward. But first, she had to be sure.

Ava genuflected onstage toward the empty house, unburdening herself of coffee tray and donut box and unbundling herself of gloves, hat, and coat. In unison, and without lifting their eyes from the scripts they were studying, Will and Chantal rose from a pair of squat, tusk-legged ottomans, he on his crutch. They crossed the boards and, muttering good mornings, took up their allotments of caffeine and sugar and returned to their seats.

Ava gestured at the scripts they ate over. "Glad it's finally ready. I haven't seen one scene."

"We hadn't either, until we got here," Will said without looking up. His mouth screwed sideways as he chewed his inner lip.

"Where's my copy?" Ava asked.

"At your vanity."

Ava walked backstage, calling over her shoulder, "Is Edgar here yet?"

Chantal didn't miss a beat. "Why ever do you ask? Do you *need* something from him?"

Ava's heart stopped, which reflected in her step. "I—"

But before she could say more, Chantal sang-sighed, "Whatever."

"He's looking through the storerooms with Fallon," Will said through a bite of donut, catching a rogue flake of glaze beneath his chin with his script. "Scavenging for the sets."

Ava made her way to the last vanity in the dressing room, the only one with a script still in its spotlight. The cover was blank but for the title, *The Stab*. With the pages tucked beneath her arm, she headed to her seat on the stage, stopping to grab a coffee and a napkinful of donut holes, one of which she made a peruse bouche of as she flipped the script open to the start of the first act.

Chantal cleared her throat. "Ever faked it?" she asked.

Ava looked up, but Chantal's eyes were still tied tightly to her lap. Ava swallowed some of her bite. "What?"

"You know—faked it?" Chantal's eyes met Ava's. They were strangling. Ava wrenched her attention back to the script.

"What am I saying," Chantal crooned. "Of course you have. Who hasn't?"

"I fake it every day," said Will with a shrug. "Hell, I'm faking it now."

Chantal scanned his body from face to foot, ending at the crutch lying on the floor beside him. "We're well aware. Why are you even here? You're not in this play either, are you?"

Will's voice, when it was heard, was as weak as he claimed his ankle was. "I thought I'd still come to rehearsals." He shrugged. "Since I'm still part of the troupe."

"If you say so." Chantal snorted. "Nowadays anything's possible. You can be whatever you want to be, even an actor who doesn't act."

It was then that Fallon and Edgar burst from the wings, dragging two more ornate chairs behind them.

"There's so much to work with here!" Fallon called as she approached the circle of stools. "It's quite an accumulation of junk, but—just our luck—much of it perfect. Ready to start?"

Fallon and Edgar took their seats, and Fallon made a show of resting her hands flat on the cover of the script in her lap. "Before we begin, I have something to ask you, Edgar, and we're all fearfully dependent on your answer. It could mean our rise or ruin."

Ava sensed more than saw Edgar's slight stiffening.

Fallon continued. "We really need you to play a part. I won't take no for an answer." Edgar winced. He shot a wild eye to Ava and opened his mouth to protest, but Fallon cut him off. "I know you didn't enjoy playing the swan. I know you've sworn off anything but staying back-stage, but the fact is, without Will, we need another actor. I need you. Will needs you. Chantal needs you."

"How right you are," Chantal said, flirting a smirk.

Ava saw Edgar's distress riling beneath the surface. She wanted to calm him, speak on his behalf, but couldn't. Fallon was right; they need-ed this. She was as eager as the others to hear his answer.

"Ava needs you too," Fallon added, pausing for emphasis. "If all goes well, this will be the play to put the tour in the black. I've hit upon my hit. I know it."

"Who would I be playing?" Edgar asked feebly.

"A magician. It's a key role, but there are hardly any lines. I'd play him myself, in addition to my two other parts, but the plot requires each of my characters to be in several scenes with him. Besides, you're perfectly suited to the part: the brooding, the intensity, the strength, and the silence. Will you help us?"

Edgar looked at Ava. She lifted her eyebrows to try to communicate her encouragement, the troupe's need, but she wasn't sure it landed. Edgar started to speak, balked, closed his mouth, then spoke. "I can't. I'm not an actor."

"Pish posh," Fallon said, pushing up the sleeves of her tux jacket. "You act. I guarantee you do. No one's above it. We're all acting, all the time. In the drawing room, on the esplanades, in the operating theater or theater of war, et-cet-rah, et-cet-rah." The ars rolled off her tongue.

"Not exactly places I frequent," Edgar said.

Fallon dropped her shoulders, sighed. "We act every day, in every way. What are our lives but a series of scenes we play in character, a routine of repeat performances that, when altered, people are quick to call out. 'This isn't like you,' they say. 'You don't seem yourself.' As if somehow you couldn't be you. As if what 'you' are isn't whatever you make it. I mean, come on. Look at your boots, your black, your muscles, your stubble."

Edgar rasped his hand on his chin, and Ava hurt for him. He shook his head. "I can't lie."

"Did you lie when you played the swan?" Fallon continued. "Or did the role reveal something you wish it hadn't, something you can barely hold inside you? That's the lie, my little soothsayer, that clutching at secrets, that locking away of feelings we need to express. And what safer way to express them?"

Edgar stood from his chair, and with one quick motion, lifted it over his head, as though preparing to dash it to the stage. The conversation flinched.

Ava broke the silence, knew only she could save the scene. "Please, Edgar?" she said, rising. "Won't you help us?" Standing, she laid a hand on the chair and guided it back to the boards.

Edgar looked about the circle of faces. "Fine," he growled. "I don't belong onstage, but I'll do it once more." He looked at Ava. "For you." Then remembered himself, swept his glance across the troupe. "All of you. Then I'm done. I told you: I'm not an actor, and I have no desire to become one."

Losing no time, Fallon began to read.

THE STAB

Act One, Scene One

A dark stage. A spotlight comes on with a bang, its light circumscribing a seven-foot-diameter target with rings diminishing to a bullseye. Before it stands a MAGICIAN'S ASSISTANT in a showgirl costume, stockings, and heels.

A MAGICIAN in a tux, cape, and top hat stands far stage left, blindfolded. He holds a knife out to the audience, then turns his back to them and throws. The ASSISTANT twitches, tightening her lips, and the knife hits the target just shy of her wrist. The MAGICIAN throws again, making the ASSISTANT flinch. The knife hits beside her thigh, and she shifts stiffly, as if bound.

Three more throws follow in succession. Hit. Hit. Hit. In the silence after, the ASSISTANT faints, sliding to the boards. The target stands bare, five knives embedded, its chop of pocks outlining a woman's figure.

The spot switches off.

As they did each time they began a new play, the troupe read through the rest of the scenes. The others sipped and nibbled and fidgeted their way to the end, but it was hard for Ava to stay focused, to keep her mind from wandering to Edgar. Each time she looked up to check on him, she caught Chantal glancing away.

Act Three, Scene Three

A backstage dressing room, its exterior hallway visible. Inside is a tattered sofa with mismatched throw pillows, a hat rack draped in dressing gowns, a vanity spilling over with products, and a table covered in props.

The MAGICIAN approaches the dressing-room door from the hall. He carries a tray bearing sandwich, teapot, cup, and saucer. He pauses, shifts the tray onto one hand, and uses the other to fish the key from his pocket.

Inside, his imprisoned ASSISTANT is napping on the couch. Awakened by the magician's approach, she stands and backs to the rear of the room, wrapping her dressing gown tightly around herself and tying it securely closed.

The MAGICIAN unlocks the door and enters. He places the tray on the sofa and approaches the ASSISTANT, but she continues backing away until she's pressed against a prop-filled table. He places his hands on the points of her jutting elbows and turns her body square with his, trying to get her to look at him. She turns her face from him.

The MAGICIAN turns his ASSISTANT's face back toward him, then pulls her close, pinning her arms between them. He kisses her.

Ava shot a look at Edgar, but he didn't meet it. There'd be a kiss—in public and in front of the troupe—but under the cover of their roles, she told herself, it wouldn't matter who saw.

The ASSISTANT resists, pushing weakly against the MAGICIAN's chest. She breaks one arm free and flails it blindly behind her through the tabletop's props, groping for anything she can use to escape. She grasps something, holds it behind her. The audience can see it's one of the throwing knives.

Ava crossed her legs.

With the MAGICIAN's lips still pressed to hers, the ASSISTANT thrusts the knife into his chest. He pushes her away, throws his head back, and puts his hand to the wound. When he removes it, it's covered in blood. He looks at the ASSISTANT and drops to his knees. She presses herself back against the table for just a second, looks at the knife still in her hand, throws it down, and runs from the dressing room.

The MAGICIAN falls to the floor.

Chantal gasped. "What a great death, Edgar!"

This time, Edgar looked up at Ava. She felt the blood drain from her face.

"What's wrong with you?" Chantal asked her. "Jealous?"

Ava slapped her script onto the planks of the stage and ran for the dark of the wings.

&

The cold cut through Fallon's tuxedo. It lingered in the silk lining even after she'd climbed into the baggage car, which was dark, lit by a single stripe of light from the narrow gap at the top of the door she'd slid closed behind her. There was a scuffle from the direction of the large worktable.

Fallon squinted. "Hello?" There was no answer. For a second, it was like writing.

Ava's voice flew forth like an arrow, struck. "You stole our moment?"

Fallon could make out Ava's limned thinness. Working quickly, she crafted, then revised a sentence, but as she inhaled to speak it, Ava launched in.

"You see something you're not supposed to, then share it with everyone else on Earth? What the fuck is wrong with you?"

Fallon held out a hand to Ava, as though approaching something wild. "Now, I didn't mean to see that moment between you and Edgar." She took another slow step forward. "I went to get something from the dressing room. The door was wide open. It happened in front of me. I didn't do anything wrong, Ava." Fallon cited Ava's name to remind her she was tame.

Ava's face stayed in shadow. "Seeing it is one thing; writing it into a play is another. And asking me to act it before an audience—to *reenact* it, with Edgar, no less—"

"It's too good of a scene not to use." Fallon shrugged. "I couldn't let it go to waste."

"A great scene? It's my life. That moment can't go to waste. It's already happened. It's already changed me. It changed things between Edgar and me, and despite that moment, despite my doubts—"

"Don't forget your secrets."

"Jesus, Fallon. Okay, sure, those too. Despite it all, he loves me. That day and many days since, I've pushed him away, but unlike Ben, he hasn't gone. Now you want me to reenact the whole thing onstage with him for anyone who buys a ticket?" Her eyes were glassy with tears that wouldn't crest the rims. "It's my moment. Not yours."

Fallon stepped forward, and the strip of light slipped down her forehead, fell across her eyes. She wore it like a blindfold, unable to see Ava through the glare. "No," she said. "I've transformed it into something else entirely, something new. It's my moment now."

Ava went to speak, but Fallon cut her off. "Look, my little Athena, no one knows the scene is based on yours except you, me, and Edgar, and God knows I won't tell. I'd rather the others believed it sprouted from my head fully formed. I suppose I could rewrite that climax today, the day before the opening, like you're asking, but Chantal and Will will be bound to protest and ask why." Fallon paused pointedly. "What would I tell them?"

Ava shuffled in the dark.

Fallon continued. "It's a powerful scene, if I do say so myself, and only you and Edgar can do it justice. The tension between the two of you is palpable. Even the people in the last row of seats will be singed by the heat of that kiss."

One of Ava's wrists emerged into the slice of light, then the other. She lifted a length of lace from the worktable, winding and unwinding it about a finger. "I hate the way you sprang that part on him at the read-through. He was so thrown."

"And you helped me convince him. You played your role, like you always do, because you know exactly how badly we need this. If we don't strike on something soon, I can't hold the troupe together. This play will sell, Ava. I know it; you know it. It has everything: trouble in love, scandal, magic, and something honest. How can it fail?" Fallon brushed some dust from her sleeve. "Can you do this for me? For all of us?"

Ava's throat floated into the light, then her mouth bobbed up from the darkness, painted red. "There's something about Edgar onstage, isn't there? That swan. I loved watching him. I suppose it won't be so bad, kissing him." The lipstick smeared into a smile. "Kissing him freely, in front of everyone, anyone."

The rest of her face emerged into the light like a moon from cloud cover.

❧

The fox's eyes burned on Ava, trying to read her intent. She squatted, stretched to proffer the piece of cheese. The fox was riveted, one foot lifted frozen. It sniffed the air, leaned forward from its crouch.

Staying low, Ava shuffled back a half-step down the sleeper car's corridor, then another. The fox followed hesitantly, slinking along the wall. The gears of its shoulder blades cycled. Nervousness bellowed its ribs.

When Ava backed over the threshold of the vestibule, she hooked right, glancing over her shoulder to watch for the edge of the metal stairs. The fox hesitated to leave the corridor's carpeting, and Ava tossed the piece of cheese toward it, holding out another as it ate. She took one step down, then a second, tempting the animal. They were at eye level, its gaze shifting between Ava's face and the food, when Ava dropped off the third step into the rail yard's gravel. At the crash, the fox scurried back.

By leaning into the car again and extending the cheese, Ava reset the lure. She fished the fox downstairs into the sunlight. Foot by foot, she drew it alongside the train's steel wheels then, inch by inch, into the woods at the edge of the rails. When it was a good way in, Ava tossed the piece of cheese into the dead leaves with a handful more and jogged back to the train. Then, stepping over a sticker that read Watch Your Step, she climbed back into the vestibule. She locked the door to the staircase behind her, setting the fox free.

The leather roll of knives was still under Edgar's bed, lying in wait. He knew he had to use them. Having inspired Fallon to create the play, they would best fit the part.

Edgar was getting used to the way Fallon broke each member of the troupe into blazon, rifled through, and reassembled them in the facade of her fiction. Details were magnified, refracted, or erased, the way he'd lend the second dimension a third. He understood her scavenging, but that didn't mean he liked it, not when the details were his. He knew, though, that this was how art was made, that hanging a painting wasn't the same as telling. He wished it was. At this play's heart, at least, was a moment of truth.

Leather roll in hand, Edgar headed to the baggage car, where he unfurled it on the weathered worktable. Five tips glinted. They'd do nicely, but for the climax, he needed a trick knife. He unsheathed the fourth blade, examined it. Working at the table, he used it to shear a strip from a block of pine, then another, removing everything not-knife. When the shape was replicated, he separated the handle from the blade and hollowed it. The handle he painted black; the blade, silver—so it was indistinguishable from the one that carved it. Near its tip, he shaded the blade with dark fingermarks, attached a spring at one end, and anchored the other inside the trick knife's hollow handle along with a weight.

When the work was finished, Edgar could hardly tell the knife and its replica apart. With satisfaction, he ran his finger along the dull blade of his copy, then stabbed it into the worktable, so it seemed to penetrate the wood.

❧

"It's me, but it's not me, when I'm acting," said Ava. "It's me, but it's someone else too."

Edgar hooked a boot under the stool she sat on and dragged it across a few of the stage's aged planks until it bumped his. He kissed the shallow furrow between her brows, then mirrored her and furrowed his own.

"Look, it's not you. It's me." He tried to hold a straight face as he said it, but broke into a smile. Then he turned serious. "I'm leaving the troupe at the end of the season. Come with me."

"Where?"

"Does it matter?"

Ava's eyes shifted focus. She fussed with the edge of her script. "What would I do there?"

"Be with me."

"Oh, Edgar, I—" She fell silent.

He ran his knuckle across her clavicle and down her arm. "Aren't you tired of this life? Of the traveling? The train? The people? We should slow down for a while. Besides, there may not even be a troupe next season, the way Fallon's talking."

"I've been with the troupe so long. I suppose I'm not able to see myself doing anything else."

"Is that any reason to keep doing it? This isn't for me. It isn't for us."

From the mezzanine came a heavy thump, which made Ava jump, knocking from her the confession that had been perched at the tip of her tongue.

"I love you," she whispered, then paused, shocked. As though watching her words take flight, she looked up at the empty mezzanine toward the source of the noise.

Edgar took her by the shoulders, tipped her back across his lap, but she delayed him by holding up a finger.

"Hello?" she projected into the rafters. A second passed. There was no answer.

Edgar leaned down and kissed her. "*I* love *you*," he said.

Ava hushed him, smiling. "Someone could be up there."

Edgar righted her, stood. "I hope they are." Opening his arms with a flourish, he turned to face the sea of seating. "Ghosts of the theater! I want you to know—" His volume increased. "That I, Edgar Cosentino, love this woman, Ava Vale. I love the sfumato of her hair and the impasto of rib on her skin, the chiaroscuro at her clavicle and the glint of her tooth. If she will but love me a fraction as much, I'll die a happy man."

A solemn bow ended his solemn vow.

He turned back to Ava. "See?" he said. "There's no one"—creak—"there."

Ava gave another wary look up at the mezzanine as Edgar sat and dipped her over his lap again.

"Good thing we're alone," he murmured into her neck. "We can do *this*." He kissed her. "And *this*." He kissed her again, then pulled back to study her face. "Or can we do this in public now too?"

She shook her head nearly imperceptibly.

"What if we were rehearsing the third act?" he said, energy flagging. "We'd have to be kissing."

She gave another slight shake of her head. "We don't rehearse kisses, remember?"

"Maybe we could, just this once," Edgar said. "I have the feeling I'm going to have a very hard time learning that part." He kissed her, and the kiss was real.

"Speaking of acts, we should get back to it," Ava said.

He let her up, switched her for script in his lap.

"Where were we?"

Edgar reached for her. "We were right here."

Ava pulled away. "No, no, no. We need to rehearse. What do you want to go over first?"

"What I'm not sure about, honestly, is the whole thing."

"The whole play?"

"I don't know how you do it, lying every day."

Ava stammered. "It—it's not supposed to be a lie. Not exactly. You're playing another person, but it's *your* truth. You bring to it the truth of your experience. In that way, every performance is honest, you know? Like, you may not have been a magician holding your assistant captive, but to create truth in the moment, you bring to it the closest thing you can, from the most honest part of yourself. You have experienced love, wanting to keep that person, right?"

One of Edgar's eyebrows raised. He reached for her again, but she playfully swatted him away.

"Take the first act, for example," Ava continued, "when I have to cry. The character is crying because she's being held against her will. I don't know what it's like to cry for that reason, but to bring truth to the part, I remember something that made me feel trapped, hopeless. I bring my own emotion to the role, but in the context of the play, the audience sees it as the assistant's. I play to the higher truth, the truth of the play. That way it isn't a lie."

"You're lying with me, aren't you?"

Ava blanched, stammered a denial as she tried to read his face.

"Well, you should be. We could be *lying* together right now."

He kissed her again, then lifted the hem of her shirt. Ava lifted her arms, let him, tried to ignore the second creak, then click, that wafted down from the mezzanine as Edgar pulled her from her stool.

The door to the mezzanine closed behind Chantal, and she hustled through the dark lobby and out the theater's front double doors into the street like someone who'd just seen a show.

Like someone who'd just seen a show, she sighed on the sidewalk, wished it had happened to her. On the stage of her mind, she replayed what she'd seen, remembered she was part of the cast, could change the course of the story.

February 24

The morning was gray; the sky, heavy. Fallon crossed the tracks into town, the side that was supposed to be right but felt wrong. The strip of Main Street businesses stood before her, but she could hardly see beyond *The Stab*. After working so hard on it, she was spent, but she still needed one more play to close the season. Feeling like she'd never be inspired again, Fallon pulled a water-damaged guidebook from her back pocket. The pages, now dry, were wavy and swollen, bulging its hard cover.

Due to its strategic positioning at the convergence of two rivers along the main highway from northern to southeastern France, Roman statesman Marcus Vispanius Agrippa made Lyon the starting point of the most important Roman roads throughout Gaul. It was later made capitol.

Fallon yawned. Breakfast was in order; perhaps she'd overhear the tickle of her next play. As she crossed the empty street to the diner, a frigid wind whipped through her tux, and she wrapped the jacket tighter across her chest so the front of it crossed just beneath the midnight-blue scarf she'd thrown over.

A dusty black pickup was parked in front of the diner, and from the corner of her eye, Fallon spied a streak of red. Moving closer, she saw that the truck bed was filled with dead coyotes stacked three deep, topped with the mangled body of a small red fox.

The bell on the diner's door rang, and four men in camouflage emerged, heading Fallon's way. "Looks like snow," one said to another as they passed.

She looked back over her shoulder at them before reopening the diner door, once more setting off its bell. As she settled into a booth along the front windows, she warmed one of her cold hands by sitting on it, reopened her book.

During the Second World War, occupying German forces used Lyon as a stronghold, and the locals used secret passages to escape Gestapo raids.

Loaded with the men, the truck was pulling away. Fallon thought about camouflage, hiding in plain sight. Maybe theater was similar: the actors onstage, but no one seeing them as themselves.

The bell on the diner door rang again, resonated. She reached inside her jacket, pulled out her black notebook, and wrote.

Edgar rasped his stubble. Staging the knife-throwing would be tricky. He wasn't sure how magicians pulled off the illusion, if it was one. The troupe's would have to be.

Edgar set the script on the baggage car's worktable. He turned on the saw and took a long piece of lumber from the pile beside him. When he pressed the wood into the blade, it screamed.

Good, Edgar!" Fallon called. She stood from a second-row seat in the empty audience. "Grab her, yes, and pull her toward you. Rougher—you're a villain. Good! Then you kiss her, and she—no, no, no, no, don't *really* kiss her. We're rehearsing!"

Fallon put the heel of her hand to her forehead. "Okay, Ava, I need to see you struggling. Go bigger. Now grapple on the table behind you. Your hand closes on the knife, and you thrust it into his chest to make your escape. Excellent!"

Fallon hopped over the first row of seats and approached the stage. "Now let's talk about the opening scene. Edgar has something to show us."

She gave Edgar a nod, and the rest of the troupe gravitated near her as he exited stage right, disappearing into the dark. A beat later came the approaching squeak of metal castors, the thunk, thunk, thunk of something heavy rolling across aged planks. A large wooden target entered the scene, pursued by Edgar, who wore a black cape. The target came to a stop center stage, and Edgar stepped before it.

"I'll require the help of a beautiful assistant," he said, holding out a hand to Ava. Fallon saw Chantal roll her eyes. Ava acquiesced, and Edgar drew her into the danger posed by the target's black-and-white rings, carefully positioning her in front of its red bullseye.

"Make sure you feel for these nails beside your ribs, so you know you're in the right position," he told her. "Otherwise, you could get hurt." He lifted her thin arm. "Rest your arms along this series of nails, and open your legs until they're flush with these." Edgar shifted her booted foot out with his until she became Vitruvian. "Feel them?"

She nodded.

"Do you trust me?"

Her eyes met his.

"Don't move, no matter what happens."

Edgar grabbed a wooden crate that had ridden in on the base of the target and walked to the edge of the stage. From the crate, he removed his leather knife-roll. The crate, set upside-down beside him, made a makeshift table. He untied the roll on it, revealing the line of knives, and removed them from their pockets, stabbing four into the top of the crate so they stood at attention. The last he held in his hand, then he swung around, cape to the audience, and lifted the knife to his ear by its blade.

"Uh." Ava balked from her spread-eagle. "I've seen exactly how good you are with those knives, and I—"

Edgar threw, and the troupe winced in unison as the blade slapped into the target close to Ava's wrist.

She wriggled. "Edgar?"

"Stay absolutely still!" Edgar pulled the next knife from the line, wielded it back, and threw again. This blade hit closer, just inside Ava's thigh.

Will spoke up. "Edgar, this is a bad idea." He hesitated to step into the line of fire.

Fallon put a hand to Will's chest. "Let him finish."

"Agreed," Chantal said. "I've been waiting so long to play lead."

Edgar threw the three remaining knives, dispatching blades near Ava's hip, ribs, and throat. As soon as the fifth knife hit, Ava scrambled away from the target.

Fallon smiled a wicked smile. "How ever did you—"

Edgar walked across the stage to the target and wheeled it around. Standing on its platform was a man in overalls, one of the theater's stagehands.

"The daggers are loaded behind the target, see?" Edgar explained. "They're cocked back in this rubber strip, like a stone in a slingshot or an arrow in a crossbow. I fake a throw and, with my back to the audience, drop my knife into this pocket inside my cape. Then Darrell here"—the stagehand gave the salute of an ammunitions man—"watching through a peephole in the target, releases the knife, and it shoots out. I never throw the knife, but the audience, seeing the cause and effect, imagines the throw for themselves."

Fallon laughed. "You've outdone yourself, my clever Odysseus." She gave Edgar a kiss on the cheek.

Waving her away, he wheeled the target back to its mark and stepped in front of it, covering the bullseye's red heart with his own. "To be honest, it's a little selfish. It feels so good to actually hit the target with these things." He held up a knife. "Even if it is a trick."

The others had gone. At the edge of the stage, Edgar's leather knife-roll remained open on the wooden crate, one knife missing. He was putting the finishing touches on his target. He had to make it look used.

The dusty CD player sat on the boards near Edgar's boot, and he turned the volume dial until the opera was loud enough to throb his chest in prestissimo. It felt good, something like love. He raised the knife and stabbed the target as hard as he could, which felt even better. With effort, he pulled the blade from the wood, leaving a blank in the paint. Then he stabbed again.

At first, his tempo was set to the music's, then his metronome surpassed it. The hits grew more urgent, irregular. Edgar was sweating; his force made the blade hard to extract. For the next few hours he worked, outlining a woman's silhouette in chipped paint, stabbing everywhere but her.

๛

A fly tickled Ava's hand, the one that held her pencil. With a twitch, she sent it back into the air of the observation car and turned the page of her physics textbook.

The Double-Slit Experiment
Shoot a volley of electrons at a metal plate with a single slit, and they land in a band pattern on the wall behind, indicating travel as particles, in straight-shots. Fire at a plate with two slits, and you might expect them to land on the wall in two bands, but instead, the electrons create a striped interference pattern, as though traveling in waves. Concentrated stripes mark where the peaks of the paths crash into each other and amplify, and gaps between them show where the troughs collide and cancel each other out.

One might make the wise hypothesis that the electrons were interfering with each other through the air, as they passed through the slit, yes? Reduce, then, the volley to a single bullet. As you could expect, one electron shot at a plate with one slit marks the wall behind as though it traveled in a line, indicating yet again that it travels in a straight shot, as a particle. However, when a series of electrons is shot one at a time at the plate with the double slit, something strange happens: they accumulate on the wall in another striped interference pattern, indicating that the particles are traveling in waves.

How could a single electron interfere with itself? And why does the pattern imply it is carrying out all possible paths—traveling through not only the first and then the second slit, but also both slits and neither, all at the same time?

The experiment gets even stranger when an instrument of observation is introduced in an attempt to determine the electron's path of travel. When such a device is placed near one of the two slits and a single electron is fired, the particle reverts to its straight-shot band pattern. It goes back to acting like a particle.

This is the case no matter how minute or how quick the method of observation. It occurs even when the measurement is faster than the amount of time that knowledge would take to reach the parti-cle—in other words, even when it isn't possible for the particle to somehow perceive it is being observed. Being watched changes its behavior.

The phenomenon has been observed with increasingly larger particles: electrons and photons, initially, but then atoms and, more recently, even groups of up to 810 atoms. (See also the quantum Zeno effect, in which continuous observation protects a quantum state from decay.)

Ava lifted her thumbnail to her mouth and gnawed on its rough edge. The very act of observation, then, disturbed. An audience changed everything.

All possible paths were open when no one watched. They could even be taken simultaneously. But the force of a witness whittled one's options to a single position, changed a thing into something different: a thing seen.

Fallon had seen Ava and Edgar's kiss. This had changed it. And re-enacted before an audience, it would change again.

The fly's buzzing stopped, and a twitch of Ava's pencil set it back in motion. Then Edgar entered, taking his usual spot on the wingback nearest her. Ava lowered her thumb from her mouth, rubbed the nail's still-rough edge discreetly with a finger.

Chantal had to go out, to get some attention. It wasn't that Edgar hadn't wanted anyone; he just hadn't wanted *her*. But someone out there would; they'd choose her over all others. Wrapped tightly in the arms of the sleeper car's small bathroom, she leaned toward the mirror over the sink and outlined an eye in liquid liner. Where her pelvis met porcelain, a chill spread.

"Ugh!" Chantal recoiled. Her polyester blouse was drinking the sink's wet edge. She grabbed a frayed, bleach-stained towel from a hook,

wiped down the sink, and leaned again, wide-eyed, to resume her trac-
ing. At the outside edge of her second cat's eye, the brush tip flicked
the line too long.

"Shit!" She reached inside the makeup bag set at the edge of the
pedestal sink and dug for remover. Her effort grew more desperate, and
she pawed more and more flailingly. At the bottom of a downswing, her
elbow cracked against the metal edge of the open shower door behind
her.

"Goddammit!" Chantal pulled the elbow to her like an injured wing,
knocking the makeup bag off the sink in the process. It splayed vials, compacts, lipsticks, and brushes across the linoleum floor. "Fuck,
fuck, fuck, fuck, fuck." When she went to pick up the makeup, her butt
bumped the wall behind her, bouncing her forward, into the sink.

"Ow!" She rubbed her head. "Fuuuuuuck! I can't even goddamn
move in this fucking shithole!"

Chantal yanked the bathroom's accordion door open, and its bottom
track jammed, leaving barely enough room for her to squeeze through.
She sucked in her stomach, squashed her breasts as flat as they'd go,
and shimmied through, red-faced. Then she was gone, the car rocking
in her wake.

❧

The coffee was scalding. Even so, Will swallowed it. He distracted himself from the sear burning down his esophagus by taking a large amount
of inner cheek between his back teeth. This made him, for a second,
forget he should be limping, but before he could hope no one had seen,
a black-jacketed arm shot out from Fallon's compartment, grabbed his.
He turned to face her, and she held up a scroll of rolled paper.

"I wrote you a part," she said.

Will blanched, reddened, turned purple. "You can't expect me to go
on tonight!" he said. "I haven't rehearsed! And my ankle's still—"

Fallon shook her head. "I wrote you an ending."

"An ending?"

"A way out of your trouble."

Will shifted his weight to lean against the corridor wall.

Fallon continued. "The men who are after you, they said they'd show
up at tomorrow night's performance, right?"

Will nodded.

"So tomorrow night, when we go on, you'll hang back here. The men, I'm sure, will force their way backstage afterwards, but you won't be there. We'll tell them you've left the troupe, invite them to search the place."

Will pursed his lips, puckered them off far to one side as he gnawed on the inside of his cheek. "But they'll just come back to the train, look here."

"And that's what we want!" Fallon lifted a long finger.

"We do?"

It was Fallon's turn to nod. "Because you won't be here either. You'll be vanished"—she brought her hands together, then fountained her fingers up and apart—"into thin air."

Will came off the wall squarely onto his feet. "You want me to hide somewhere in town? They'll find me within an hour. There's nowhere to go."

"And nowhere's exactly where you'll be!" The fire in Fallon's voice blazed, and everything Will said seemed to stoke it. "We'll have Edgar paint you. He'll camouflage you into the back wall of the baggage car, in head-to-toe trompe l'oeil."

"Seriously? That might work in a play, but this is my life, and I really think it's at stake."

"You know what I think?"

"God help me."

"I think it'll work."

"But what if—what if they start moving things around, feeling the wall?"

"Why would they, when they plainly see nothing there? There's nowhere to hide. Why would they doubt their own eyes?" Fallon smiled. "This will work. I know it."

Later that evening, when it was time for Will to head to the theater to watch the others put on their performance, he had trouble crossing even the threshold of his compartment.

He stood by the accordion door, a hand poised on its handle. Feeling for bumps on the inside of his lip with his tongue, he suctioned in his cheek and bit off anything uneven. His pursed lips worked far left, then far right. The trouble was, the more he tried to chew smooth, the more his cheek needed chewing. From every little ridge sprang two. Mitzi was coming for him in less than forty-eight hours.

The brass pull of the drawer holding the bracelet was like a bracelet itself, only halved, its less-precious metal advertising the contents of the drawer behind it. Will knew it was a terrible hiding place, especially for jewelry, but it was too stressful to continue keeping it in his pocket. He drew a slip of paper from his upturned hat.

"Jerk th—juh—jerk the-the-the dart—the dart—from the cork target." He shook his head, tried again, popping his consonants. "Jerk the duh-dart."

He reached into the hat again. "Sever the twuh-twuh-twine with a quick snip—quick snip—quick snip—of the knife."

Edgar's final scene in the first performance had, at last, arrived: the scene where he'd kiss Ava. On his tray, the teacup trembled in its saucer. He took a breath, then plunged from the wings. This put him onstage beside the set's closed dressing-room door, so he had to enter the scene again, walk into a room like the one backstage he'd just left. The house was decent, not packed, but still, the bath of attention was scalding.

The cup trembled harder as he shifted the tray to his left hand, swept his cape back, and rummaged in his pocket with his right. A key was retrieved to unlock the door marked with a star, the one between him and Ava. When Edgar entered, she gasped, wrapped her silk robe tighter about her, and knotted its belt. He lifted a foot to step toward her, stopped.

His cape had caught on a nail protruding from the stand-alone doorframe. Carefully holding the tray away from his body, he yanked the fabric. There was a ripping, and the doorframe jerked toward him, threatening to tip. The audience gasped, but the door rocked back, recovering in ever-tightening arcs until it shivered to a stop. Edgar set the tray on the sofa. He approached Ava as she backed to the table of props along the far wall.

Just as his fingertips brushed her silk robe, a faint siren wafted into earshot, the way a thought bubbles into consciousness. Its long note rose, drew a vibrato coxcomb or comb's teeth at its peak, then slid down again. Another wave of it crested, coming closer, and the house's attention bit down on the harbinger.

MAGICIAN

Still not hungry?

Edgar said it in his most villainous voice as he reached for Ava.

MAGICIAN
I know *I* am.

He padded the points of her elbows with his palms and searched her face for some slight sign of love, but she had turned away defiantly, crossed her arms.

There was a squeak from the back of the audience. Edgar looked across the house in time to see a wedge of light span the aisle from the opening lobby door. With it, the siren leapt louder, then muffled as the door swung closed.

Trying to ignore the distraction, Edgar grabbed Ava roughly by the nape and hip and shook loose her haughty posture. But before he could kiss her, the siren passed the building, sliding down a half-step and flattening the energy of the scene.

One of the lobby doors reopened, and a man pushed his head and shoulders into the theater, shifting the stage to the back of the house.

"Something's going on at Hendrick's!" he called. The door swung shut.

A murmur began. It changed the scene the way a key change changes a mood.

The man reappeared, yelled, "The diner! It's on fire!"

Several people stood, side-stepping down their rows. Others stood to let them pass, only to succumb themselves. The murmuring rose to full volume, and the opening and closing lobby door became a lighthouse, pulsing a beam of warning for Ava and Edgar, who could do nothing but watch. For them, lashed to the cast, the siren song was dampened. They stayed onstage, didn't run aground. The show, though, had sunk.

In the wings, Fallon threw up her hands, drawing parentheses in the air around her.

➊

February 25
THE MIDWEST CHORUS | THEATER REVIEW
The Stab
The Troupe Adores
The Mirage Theater
Lyon, Wisconsin

Remaining performances: tonight at 8 p.m., tomorrow at 3 p.m.

In *Winter Notes on Summer Impressions*, Fyodor Dostoevsky wrote, "Try to pose for yourself this task: not to think of a polar bear, and you will see that the cursed thing will come to mind every minute."

In 1987, psychologist Daniel Wegner tested the idea. Recorder in hand, experimental subjects entered a room and reported everything that came to mind. Some were told beforehand to think about a white bear; others, anything but. The groups later swapped roles.

Those told to suppress the idea, as Dostoevsky well knew, thought about the bear more frequently than those told to think of it. But several other interesting findings were made. When those suppressing the thought were then allowed to express it, the idea came forth with even more urgency. The study also determined that many suppressors, grasping for other objects or ideas to displace the bear in their minds, inadvertently bonded the unwanted thought to each, increasing its frequency.

Psychologists suspect the white-bear problem is also at play when one is told a secret. In a later experiment, Wegner had two male-female teams of strangers play cards, asking one of them to play footsie under the table without telling the other. At the end of the experiment, the flirts had developed such a strong attraction that, for ethical reasons, they were asked to leave separately.

Now, I task you: try not to think about a pin.

It was early, and the baggage car was silent. Chantal spread Edgar's cape in the spot of light that fell on the worktable from the bare bulb overhead and examined its fabric until she found the tear caused by the nail, by Edgar's frustration and fear, by his love for Ava.

He had been careless, but it could be fixed. She removed the pin from between her lips.

Edgar considered the baggage car, saw it differently now that it was to be scenery. He paced the cleared, narrow space before the battered, paint-spattered worktable. Behind him, along the car's length, hung the painted backdrop of a hotel room, the one they'd used in *The Slip*. Crossing it bed to desk, Edgar rasped his stubble.

Placement was crucial to the illusion. The viewer would have to be corralled into position, forced to see Will (*not* see him, rather) from a certain angle. Viewed from the wrong place, his profile might be discerned against the wall or shadows might be misaligned, shattering the illusion. Most of all, the spot would need to look exposed, above suspicion, so no one would be tempted to look closer.

Edgar's eye was drawn to a place near the back wall's far left corner, where a space for Will could be cleared. Because it was close to the end of the car, its sightline from the door marked Private was limited, and the long view from the door to the sleeper car was blocked by the worktable and stacked-up set pieces, forcing a fairly straight-on viewing. A few framed paintings could be leaned against the wall there, and Will's legs could be camouflaged into them. To discourage close inspection, an almost-empty costume rack could be rolled in front of Will as well.

It would be a long day, if Edgar was to finish by the evening's performance, but it was doable. He waded into the piled props, lifting and shifting pieces as he made his way to the spot against the wall, when some dust tickled his nose. He froze, sneezed.

Chantal piped up from where she sat behind the worktable, his magician's cape draped over her arm. "Bless you." She fingered a rosary that was mixed among the tabletop's flotsam.

Wiping his nose with the back of his hand, Edgar mumbled thanks and resumed his lifting and shifting.

"What are you looking for?" Chantal asked. "I thought you were done with this week's set."

"I'm working on something extra," he said over his shoulder.

"What is it?"

"I'd rather not get into it."

"Well, aren't we mysterious?"

Edgar tried to regain his focus, but he heard Chantal inhale as though to say something, then let the air out and inhale again.

This time she said it. "Do you think Ben'll be back next season?"

Edgar had reached the back corner of the car and was piling the props and scenery there into a tower behind him. "I don't know. Surely, Fallon's hoping for it. She's feeling the loss of him."

He almost asked if she knew anything about Ava and Ben, if they'd ever been together, but remembering his promise to Ava, he stopped himself. The question was bound to make Chantal suspicious.

"She's not the only one feeling Ben's absence," Chantal said. She grabbed a wire hanger from the costume rack behind her and forced its shoulders under the cloth of the cape. "Do you think they'll patch things up?"

Edgar stepped back to appraise the corner he'd cleared and lifted a hand to the back of his head, still distracted by his work. "Ben and Fallon?"

"Ben and Ava."

Chantal had his attention.

"Oh," she said, picking lint from the cape. "I thought you knew."

Edgar turned toward her. "Thought I knew what?"

She hung the hanger on the rack. "Ava's married to Ben, Edgar. Didn't she tell you?"

Chantal's pulse pounded. She'd watched Edgar, somehow small then, amid the sea of detritus, turn toward her like one woken from a dream. He stared over her head toward the door to the sleeper car and seemingly down its dark corridor, rubbed his mouth with a loose fist, then moved quickly toward the vestibule. A few heavy steps rocked the car. Another came as a spray of gravel.

Following the crash, Chantal moved quickly back through the sleeper car, past the others' closed compartment doors and into the observation car. She stopped behind its last seat and stood in the dim dawn light, looking down the length of the track. Edgar, head lowered, was walking with purpose down its center. For a long while, Chantal watched him shrink in the pane and rise on its surface until he became the dark point where the rails met.

Sunrise bruised the sky's gray-flannel cloud cover. Edgar didn't look back. He knew he'd no longer see the train.

The weight of Chantal's news pressed on his chest like a breath he couldn't exhale, at least not where people might see. On either side of the track was a forested margin. Veering off the rails, he pulled aside a branch of the trees' curtain and stepped backstage into the woods.

An animal sound, an almost-sob, clawed out of him, and Edgar dropped into the bracken. He forced the air from his body with a yell, fogging the morning air, until there was no sound left, until his lungs burned. When air rushed back in, he did it again. From far off, the wail of a train's horn rose and held until its own breath gave out. Panting, he listened.

Edgar spent hours in the cold, feverishly going over everything Ava had ever said, all the lies and all the times she could have confessed. No matter her excuse for hiding her marriage, he'd never again be able to believe her. Their love had felt so real; what else wasn't? Edgar's mind stretched to everything that would have to be reexamined, guarded against. The only thing he could trust was the hurt. The hurt felt real, and in it, the world did too. He was womb of it—the cold in his lungs, stones on his knees, the scratching of branches—and only he could unmake it. He wished he didn't exist.

When the shadows were almost at their shortest, he let the forest slide from his shoulders like a cloak, stepped back on track and walked along it, his foot kissing the rail. Its touch sped ahead through the steel like the sound of an oncoming train on its way to a crouching train robber's ear to where Ava was walking into town, the heel of her worn black ballet flat missing the rail by a hair's breadth.

The playwright paged through her notebook.

A lie is born of lack. Someone wanting, wanting someone else to see them so. A lie has ego, id. It's scared and selfish, shared between two people. It's flourished truth stretched thin, wholes created to mask holes.

A liar wants to play a different role, paints a dearth with words and stars themselves (at least as long as it's believed). It's how someone halving can appear to have. It's something given that can take.

In Rome, EDGAR is betrayed. It isn't the thought of what she's done; it's the lies, a silt of them accumulating in strata for more than 300 days, in retrospect, so that, unbeknownst to him, the layers between have been piling thicker day by day, hour by hour, pushing them farther apart.

There were the lies that counted, the big ones. Then, more insidious, there were the countless little lies it took to keep the big ones afloat, so that when he looked back, he found he didn't know anything about her, where she'd gone or what she'd eaten, who she saw or what she'd done on even the most mundane of days. He'd lived with her for years and didn't know her. The thought of sleeping beside her, a stranger capable of he-didn't-know-what, frightened him.

The truth came out—haltingly, gingerly, unwillingly—like pulling a stuck stopper. Then there was a whirlpool rush of it as she told him, his punched gut her comfort. He'd been winded, then terrified of what she was or wasn't. She'd made his past year a fiction. At night, he lay in bed and tried to reconstruct the truth, examined the scaffolding and pulleys and trap doors behind every moment they'd had. What hurt most was that he'd been true.

Having read the last line of the act she was practicing, Ava dropped character. The boards of the stage rang hollow. She step-scuffed and scuff-echoed across them before the empty seating, the flame of a cardboard coffee cup warming her hands. She had come on the pretext of rehearsing, but the only lines sticking in her mind were those of Edgar's offer.

Could she leave the troupe? It would certainly behoove her to. It was too late to tell him about Ben—he'd never forgive her—but if she left with Edgar at the end of the season, they'd leave everyone who knew she was married. Free of it all, she could make a fresh start, quietly get a divorce. But it was the very freedom of leaving that made her balk.

Her position in the troupe was her proper place in the solar system, set the course of her days. She orbited the planet of each play, its pull of readings, rehearsals, openings, closings, and travel from town to town. There was a larger orbit to the schedule of seasons too, each ending in time for the next. In truth, the troupe kept her swept up. But Edgar had swept her away.

At the thought of him, the thought of his choosing her, the fire behind her locked walls flared into an inferno, and Ava's deadbolt broke. Nothing would matter if she didn't love him. She'd go, wherever he went. The flames within her billowed *find him, tell him,* but she tamped them down. She'd save that for tonight, after their performance, after their first kiss in the open.

Ava crossed the stage to the sofa in the wings where she'd left her things and wrapped herself in coat and scarf. With script, coffee, purse, hat, and gloves in hand, she opened the backstage door, then stopped short. It was snowing. Flakes paled the parking lot in swaths and highlighted the bare black boughs.

The last time she had seen snow was the morning she left Ben or Ben left her. There had been a dusting overnight, just enough on the lawns to dull the color of each blade, a thin skin barring blood from air.

That whitewash had been like the blank last page of a script, resonating with ending. There had been nothing to do but close it. Now she was picking up where her love had last left off, as if that drab, too-warm winter between snows, between loves and lives, had been a scene that could be cut. All was set right again, the story once more moving forward. As she watched the flakes fall, an ache accumulated in her throat, such tenderness for the playwright. Stepping out onto the tabula rasa, Ava made the first mark on its canvas, printed a new script on it as she walked back to the private cars.

Edgar faced the blank canvas of Will's ass as Will stood, nose to the back wall of the baggage car, wearing a nude-colored bodysuit. Edgar's paintbrush worked over the fabric stretched taut across one pudgy buttock, recreating the flowers in a still life leaned against the wall of Will. Will squirmed, ticklish.

Edgar set his jaw. "Hold still," he said. "Keep your body flush against the nails I placed, otherwise you won't line up right when the time comes."

As Will realigned his arms and legs, Edgar lifted the brush from the suit. When Will was still again, Edgar threw himself back into the blooms as though he could paint Ava out.

To make it look real took real art. Art was the difference between a still life and a vase of flowers arranged on a table, between the story of what Ava had done and the brunt of it. Her lies were art too: a portrait of something she wanted.

"This is never going to work, is it?" Will said, speaking into the wall.

"People believe what they see," Edgar said through his teeth. He touched brush to buttock, ran the long line of the picture frame down the back of Will's leg.

To restore the troupe's confidence after the previous performance's interruption, Fallon had scheduled a midmorning dress rehearsal. The cast had bundled up, trudged to the theater through snowfall, and made it through the thing completely—sans kiss, of course. But through scene after scene, Edgar could hardly look at Ava.

In the dressing room, he peeled off his dark, false mustache, twirled the cape from his shoulders, and crossed briskly past her to the open door. Down the hall, Fallon—to almost any eye a man, in costume— was gesticulating madly. Will and Chantal played audience, Chantal also in costume: the baggy slacks and cardigan of a reporter. When she began gesticulating as well, Edgar knew he had time.

He turned back to the room. Ava sat in the light of its largest station. She'd set the weight of her sequined headdress on a stand, and in a wig cap, her head was tilted back, the better to see her lashes. She carefully removed a falsie and, with it, lashed a blank eye on a white plastic tray. Then she caught Edgar's.

He couldn't see her face for the one beneath. The pain of it was terrible. He had to buy time to process what he'd learned, decide what to do.

"I can't tell whether something's wrong or you're leaning into your character," Ava said, still looking in the mirror. "I'm hoping it's just the latter."

A drooping strip of wallpaper crinkled as its glue sighed another inch down the dressing room wall.

Edgar cleared his throat. "Fallon asked me to help her and Will with something tonight," he said. "I've been busy with it, and it'll take most of tomorrow too."

"So I won't get to see you?" Ava said in a low voice, glancing at the open doorway.

Edgar shook his head.

"What kind of help?"

"I'm not supposed to say. I promised I wouldn't."

"Someone's getting good at keeping secrets," Ava said.

Edgar thought she winked. He rasped his stubble, then saw she'd closed the eye to peel the other falsie from it. "Not that good, apparently. I said something."

"Well, don't worry. I won't," she said, still looking into the mirror. Unscrewing the top from a bottle of makeup remover, she stopped the opening with a cotton ball and turned the bottle over, then used the cotton to wipe the red from her lips. "Just don't tell Chantal. It'll be halfway around the globe by morning."

Edgar nodded, walked to the open doorway, then turned back for one last wincing look at her before leaving. She was wetting another cotton ball, one eye black with shadow.

The snow continued all day—heavy, wet flakes that blanched the landscape and made it impossible to see farther than a few feet. Through its swirling blankness, Fallon crossed a field alone on the way back to the private cars, but she wasn't lonely. She loved to squeak-step through a fresh drift, where no one had yet gone. The marks she left showed her companionless, sure, but showed her to another. They were evidence for some later passerby who might walk beside the tracks for a while, wonder who she was, where she'd come from, and where she'd gone. Following long enough, they might even find her.

When she reached the train, Fallon climbed the vestibule's steep stairs. She removed her midnight-blue scarf and stomped the snow off the green wellies she wore in this sort of weather. Will was waiting for her on the observation car's tapestried sofa.

"The theater manager just called," he said, looking up from his phone and chewing the inside of his lip. "He's not going to open the theater tonight, because of the blizzard."

"I thought this was the Midwest," Fallon snapped. "They don't cancel shit for snow."

Will massaged his ankle. "He said it's supposed to go on all day. They're expecting at least three feet, and visibility is near zero. He didn't think anyone would brave it."

"Of course they'd brave it. What else do they have going on?"

"He said he couldn't open the theater tonight anyway. He's snowed in on his farm. And he has to tend to his sheep, keep breaking the ice in their troughs."

"Sounds like a lot of bullshit to me." Fallon unwrapped the scarf from her neck. "Either he doesn't think people will come, or he's snowed in on the farm, or he has to tend to his sheep. Which is it?"

"I'm guessing all three?" Will wrung his script. "I'm just passing along the message. But maybe this is a good thing?"

"How is this a good thing? You know what's at stake. And we finally have the play to make us."

"I mean, good for *me*. It means Mitzi and his men probably won't show tonight."

"Well, thank goodness for that," Fallon said, touching a hand to her chest facetiously. "I'm so glad you'll live to see another day. I'm sure the poverty and anonymity will be well worth living for."

Will rose from the sofa, began hobbling in the direction of his compartment.

"Snow dresses the world differently, you know, hides its flaws,"

Fallon called after him. "It drapes the world in sheep's clothing, covering its chaos and cruelty, playing pure. Under that downy perfection is nothing but mud, thorns, sticks, stones, trash, dead leaves, dog shit, and piss. Snow," she said disdainfully. "Everywhere you step, you muss that facade, reveal its falseness. How can anyone sit in a theater and believe?" Fallon reconsidered. "Then again, why do anything else?"

෨

February 26

Edgar awoke off key. The orchestra of a headache was tuning in dissonance, preparing to perform. For a second, he felt buoyed despite it, thinking he had Ava. Then, remembering, he lifted a hand to his temple and closed his eyes. The morning light streaking his compartment backlit the scrim of his lids, and Edgar saw red.

Although he was using his own knives in the play, he hadn't dared leave them behind in the theater. He swung his still-booted feet off the bed and reached underneath for the leather roll. Yanking the thong loose, he slapped the roll open on his navy blanket, revealing the five knives: a fist with which to hold or hit.

Edgar unsheathed the leftmost knife, the most sinister, and felt its tip. Against the soft wool, it looked sharper. He lifted the back of his tee shirt and tucked the knife's hilt under his belt at the small of his back, so the blade lay cold and flat against his skin. Then he pulled his shirt over it.

Outside, the snow had accumulated into thigh-high drifts, and the air was whitewashed with flakes. For the first time that year, it was winter, and Edgar was glad he'd rummaged up his one thick wool sweater, even though its cowl neck itched like mad. Scratching underneath the rim of it with icy fingers, Edgar dredged through the snow at the edge of the rail yard and then along what he guessed was Main Street's sidewalk. His eyes, though tethered to the snow, saw none of it, and his thighs burned with cold. When he arrived at the theater, he wrenched the stage door open, and its slam against the brick wall of the alley ricocheted backstage. His bootsteps echoed the sound across the stage to the prop table, where he lifted the carved-pine trick knife and examined it beside the original he retrieved from the back of his belt.

Side by side, they were nearly identical. Taking one in each hand, he stabbed them into the tabletop. The tip on the right stuck into the wood; the other's blade retracted. He tucked that one into his belt, pulled the other from the table, and set it on its mark. If he wanted something real, something to cut through the lies, tonight he'd have to create it.

Will couldn't sit. He paced the observation car between the others in their usual seats as the final touches of paint on his bodysuit dried. The energy was catching.

"Stop that!" Fallon snapped. "And stop chewing your inner lip—out of the corner of my eye, it looks like you're saying something." She scratched out something in her notebook with the frenzy of someone trying to start a fire.

"Where's Edgar?" asked Ava from behind her script.

"You're always so keen to know, aren't you?" Chantal asked.

"That little rabbit had better be at the theater," said Fallon.

Will's lips screwed left as he stretched to chew a bump on the inside of his right cheek. He tried to think of Claudette, for courage. "Can we go over this one more time?"

The others rolled their eyes as one. Fallon conducted as they recited rote together.

"We'll leave the private cars unlocked. If anyone asks for Will, we tell them he stayed behind in the train cars. If they ask to search backstage, we let them. The hope is they'll come here, search the cars and, unable to see Will in his camouflage, move on."

Will nodded. The bracelet was on his wrist beneath his bodysuit, and he ran a thumb over the cloth that veiled its faces. With his tongue, he felt a bump on the inside of his bottom lip and bit it off, creating two more in its place. There was a faint taste of blood. The situation was eating away at him.

Three long steps carried him to the ottoman, where he'd set down his top hat. He drew out a slip of paper.

"The knife—knife—knife was hung inside its bright sheath—bright sheath."

The Stab was underway. Adrift in the dark, the audience haunted the performance. They longed for life, remembered what it was to love and fuck, breathe and eat.

Watching, they leaned in at the light's lip, toed the edges of the text, but they couldn't affect the events, couldn't prevent a disaster or rush the love they rooted for; for the players, even when hearing their rustles and coughs from the darkness, pretended they weren't there.

Edgar stood at the control panel, waiting to go on. He wiped sweat from his brow. He twisted his thin mustache. Pang, pang, pang, went his heart. Bang, bang, bang.

Fallon and Chantal finished their scene. As they exited, Edgar lowered the lights. He and Fallon jogged onstage in the dark, swapped the desk, filing cabinet, and rolling bulletin board for a dressing room door and sofa. Together, they carried the prop-littered table to its mark.

Back in the wings, breathing hard from the exertion of the stage business, Edgar watched Ava, on the other side of the stage, enter and take her place. For a second, he missed her, then reminded himself that the Ava he'd known had never been. He flipped the switch. The lights came on. The heft of the tea tray made him feel hollow, throwaway. He stepped into the light.

∂

Behind the freestanding door, Ava waited in the staged dressing room for Edgar to enter. Last night, for the first time in a long while, they hadn't met, so when she heard the knob rattle, saw him coming closer in his cape, she wrapped her robe about her and backed into the prop table with a trill of excitement in her chest not far from the fear she was supposed to be portraying.

Edgar placed the tea tray on the sofa, spat out his line. "Still not hungry?"

There was genuine nastiness to his voice. Ava was impressed.

As Edgar came closer, she stretched taller, still gripping the robe closed at the collar, and turned her face haughtily toward the audience so they had a clear view of her expression. Edgar put his hands on her elbows, turned her roughly, and gripped her by the nape of the neck, the small of the back. Leaning over her, he pressed her against the table until its edge cut sharply into the back of her thigh.

This time, no interruption intruded. No distraction happened. The rams reared back. Edgar's expression was one of conquer, one of loss, beautiful in its trueness. Ava inhaled his exhale. Then the rams fell forward. The kiss crashed. Behind it was all his all for her. She couldn't breathe for the fierceness.

The black backs of Ava's closed eyelids starred with sparrow-carried flames, and her gates swung open, revealing the wreckage within. She fumbled her hand on the table behind her, closed her fist around the knife, and lifted it to glint in the spotlight before pressing it into Edgar's chest.

But something felt wrong. Right, rather—not false. It met resistance. Ava tried to pull the blade back, but Edgar held himself tightly against her. There was a wet warmth, then he slumped to his knees, blood bright on his white shirt. She dropped the knife.

Fallon ran to the control panel and flipped the switch that lowered the curtain. She was winded with surprise. Something she'd created had made audience of her. Something she'd written had become.

The funny thing was, the house hadn't noticed. They sat rapt, glassy eyed, chewing their gum like cud. The troupe worked hard season after season to make each scene ring true, and the audience saw all the flaws. But when something real played out, the house took it for fiction.

The train shifted beneath Will, and he lost his footing, caught himself with a step back from the baggage-car wall. Outside, a crew called out to one another as they connected the private cars to the train. Will heard the bang and clank of chain, the sounds of men at work. He touched his wrist to reassure himself that the bracelet was still safe beneath his bodysuit, then stepped his nose back to the wall and repositioned his limbs on the nails.

Disappearing again, Will waited. His breathing quickened between his shoulder blades, where the suit darkened with sweat. Trying to slow his breath only made him huff harder. His hands trembled. When his mouth began flooding with saliva, he quickly stepped back from the wall, but the vomit came before he could bend over. It ran warm down his chest, and the smell turned his stomach. He reached for a nearby plastic witch's cauldron, vomited once more inside.

Will looked at the mess running down the soft paunch at his waist, and his trembling switched from fear to rage. He couldn't keep living like this, running from Mitzi, running from himself. He couldn't keep escaping into role. He resolved to doff it all.

Peeling the spandex from around his face, Will pulled down the hood of the bodysuit, stretching it over his shoulders to his waist, where it dangled. Without one hint of a limp, he strode across the baggage car and into the sleeper car's small bathroom, where he stripped off the rest of the suit. Ten minutes later, the bathroom's accordion door yanked open without a single catch, and the narrow corridor clouded with billowing steam. Through it stepped Will, dripping wet and naked, save his glasses and the bracelet. He marched to his compartment and dressed himself as Will in his blue button-up shirt, tan corduroys, and dusty Chucks, unclasping the bracelet from his wrist and slipping it into his pocket. On his way out of the car, he stopped in Chantal's compartment to take a look at himself in her full-length mirror. He could taste every word of a speech for Mitzi.

Will made his way back through the baggage car, and a glance at the spot Edgar had prepared for him filled him with shame. He opened the door marked Private and made his way through the empty train to the bar car, choosing a stool at the mahogany bar.

Art rose from behind it like a Marrakesh cobra. He had yet to put on his apron and was, shockingly, without his curtain beard, but Will couldn't get distracted. Not now.

"You're the first aboard," Art said, his voice unusually gruff. As he continued, Will saw him soften into his bartender persona, one designed to garner tips. "No part in today's play? Shall I pour you a beer?"

Will shook his head, asked for a scotch, a double.

"Scotch?"

"You heard me."

Art shrugged and reached for the bottle. "As I always say, 'Towering genius disdains a beaten path. It seeks regions hitherto unexplored.'" He poured the glass high.

Will slid it toward himself, took a swallow. His stomach was calm, his palms dry. There were no nervous ticks or talks. He settled in to wait, keeping his attention peripheral—on the doors at either end of the car.

Night Travel

From the tracks came a scream, a relentless, endless screeeeech, which violated the body like a blade, entered the ear like an icepick. The train's mechanics were unsuited to curves. Locked metal on metal, its wheels ground round the bend at speed, so that all the train was, was pain.

❧

At her mirrored desk, Fallon scried, conj(ect)ured.

> *WILL tears at his hair. Dropping to his knees, he pulls on his shirt and clutches his chest. He forces a sob, and a spray of spittle glints. A line of spit stretches between his top and bottom teeth, then breaks, landing on his chin.*

BUD MONCRIEFF
No and no and no and no and no!

> *In the weak circle of light from a plastic lamp clipped to the arm of his director's chair, MONCRIEFF removes his reading glasses from the end of his nose and throws them down onto the script in his lap. They launch off the paper as if it's a ski jump, then skitter frictionlessly across the plywood riser that serves as a drama-room stage.*

MONCRIEFF
You. Are. Enough! I don't want to watch pre-sen-ta-tion! We've no use for facade! When you are you, the room lights up. When you're an *ac-tor*, no one's excited. Be Will! That's who they want to watch! (*He sweeps an arm over the class, who don't look up from their script-margin doodles.*)

WILL
(*Slumping and letting his hands fall to his sides, his angst softening*) But I've never—

MONCRIEFF

You've never this; you've never that. You've felt, haven't you? Haven't you ever wanted something? Wanted it badly? That's all you need to know to play this scene. Embrace all of yourself! You contain multitudes, as Walt tells us. If you are not yourself, onstage and off, you are no one.

(*He pauses, and there is the sound of pen scratch.*) You can change your world if you change your reality.

WILL

Change reality? But, how—

MONCRIEFF

Just believe. Then so will they.

❧

Will's scotch on the rocks sweated full on the mahogany bar beside the bracelet. The car was filled with departure buzz, which was likely usual but which he usually never saw. Passengers passed through, some stopping for a drink on the way to their seats.

Having never met Mitzi, Will scanned every entrant for menace. Three women came in together, another alone. There was a father with a boy who spun on a stool and drank soda, a group of college-aged bachelors, an old man, a couple who saw only each other, and another who saw everything but. When a man in a suit made his way to the bar, Will stiffened, but the man merely started up a friendly chatter with Art.

Then four thick, hairy, beringed fingers came around the door marked Private, followed by four thick, hairy men. The man in charge was shorter than the others. He cracked his knuckles, threw a left hook to shoot a wrist beyond its velour sleeve, and checked his watch. Its gold glinted with the twist. The men's lines of sight swept the car like search beams would a prison yard, which set off an alarm of blood-rush to Will's head. He could almost hear the hounds howling, had to take a deep breath. He wasn't sure if he was ready, but he knew enough to act as though he was. He sat up straighter, pushed away his scotch, and swiveled to face the men. His lips itched to screw, his teeth to chew his cheek, but he wouldn't. He didn't.

One by one, the looks of Mitzi and his men lit on Will's face. The first beam glanced and ricocheted. The second punched, stung. The third rinsed over, but Mitzi's saw deeper—it burned. Will met it. He had never felt more like himself. He hunkered his mind in his body, sat down in it for once.

Then Mitzi's eyes broke away. "Is he here?" he snarled, flashing a filling. He turned to his goons with impatience, met three blank faces. "Well? He wasn't at the theater. You said you've seen him. Whet your memories, boys, or I'll give you something to remember."

Three beams made one last sweep. Three pairs of shoulders shrugged, Will in shadow.

"He'd better be in the dining car," Mitzi growled.

The goons grunted, followed him cross-car. They passed Will: one, two, three, four, then the vestibule door shut behind them. Will swallowed his speech. His mind whirred. The only time the henchmen had seen him was onstage in *The Slip*, when he'd worn a wig and a prosthetic nose. As usual when he was onstage, he'd also been without his glasses.

Will laughed aloud. They were looking for someone else.

Chantal pushed away the dining-car china and lifted a clamshell compact from the white tablecloth. Her lips filled its mirror as she painted them with pink gloss. When she backed the mirror away to see her whole face, the reflection of a man appeared behind her. She winked, but he looked away. No matter. They couldn't all be expected to bite.

Before clicking the compact closed, Chantal quickly checked her eyeliner out of habit, but when she met her own eye, she wished she hadn't. She felt a stab of guilt about Edgar, could hardly believe that on top of lying to him (and with him), Ava had attacked him. You never really knew what someone else was thinking, Chantal thought. Still, she couldn't help feeling slightly responsible.

The train must have been approaching a crossing; its horn sounded, and the volume increased as the door to the vestibule opened. A man entered, stopping Chantal in her tracks. He was burly, manly, and the three beefcakes behind him told her he was important. He made his way to the table beside her, and when he reached for the seat, his wrist showed gold. The man smiled, smoothed his balding head with a hairy hand. There were rings on every finger. Chantal uncrossed her legs.

Silence cut the buzzing. Then Edgar's leg twitched away a fly. It was what the dead felt, he thought, or the dying, too weak to shoo them away.

The eye of the red velvet camera obscura gaped, and gray morning light peered into his compartment. In bed, Edgar rolled over, wincing, holding a hand where his heart-scar had been re-broken open. The stitches felt tight, and his left pec was sore. They'd said he'd been lucky; his rib had taken the brunt of the blade. He was alive. The funny thing was, he was glad.

Edgar sat up. Fallon had offered to enlist someone from the theater to help with this week's play, but he'd insisted on working. It was a standard, with a standard set to match, needing him to control only the lights and curtain. He needed to take his mind off Ava.

At the thought, Ava's image, inverted and shrunken, walked onto the wall of his room. He'd heard from Chantal that Ava was as mad at him as he was at her, but he wasn't sure that was possible. He would carry her deception for the rest of his life, the way a black hole carries its singularity, this heaviness and absence (somehow both) at the core of him.

Lightning flashed like far-flung paparazzi. The world lifted its head to look.

BERLIN, INDIANA

February 27

Ava woke from a dream in which she'd found a new room in a building she thought she knew well. There was a warm weight on her thigh. She thought of Edgar, but when she stretched an arm across the sheet where his chest would have been, it was all smooth coolness, something that once would have pleased her, but which now felt like lack.

When she opened her eyes, two green eyes glowered back. The fox sat against her leg, looking down its nose at her.

Ava's head ached from crying. She'd been starting and stopping all evening in her compartment, as the train stopped and started its way from Lyon to Berlin. It wasn't like Edgar at all, what he'd done. Ava should have told him about Ben, of course, but the Edgar she loved would have come to her when he found out, no matter how angry. He wasn't who she thought he was, who she'd thought he'd be.

Held up on waitresses' trays, satellites of gravied biscuits wheeled about the busy diner's central tables. Glasses and coffee mugs clunked onto tabletops, silverware clattered on the thick ceramic dishware, and the townsfolk—here Fallon returned the nod of a man in muddy boots— kept up a buzzy cheerfulness that would have been impossible for a Monday anywhere else. Fallon was the only one in black. She glanced up from the beaten Berlin guidebook limply spread-eagle beside her plate and looked out the front window to avoid the stares of her fellow diners. There wasn't much to look at. Of the buildings across the street, only one wasn't boarded up: the Mykonos Restaurant, which saluted her in blue and white.

Fallon opened the book to its index and ran her finger down its list. *Mykonos Restaurant 147*—it was there. Crunching another bite of toast, she flipped to the page, leaving buttery fingerprints in the margins.

The plaque outside the Mykonos commemorates an assassination which took place there on September 17, 1992. An Iranian tied to the Iranian-Kurdish opposition had recently purchased the restaurant from a Greek but had yet to change the name. That night, during a political meeting in the back room, two masked men burst into the restaurant and sprayed the place with bullets. Three opposition members were killed, and others were injured.

The waitress sloshed coffee from a carafe into Fallon's tea. "We were just wondering—are you part of that theater group comin' through town? You don't look like you're from around here." She smiled.

This was a first. Fallon masked it, daubed her mouth with her napkin and answered. "I am."

The waitress nodded over Fallon's head, triggering a burst of activity from two more by the kitchen door. "We didn't want to bother you."

Fallon gave a weak smile.

"It's just—" The waitress looked to her colleagues for courage. "We'd love to see the show, but with it being sold out and all—is there any other way we can get tickets?"

"A sold-out show is a sold-out show, I'm afraid," said Fallon. "I'm sorry, but there's nothing I can do." Her voice was calm, but as she spoke, she lurched out of the booth, fumbling to stuff the guidebook into her back pocket while removing a money clip inside her jacket.

"Did that actress really stab that man?"

"Maybe you can catch us next time we come through?" Fallon said, tossing a twenty-dollar bill on the table.

The girl picked up the twenty. "But, ma'am," she protested. "This isn't—"

"Keep the change, my little piggy bank!" called Fallon, rushing out the door.

As she jogged down empty Main Street to The Majestic, her long strides dashed the shallow snow remaining on the shoveled and salted sidewalks. The rest of the cast wouldn't arrive at rehearsal for another half hour, but she had to see for herself.

When Fallon neared the last block, she stopped, gawked. The theater's front was plain, built of institutional brick, but on its far side, before the box office, was a crowd. There was a sandwich board out front: SOLD OUTHOUSE. She laughed, then laughed again. It was true. Fallon's stomach frilled with pleasure.

That pleasure, though, was dampened by the thought that this success was due more to Ava and Edgar's drama than her own. Still, Fallon had had a hand in that. She'd brought Ben up in his craft until he was ready for the limelight, and she'd encouraged him to leave. She'd hired Ava, then Edgar, had thrown the two of them together. She'd witnessed the stab-kiss and written it, then kept their secret. Without any of these plot points, the scene couldn't have played out. It was some of her best work, and it was finally paying off.

The diner was nearly deserted. It was too late for lunch and too early for dinner. Ava pushed the back of the thin pressed-tin spoon into the soup's surface and let it fill with broth. As she lifted it carefully to her mouth, she flipped over a folded copy of *The Midwest Chorus* left on the counter so she could see above the fold. What was there made her gasp and inhale soup, coughing as though she were drowning.

"Are you okay, honey?" asked the cashier.

Ava nodded between hacks. Her eyes were watering. She looked again at the blurred black-and-white photo of her stabbing Edgar in halftone. She blinked, and a tear welled over the lip of her lid, fell onto the lid of her lip.

How could he have betrayed her like this, switched out the knife? She could have killed him. She could kill him. He'd ruined everything. Because of what he'd done, Ava couldn't ever trust him again, could never love him as she had.

And now the world knew. It knew about her, about Ben, about them.

February 28

Everything was different. The troupe hadn't gathered in the observation car as usual before the first performance, and getting ready at the dressing-room vanity, Ava was nervous. She was hoping she wouldn't see Edgar. To top it off, she was wearing a crown.

"Now look down," said Chantal. She stroked the mascara wand along the underbelly of Ava's eyelashes.

Ava jiggered her heel on the floor, picked at her cuticles. She couldn't stop thinking about all the eyes that would be on her. The eyes that, for the first time, would be looking at Ava—Ava the murderess, or whoever they thought she was. She tried to tell herself that, in a sense, their Ava was just as much a character as any other role, but it wasn't so easy to believe.

"Look up," said Chantal, bringing her face even closer. Each syllable smelled faintly of mustard. Ava complied, showing the whites of her eyes.

Chantal ruffled Ava's lower lashes with the wand. "You know, I can't help but feel a little responsible for what happened last night, since I was the one who told Edgar about Ben."

Ava's irises lowered again.

"I didn't know he didn't know," Chantal said. She shrugged. "You should have told me you two were a thing."

Ava wanted to be angry. Sad, even—something. But all she felt was empty. All that remained of her was smoke. Smoke and ash. Black.

"Now look what you've done," Chantal said, dabbing a smear of mascara. She soaked a cotton ball in makeup remover and wiped its cold wetness beneath Ava's eye. A tear of it ran down her cheek.

"Oops! Don't worry. It'll be fixed in a jiffy." Chantal reached for a tissue with a flourish of her wrist. Something flashed on her hand, giving Ava the shock of meeting an old friend on the street, in a town she'd never expect to. It was her wedding ring. Or was it?

The sapphire rode Chantal's finger from the vanity to Ava's cheek and back, shattering the beam of light overhead into a clustered constellation that travelled the walls with every daub of powder. Was the ring hers? It was. Ava was sure of it. It had to be, but on its new hand, in its new role, it somehow looked different than she remembered. Like her, it had a new life, was matched to another. How many more would there be?

"That's better." Chantal pulled back, appraised her work. "You're ready to go on."

At the thought, Ava's stomach turned. She lurched for the trash can.

Through a gap between the closed curtains, Will peeked out at the packed audience. The theater's concrete floors and molded-plywood seats bounced their noise about, keeping it on its feet, and the full house sounded like three. The buzz of conversation had a new charge, an energy he'd never felt before. He made his way back to the dressing room and drew a slip of paper from the upturned top hat.

"The room was crowded—was crowded—with a wild mob."

A black plastic trash can stood ready near the vanity. Will eyed it expectantly, but besides a touch of flutter, his stomach held. He reached back into the hat, and its cool silk lining soothed the back of his hand. The paper he drew out was crumpled.

"These words—" Will's stomach butterfly-kicked. "These words were the cue—words were the cue—for the actor to leave."

The ritual was winding him up, but he needed to wind down, keep his calm. "Fuck it," he sighed. The flutter foundered. "Fuck it all to hell." It settled. "Who even gives a fuckity fuck fuck about this shit?"

Will let the slip slip from his fingers. His pulse slowed, and the muscles on the sides of his head—muscles he never before realized were there, let alone tensed—relaxed. For a second, he felt his self drop into his body, felt the weight, but as soon as he did, he didn't.

"Fuck it." With an exhale, Will plunged down again like a Finn into a hole in the ice. It was shocking, but he'd never felt more himself. He tried to hold himself under but buoyed. The touch of calm stuck, though. It wasn't preparedness. He wasn't confident he'd fully memorized his lines or that some disaster wouldn't befall him, but he knew no matter what happened, life would go on, just like it had after Mitzi. He would be fine.

Will made his way back to the stage and peeped again through the gap where the two halves of the closed curtain met. The crowd was roiling, but Will willed himself to see—instead of conspiracy and judgement—enthusiasm, people looking forward to the show. He took a deep breath, willed himself to believe that his nervousness—the rapid heartbeat, butterflies, and trembling hands—was the feeling of excitement.

The feeling reminded Will of Claudette, and the bracelet strained his pants pocket, seeing 360 degrees. Its mettle made him braver. The bracelet was his rabbit's foot, his lion's mane, his shield and his sword. It was his key to her, and he knew she'd return so he could turn it.

The lights dimmed, the audience quieted, and Will entered the first scene, went onstage for the first time as Will. He entered as Will and was seen as not-Will, a character whose presence made Will disappear. Nothing but a general was seen. Both he and the audience believed.

༜

March 1
THE MIDWEST CHORUS | THEATER REVIEW
The Singed Songbird
The Troupe Adores
The Conflagration Theater
Berlin, Indiana
Remaining performances: tonight at 8 p.m., tomorrow at 3 p.m.

All we saw was Ava, but it may not have been the Ava Ava is. We'd come to see Ava, and we saw her, Ava, underneath the makeup, under the crown and the gown. Instead of a queen, we saw devious Ava costumed, Ava pretending to order a siege.

As we watched a queen's vengeance, the city burning behind her, we saw Ava's malice for Edgar. We saw the cardboard forest, the fabric fire, stuffed doves ascending on wires. The props looked like props.

We wanted only what we couldn't have: more Ava, more Edgar, more of the knife and the train, to see for ourselves the drama behind the drama, the thoughts in the minds of the players, the truth of the affair that ended in tragedy, the hit The Troupe Adores can't give us.

❧

During the final performance, Ava sweated onstage beneath her crown, turning in the heat of the lights and eyes, like meat on a spit. The beast seethed, restless in its seats. It was hungry. She could feel its want.

Some of the fans were unwrapping sandwiches, some were talking and pointing in her direction. Some crumple-clutched programs they hoped she would autograph after. When she'd arrived late at the backstage door the past two afternoons, a crowd had descended on her, gnawing and tearing at her behind the flash of cameras. She'd fled into the darkness backstage from the very thing she'd been working toward for years.

❧

Even Edgar saw only Ava onstage and saw Ava wrong, as something she wasn't. Behind the spotlight, the darkest spot in the theater, he watched her, the chest of his white tee blooming with a blur of blood.

Night Travel

At the center of the train, somehow astride the mechanical clamor, was a stillness, a silence, broken only by the rustling of newspapers. Between pages, the passengers looked up, saw their destination inevitable through each field and forest, house and town. They watched the passing landscape being sucked in, churned, and stretched into a blurred line, then tossed and forgotten behind them.

Will knocked back the last of his glass and, with it, a large cube of ice. Its cold was scalding, and he moved it around on his tongue, clicking it against his teeth like a stick across a picket fence.

"Ready for another?" Art asked.

Will gave a nearly imperceptible nod, and Art reached beneath the bar for a new bottle.

"One more ginger ale, coming up." The metal cap hissed as it was pried off, then clinked into a heap of others in the trash can beneath the bar. Art freshened Will's glass with a scoop of ice and poured the soda. "Keeping sharp tonight?"

"To be honest, I've never liked drinking much—it always seemed like something I *should* do—but I've decided to be more like myself from now on."

"You know I'm one for honesty. And as I always say, 'I don't think much of a man who is not wiser today than he was yesterday.'"

"Speaking of yesterday and today—" Will said, tipping his drink toward Art's shaven face. "I see you're a changed man."

Art rubbed a palm over his smooth cheek and chuckled. "It certainly feels that way. I'm still getting used to it myself."

"You looking for work other than Lincoln now? I don't need to worry about competition, do I?"

"Nah, who else could I play? I just had the urge for a change. Besides, Lincoln went beardless at times in his life, and this way, I don't have to keep dying my facial hair."

Art looked past Will to a man at the end of the bar and, in one practiced motion, flipped over a fresh glass and reached for a bottle of gin. He inverted it for a precise *one-thousand one, one-thousand two*, added tonic from a nozzle, and garnished the drink with a wedge of lime.

Will was watching Art work, when a hand slapped his honey-colored wallet onto the mahogany bar top. He slapped flat his back-right pants pocket.

"Missing something?" asked a woman behind him.

He thought it was his, at least. The leather was worn in the way he'd worn his. He touched the split beginning on its spine, the spot where the ridge of a credit card within had worn off the dye. He opened the wallet and slid the ID out of its slit, just enough to find himself looking back.

It could only be her. Will wheeled around on the stool to face the pretty face of Claudette Rex.

"Had you given up on me?" she asked.

Will didn't know what to say. He had and he hadn't. He'd hoped and feared.

"I tried to meet you in Paris," she said. "But I saw one of Mitzi's goons outside the theater and another outside your train cars. He hasn't been giving you any trouble, has he?"

Will shrugged.

"Do you still have it?" Claudette said.

Will nodded. He sat up to access his front pocket and slid the Janus faces from it. The metal was warm, and he placed it into Claudette's cold hand.

"Thanks for looking after it for me. I won't soon forget."

"Is it worth a lot?" said Will as he slid his wallet back into his pocket.

"In my line of work, I've gotten pretty good at sniffing out fakes."

"I sometimes wonder if I'm one, or if I've been one for a long time, anyway."

Claudette clicked the bracelet closed around her right wrist. "It's not polite to make appraisals outside of a jewelry shop, but I'd say you're as true as they come."

Will tried to believe what she'd said. Then the confession rushed from him. "I have to say something." He stopped himself, took a breath. "Or, rather, I have something to say. I slept with someone, while I was waiting to see you again. I didn't mean for it to happen, and I'm sorry it happened, and you mean much more to me than—"

Claudette stopped him with a hand on his thigh. "Oh, sweetie."

Will put his hand over hers. "Have you ever thought about acting?"

"I don't think that's a good idea," Claudette said, removing her hand. "An actor works in the spotlight; in my line of work, I work everywhere but."

"It could be good cover," Will suggested.

"Nothing's better cover than the dark."

With that, she disappeared like the wallet from a pocket: his, which was gone again. For once, it had been thick with bills from his cut of the last two performances. Will took a step toward the door to catch up, let her have it, then threw up his arms, spun abruptly on his heel, let her have it.

The observation car was the brumous night's womb. For the first time in a while, Ava sat facing forward. Other than the snow, which appeared as a faint haze, all she could see in the darkened windows was the car's interior. She'd grown accustomed to herself as overlay, existing only ghostly in this reflected existence of the train, the troupe, the tour, and the world of make-believe. She had almost believed in it.

On the glass, the reflected white pages of her open physics textbook blended with the snow, until the book's text appeared printed upon it. Ava tried to read the equation in reverse:

$$r_s = \frac{2GM}{c^2}$$

It described a black hole, its point of no return. Facing forward, she could feel the gravity of her own situation, the tug of the past. She almost wished she could go back but, like a character in one of Fallon's plays, her plot had reached its event horizon, and there was no escape now from the descent to ending, that last long draw within.

There was hope, though, in singularity: a center at once infinitely massive and infinitely small. It seemed the same as that from which the big bang sprang. Could creation be born of devourment? She penciled an ouroboros in the margin, imagined the end, instead, as the beginning, the energy the black hole swallowed banging forth into a new universe in a parallel dimension, starting anew.

The sun was coming up, and Fallon felt like she'd been writing for months. In the wee hours between Berlin and Warsaw, the story of the stabbing, of Ava and Edgar, tumbled from her onto the page. The weight of the words rolled about on her tongue, even unspoken.

The story was one Fallon must have been subconsciously shaping since she first witnessed Ava and Edgar's strange kiss, maybe longer. Now she made of it what she wanted: Ava was Ava-er; Edgar was more Edgaresque; and their love was deeper, as was their pain. It had begun as a play, but a play was limiting. Only so many could see it; only so many could sell it. Playing on the page, she decided against the stage for the stage of the mind—a novel. Fallon would adapt a play from the story later, make it next season's sole production. She had created herself, and she'd play herself, but she'd find a new Ava to play Ava, ask Will to play Edgar, expand the cast and crew, add another train car or two.

In the bar car earlier that evening, Fallon had been shocked at Art's beardlessness. She couldn't help but wonder if it had anything to do with what she'd written. He'd been wearing his usual uniform, not a Hawaiian shirt, of course, but still. The coincidence was strange, like that sparrow weeks ago.

The sway of the moving train rocked Fallon's attention back to the page, and she scooted her director's chair closer to her makeshift desk, moving the table's leg deeper between her own. It was worth a try. After all, as Art always said, "The best way to predict the future is to create it."

Heavy with ending, Fallon gazed at her face for one long minute in the desk's mirror, willing. Then she scried, conj(ect)ured.

February 29

Lying on the green roof of the observation car, Ava rose onto an elbow, shook a cigarette out of the pack beside her, lit it, and lay back down. A puff rose from her mouth into the night sky as though she was the train's smokestack. As she lifted the cigarette to her lips again, the rail yard's gray gravel crashed, and the car began to creak with the weight of someone climbing the ladder. Ava began to worry. She scooted herself to the far end of the car.

Soon, Edgar was stepping onto the roof's wooden lawn. He halted, grimacing, and lifted his right hand to his heart, which was marked on his white tee with a small bloodstain. After cautiously rolling his left shoulder, he continued to Ava's end of the car, sitting at its edge and dangling his feet over.

Without looking at him, Ava offered the pack of cigarettes, and he took one. She passed him the lighter. They sat for a moment, smoking in silence.

"I never meant for you to find out that way," Ava said.

"Seems you never meant for me to find out."

"I convinced myself it was better for you, that it didn't matter, but I see now that was only better for me."

They inhaled and exhaled.

"Why did you do it?" Ava asked.

"Partly because I was tired, too tired to face another day. And partly to force your hand, truly feel the hurt you caused me. I wanted something to be real, anything, even if it was only pain."

"By making me kill you?"

Edgar shrugged. "I felt you already had."

"But this *is* real. What isn't is my marriage."

"It's real on paper, right? It's real in the eyes of the law."

"Yes, *only* on paper, *only* in the eyes of the law."

"*Only* on paper?" Edgar said. "What's put on paper is as real as you or me. It has a body; it's corporate, and we breathe life into it. Aren't the tears you cry onstage real? The tears of the audience? The joy you bring and theirs?"

"It's not the same. We try to make it so, but we know we'll never succeed. There's always a bit of pretending."

"Not everyone's like that." Edgar stubbed out his cigarette on the side of the train and pitched the butt into the gravel below.

"Edgar, I love *you*. I'm with *you*. Not telling you about Ben may have seemed a lie, but it felt like the truth to me. I'm so sorry." Ava stubbed out her cigarette as well, placed her hand atop Edgar's on the edge of the car. "We were lucky. I could have killed you."

She leaned toward him, and when he didn't pull away, she took a tender hand to his chin and turned his face to hers, kissed him.

"If you'll still have me, I'd like to go with you at the end of the season," she said. "We are who we want to be. We see what we want to see. The world around us is what we make of it, and I'd like to make it anew, with you. Can you forgive me?"

Edgar rolled his sore shoulder again.

"You can?" Ava placed her arms around Edgar's neck, set her forehead to his, and smiled so brightly it was hard for him not to mirror a tinge of it back.

Slowly, reluctantly, sheepishly, he broke into a grin. "Whatever your reality, I'll make it my own," Edgar said. "Your truth is the one I want to live." He kissed her, a kiss weighted with forgiveness and apology both.

As though stars started falling from the sky, it began to snow.

Fallon took a breath. It was finished. These things could go either way, but this one would end happily; it was what the audience wanted. She leaned back in her chair, stretched her long arms overhead, then bent over the makeshift desk again to read the piece from its beginning.

It was opening night. Edgar felt the night opening, saw its teeth. He was dressing himself as meat.

AUTHOR'S NOTE

The novel's opening epigraph has been widely attributed online to physicist Niels Bohr; however, I and others—including staff at the Niels Bohr Library & Archives—have been unable to trace it directly back to his writings. Because this even more perfectly encapsulates the themes of the quote and of the novel itself, I decided to use it anyway, citing it as "attributed to Niels Bohr."

The quotations spoken by the character of Arthur Conan-Doyle are Abraham Lincoln's, and the Harvard Sentences that Will Connaught uses as a vocal warm-up really were developed to test the sound quality of telecommunications systems. The Russian fable Fallon Finn-Dorset refers to draws from one in Nestor's *The Tale of Bygone Years*. The line she adds after the theater reviewer's Dante quote is from *The King James Bible* (John 1:5).